Thunder over the Grass

MALIHA ANDERSON BOOK 5

By

Steve Turnbull

Thunder over the Grass by Steve Turnbull. Second edition July 2016
Copyright © 2015, 2016 Tau Press Ltd. All rights reserved.

ISBN 978-1-910342-51-0

Published by Tau Press Ltd.
Cover by Jane Dixon-Smith (jdsmith-design.com).

Adriel, for remembering things I have forgotten.

CHAPTER 1

i

The *RMS Macedonia* thundered across the Indian Ocean on a south-westerly course. Maliha looked out through the panoramic windows that curved around the stern lounge. The room smelled of stale cigar smoke. She rested her hands on the oak rail and felt underneath it. The letters spelling out the shipbuilders Harland & Wolff were there just as they had been little more than a year ago.

When she had returned from school, on this very ship, she had worn typical European clothes complete with corset. After her encounter with Temperance Williams she had changed to the looser Continental style. When she moved home to Pondicherry she had returned to wearing saris.

After her grandmother had thrown her out she wondered why she allowed those around her to influence her choice of clothing. As a result she chose to return to the flowing, corset-less French dresses as the most comfortable. She told herself it had nothing to do with Françoise Greaux, or the fact that Valentine could not keep his eyes off her.

A few hundred feet below the ship the sea glittered in the afternoon sunshine. They passed over dark shapes beneath the water. Whales. She would like to see them close up one day.

A baby cried behind her and she turned. Barbara Makepeace-Flynn was holding the child, whom Maliha had named Barbara, in her arms. The irony of holding a black babe in her arms was not lost on the older Barbara. She too had been on this ship a year before and had treated Maliha very badly due to her Anglo-Indian birth.

But Barbara had changed and now she was entirely happy to hold little Baba, despite the disapproving looks of the unenlightened British upper class passengers. For this short journey, at least, they could be like a family even if completely unrelated by birth or marriage.

"How do you like being a grandmother?" asked Maliha.

"More like great-grandmother," said Barbara. She sniffed the air and sighed. "To be frank, Maliha, I am glad I did not have to go through motherhood. Young children can be quite disgusting." She looked down into the face of the child who had a look of concentration on her face. "Aren't you, little one? Quite disgusting."

Little Barbara groaned with an effort and then squeaked. Amita emerged from deeper within the ship as if she had been summoned, relieved Barbara of the child and took her away.

Barbara pushed herself to her feet with an effort and took up the walking stick by her chair. She came to the window. The two women exchanged another glance. The previous year it had been Maliha with the stick.

"I can see why you enjoyed the trip so much," said Barbara. "It is a relief to lose some of the weight."

"We could get you one of the Faraday wheelchairs."

Barbara shook her head. "Getting old is something that happens, Maliha. I will accept it with grace." She laughed. "Better than having a private steam engine. Have you seen them? They are quite ridiculous."

Maliha nodded her acceptance. Barbara had become her surrogate mother in the past year. The price of loving someone was knowing that one day they might no longer be around. Maliha just wished she had met Barbara earlier.

"I think I'll go and have a lie down, dear."

The Sky-liner was fully enclosed with no open decks and it was ventilated to prevent it getting hot inside. However fifty years of living in the heat of Ceylon had built the habit of afternoon naps into Barbara. A habit that she was disinclined to break.

Although Barbara was very helpful in looking after Baba, her real purpose was to be chaperone to Maliha and Valentine. Their engagement had been announced in *The Times* but that just meant they would be even more closely spied on by those seeking scandal.

Maliha was certain there was a journalist in second class following them. Thankfully that meant she was relatively safe here in first class. It was only when they went out together in the public areas that she had to be careful. She was always careful. Valentine was reckless, always wanting to kiss her and touch her, sometimes quite inappropriately.

He was like a puppy and had to be disciplined repeatedly. She smiled to herself at the image of giving him a solid rap on the nose. Perhaps she should try that.

She checked her watch, two-thirty. He had wanted her to come and watch him playing squash; there was some sort of tournament going on. She sighed. There were other things she would much rather be doing. Like reading.

But she had a duty to encourage and praise her puppy. She turned and, taking measured steps with very little bounce in the reduced gravity, headed forward and up to the main deck.

*　*　*

Amita finished changing the baby. They had acquired a separate cabin for her and the child. The baby had just been weaned from the breast so they no longer required the wet nurse. Little Barbara's care had been given over to Amita in the main. She did not mind, in fact her mistress had very specifically asked first.

It's one of the things that made her mistress special: she treated everyone the same no matter where they came from or what they were. It was a morbid thought but Amita knew that she would give her life for her mistress if she were called on to do so.

The baby was tired and, after a short protest at being laid down, curled up with her thumb firmly in her mouth. Amita put the net over the crib and pulled the cords tight. When in flight the low gravity meant a child could easily throw themselves out of bed. Precautions had to be taken.

Amita had heard the *mem sahib* go into her room and, by prior agreement, Amita knocked on the adjoining door.

"Just leave the door ajar, Amita," came Barbara's slightly muffled voice.

Amita turned the door handle and opened it a little. Then she gathered up her bag and left the room, closing the door with a gentle click.

She hurried up to the main deck using the servants' stairs. It was slower than using the main staircase but it would be awkward to meet first—or even second—class passengers. Amita was quite used to verbal abuse but it would not reflect well on her mistress.

At the top of the stairs she checked her sari and opened the door on to the deck.

The sun poured through the glass roof that encased the main deck and the promenade above it. This was her first trip on a Sky-Liner. It was true that trains ran faster in their tubes but an atmospheric could not cross the ocean. Nor did they have wide decks where people walked and talked.

The fact she received disapproving looks meant nothing as she crossed the deck and gawked at the white-painted metal superstructure, or the glass dome, or the dozens of people laughing and playing, or the children jumping higher than their parents' heads.

She saw Maliha seated on a bench overlooking an enclosed squash court. Everything was new to her; Amita knew of tennis and this was like it but the ball bounced off everywhere and the men jumped high and low to hit it. Watching the gentlemen perspire had become her favourite sport in the two days they had been in the air.

She climbed the stairs next to the bench and made her way to sit beside Maliha who glanced up and smiled as she approached, then turned her attention back to Valentine Crier who somehow looked even more appealing as he sweated.

The benches were plain wood, though polished and smooth as silk to the touch. She sat demurely with her knees together with her hands clasped over them. She watched the men jumping around inside the arena. From listening to conversations she had learnt this game was exhausting even under normal gravity.

But played under the effects of a Faraday it must be three or four times more difficult and instead of running the men would launch themselves in long flying leaps. They twisted in mid-air, turned upside down, struck and pushed off from the ceiling. It wore one out just watching it.

The final whistle was blown. Amita let out her breath in a long sigh.

Maliha stood up. Amita jumped to her feet beside her, ready to attend.

"It's all right, Amita, you can just stay and watch if you like."

"Thank you, *sahiba*."

Maliha balanced along the bench to the stairs and went down the steps with a light bouncy step. As she approached the door to the squash court it opened and Valentine came out. Amita watched as Maliha reached out and touched his wrist for a moment before dropping her hand back. He said something to her and smiled.

Amita was so pleased her mistress had someone she could love—so glad she had realised that Mr Crier was that man because he adored her—and sighed at her own lack of love. Not that she was unaware of her particular difficulties.

"Do you want to go and clean up?" Maliha asked.

Valentine shook his head and drops of perspiration drifted from his hair and sank towards the deck. Maliha took a step back.

"I should but I'd rather get a drink," he said. "When do we get in to Johannesburg?"

"About three tomorrow morning."

Maliha heard the click and glanced round. It was the man she was sure was following them barely ten feet away with a Kodak box camera. He had slicked down black hair and wore a brown suit over a creased shirt with no tie. She got a clear look at his face for the first time. She never forgot a face—it was her curse never to forget anything—and this face was one she knew.

"Ray Jennings," she hissed. "Come on, Valentine. We'll get a drink in first class."

She stormed off towards the nearest stairwell that would take her down to their deck with Valentine trailing behind.

* * *

Valentine's clothes were sticking to him with the perspiration. He glanced at the man with the camera as he set off after Maliha still gripping the squash racket. The man had a decidedly possessive grin on his face. He must be a member of the press, Valentine concluded. Maliha hated attention and especially from the press.

She was already through the door and approaching the stairwell when he caught up with her. He was sure she was approaching the stairs far too quickly. There were proprieties in regard to the use of stairs when in low gravity. Both ascending and descending too fast could result in an accidental impact with other passengers, so one always took particular care.

What one did not do was use the banister rail for support and launch oneself down a flight in a single jump. Which is precisely what Maliha did. Of course under a gravity equivalent, so he understood, of the Moon one did not fall quickly.

Hers was a graceful descent with her French gown flowing out behind her. Unfortunately it was witnessed by at least five other passengers, three of whom were dressed in a way that marked them as social superiors.

She landed and bent her knees to absorb the impact.

The door behind him opened just as she launched herself down the next flight. Valentine turned and saw the "Ray" person coming through with his camera. Maliha might not court publicity but a shot of her flying down the stairs was far from ideal.

Valentine turned abruptly and stood directly in front of the fellow blocking both his view and his progress.

"Excuse me!" said Ray and stepped to the side. Valentine went the same way. Ray tried the other direction. Valentine blocked him.

"Excuse me!" said Ray with more force and pushed Valentine out of the way. Or at least he tried to. Valentine did not move while Ray moved in precisely the other direction and collided against the wall. He lost his balance and sprawled on the floor.

Valentine relaxed and released his grip on the rail beside him. He followed Ray and grabbed the lapels of his jacket. "Here let me help you up." He lifted the man and slammed him against the wall. He jammed the handle of his racket into the man's solar plexus knocking the wind from him.

"Oh, sorry." Valentine let Ray down slowly.

Ray breathed in loudly trying to recover his breath. "You … you … can't … do … that. I'm a member of the press."

Valentine smiled and gripped the man's jacket again. He lifted him so only his toes were touching the ground. "Listen to me, Ray whatever-your-name-is. My fiancée doesn't seem to like you very much. I've found her assessment of people's character to be very accurate which means that I don't like you either."

"I'll 'ave you for assault. I'll 'ave you arrested, you see if I don't."

"Ray. You're not listening. If you disturb the life of my fiancée, or me, or anyone we know again we will have further words."

"I'm not afraid of you."

Valentine conjured all his experiences of the past year, all the terrible things he had seen done, and the men he had killed. He brought those things, that he kept hidden and suppressed, to the forefront of his mind to add venom to his tone. "You should be," he said.

Ray went white.

Valentine closed his eyes for a moment and pushed those thoughts back to where they belonged. He looked back at Ray and smiled, then let the man down. He held him for a moment while he regained his balance.

"There now," said Valentine. "Right as rain. You run along and be sure to remember what I said."

Ray scurried out through the door.

* * *

"What do you mean 'he won't bother me again'?" Maliha said hotly.

"Keep your voice down, you'll wake the baby."

She fumed and pursed her lips. "Explain yourself."

He described his conversation with Ray.

She sat down on the edge of the bed and shook her head. "You idiot."

"I don't appreciate being called an idiot. Especially not by someone whose opinion I admire," he said. She sighed again and looked over at him.

"You scared him for now, yes," she said. "But he'll get over that and just become even more underhand and sneaky."

Valentine came across and knelt down in front of her. He took her hands in his. "How do you even know him?"

"The thing that happened when I was at school. He was one of the journalists reporting on the deaths. He was the worst; he even took pictures of the girls in the dormitory."

"Really? I never heard about that."

"No," she said quietly. "I dealt with it. The girls don't even know it happened."

"But he knows it was you."

She nodded.

"So he's got it in for you."

"And now you too," she said. "I'm sorry, Valentine."

He pulled her down to his level. She resisted up to the moment he kissed her. She savoured his mouth and felt the stress seeping away. He was her therapy. He broke the kiss gently.

"You know it's really awkward kissing you when I'm kneeling on the floor like this. It's giving me a crick in the neck."

"I think you probably deserve it."

"For being an idiot?"

"You're not an idiot. You didn't know."

"Again," he said. "I didn't know *again*. You may be the cleverest person in the world but you really must learn to stop assuming that everyone sees things the way you do."

She kicked off her shoes and lay back on the bed.

He leaned over her and kissed her again.

"Go away, you need to wash."

"Will you come and scrub my back?"

"After we're married," she said. "And not a moment before."

"A moment after?"

"Get out, Valentine."

The baby started crying in the next room.

iii

Although the ship landed early in the morning the Faraday was not disengaged and the first class passengers were not required to disembark until after breakfast.

Word of Maliha's rapid descent of the stairs had clearly got around and there were more stares and mutters than usual about their party. The trip was only three days and they had not had time to become acquainted with other passengers. However, a group consisting on an Anglo-Indian with an African child, affianced to a white man who was not of the upper classes (barely even middle class) even when accompanied by a respectable widow of a celebrated General—but wasn't he the general who scandalously committed suicide after the death of his nurse?

No. Their party was not one that would attract even the casual friendship of passengers on a journey. No member of the Anderson party was even slightly concerned.

After breakfast, with their baggage packed, Maliha descended with the others to the disembarkation area and waited for the transport to the new Carlton Hotel. The klaxon sounded, warning of the imminent disengaging of the Faraday device. Maliha made sure that Barbara was sitting down before full gravity returned. Watching her body weakening was hard as she had come to rely on Barbara for so much.

Their steam carriage arrived and they climbed aboard the spacious passenger area—the vehicle was like a luxury charabanc. It had an open top but still boasted its own Faraday device although Maliha thought it was not as effective as most. Still, it helped.

The air-dock was, as usual, near the outskirts of the city and they drove through streets laid out in grid patterns. It was strange how all the British-controlled cities had the same look. Perhaps this was a little different but it was still completely European in flavour. The streets were filled with Caucasians with only a few people of darker skin both native and Indian.

The Carlton Hotel was an impressive modern structure built just a few years earlier, after the war between the Boers and the British. The British had won, of course, although the Boers had been remarkably well equipped. The fact was that the British had the best flying machines and, though outnumbered at first, as the months went on they could bring in troops from all over the world.

She sighed. She somehow felt the British would not stop until they owned the entire world, and all the planets in the Void as well.

They disembarked and headed inside. The doorman assisted them through the doors until Amita reached him. She was carrying the baby.

"Where do you think you're going?" said the doorman aggressively in his curious local accent. "You can't come in, can't you read? No blacks."

Maliha spun round. The doorman was pointing at the printed sign on the wall beside him and addressing Amita. Maliha found herself at a loss for words. Or, more accurately, found herself with so many things she wanted to say all at once that they jammed in her mind.

Valentine laid his hand on Maliha's wrist and gave it a squeeze. Then he stepped back out through the door.

"What's the problem?"

The doorman turned to Valentine, who was dressed impeccably with his crystalline English accent. The doorman seemed unimpressed.

"No blacks allowed in the hotel."

"My fiancée's maid is not a black."

Maliha could hear the dangerous edge in Valentine's voice though that was only because she knew him so well. She doubted anyone else would notice, perhaps until it was too late.

"Not the girl," the doorman said dismissively. "That." He pointed at the baby in Amita's arms.

"Are you serious?"

"The rules are the rules."

Valentine smiled and turned to Amita. "Just give the baby to the man, Amita."

"What?" he said. "I don't want it."

"Well, as you say, we can't take it inside. So I'm sure you'll be happy to look after it. She's a good little thing really."

"It's not my job!"

"Well, I suppose we'll just have to leave it by the wall. Pop the baby down over there will you, Amita?" He indicated the wall under the sign. Amita went over obediently and knelt down.

"You can't leave it!"

The discussion was beginning to draw a crowd. Inside the hotel there were people who wanted to come out and passers-by had noticed the disagreement and stopped to listen. The doorman was looking uncomfortable at the attention.

"Really?" said Valentine with convincing surprise. "Perhaps you have a suggestion?"

"Take it away," said the doorman in exasperation as if he were explaining to a child that would not listen. "Just take it away from here."

"Oh, I understand," said Valentine. "Miss Anderson, I'm so sorry, we shall have to find another hotel. Would you mind letting the manager know we're cancelling our bookings for the month? What rooms did we have?"

Maliha suppressed a look of wonderment. "Three suites on the top floor, Mr Crier. Oh dear, I expect the manager will be terribly disappointed when he finds out we'll be staying somewhere else."

All eyes turned on the doorman. He seemed to wither beneath it. "I suppose it doesn't matter, if it's a baby."

Valentine's pleasant demeanour evaporated and his voice became hard. "No, I imagine it doesn't." He turned on his heel and went back through the door.

Maliha caught the glance of disgust on Amita's face as she gathered up the child and followed.

The party arrived at the desk. Valentine was still scowling and he looked the desk clerk in the eye. "You don't have a problem with the little black baby, do you?"

The clerk shook his head.

"In that case, we are the Anderson party arrived from Ceylon."

"Yes, Mr Anderson."

"This is Miss Maliha Anderson. I am Mr Valentine Crier. Mrs Barbara Makepeace-Flynn, and staff." Barbara made a little cough. "Mrs Makepeace-Flynn will require a maid."

"Yes, sir."

* * *

The three adjoining suites had connecting doors with short passages between them. Barbara had insisted on having the one between Valentine and Maliha.

"Really, Barbara," said Maliha as they sat in Barbara's lounge with the baby, while Amita and the supplied maid unpacked. "Do you really think I would indulge in any shenanigans with Valentine?"

"Better to avoid the temptation," replied Barbara. "I know what young people can get up to when given a chance." She seemed to be remembering when she said it and had a half-smile on her face.

Maliha surmised it was to do with the intimate relationship Barbara had admitted to having before she married the General.

Maliha wasn't shocked. Given her own history she had no right to be, but her relationships had been purely in the interests of her investigations. The image of Françoise naked in bed reminded her that was not entirely true, but she pretended she wasn't lying to herself.

"I am quite eager to begin looking for little Barbara's grandparents," said Maliha as Valentine came through from his room. Once more he had dodged the idea of having his own man. He had not been brought up in a privileged environment and preferred to do everything for himself. He had had a chap when he had been working at *Sigiriya* but Jameson was long gone. It was a shame as Maliha had liked the man.

"I have to visit the consulate," he said.

"Now?" asked Maliha.

"My previous mission was interrupted."

"I hope you are not complaining about the result."

"Of course not, my dear," he said. "However that was not what I was being paid for. I shall have to see what my paymasters require of me."

Maliha frowned. "But I really need Amita with me."

Barbara sighed. "Don't worry about me. I'll just look after the baby."

Maliha stood and gave Barbara a kiss on the cheek. "I'll have them send up a nurse as well."

Barbara raised an eyebrow. "Better make sure it's one that doesn't mind looking after a 'black' baby."

"Sorry, I should have given you more warning," said Valentine. "They don't all feel the same way but I'm afraid this prejudice against the natives is quite pervasive."

"What about Indians?" asked Maliha.

"There are a lot here and they are treated better than the natives."

"But not much better?" Maliha said. "Is that what you're trying not to say?"

He nodded.

"It'll be just like being back at school, then."

iv

When Valentine exited the front doors of the hotel the doorman had been replaced by a younger man.

"Cab, please."

The fellow whistled loudly and waved his arm. Up the street the front machine from a line pulled forwards and trundled up to a stop. The man opened the door for Valentine to climb in and closed it after him.

"Where do you want to go, Mister?"

"British Consulate, please."

It was approaching noon and the sun was beating down. The vehicles, almost all motorised unlike in India, raised dust as they drove through the streets as well as filling the air with smoke, steam and diesel fumes. Johannesburg was the same bustling town as when he'd left last year. It was the heart of the diamond and gold boom. Though the rush was over people still came from across the world seeking their fortunes in the hills and rivers.

Valentine had spent the better part of four months studying the records of Terence Timmons' cargo fleet. He'd compared details in London, Johannesburg, the Fortress and Pondicherry. They did not marry up. Ships intended to arrive in one place with one cargo, turned up late with a different one. Or did not arrive at all. Not only that but Terence Timmons had been the man financing the operation of Lawrence Renfrew to extract stock market information from vulnerable wives, the so-called Guru Nadesh.

Valentine clenched his fists as the memory of how he had killed Renfrew flashed through his mind. And the memory of Maliha with the fellow.

He shook his head in an attempt to clear his mind. There were many bad memories when it came to Maliha and yet he would not have given them up for anything. He loved her completely.

The taxi steamed to a stop outside the strongly fenced grounds of the consulate a little way out of the city. The British had beaten the Boers in the war eight years before but it had been a hard struggle. The British wanted the diamonds, of course. And still just took whatever they wanted, like a spoilt child.

Valentine was proud of his country, proud to call himself British, but he was not entirely comfortable with everything that was done in the King's name. That was one of the reasons he had left the employment of His Majesty's Foreign Office. And it was Maliha who had opened his eyes.

He opened the door and climbed out of the cab. He handed over money to the driver—he still had rands from his previous visit—and received some change. The gate was guarded. The Boers did not like the British and there was always the risk of another revolt.

The Empire had given the country autonomy, while still being a vassal state, as a compromise and there had been elections a couple of years previously. Money was still being pumped into the country to help the farmers whose farms and livelihoods had been destroyed by Kitchener's scorched earth policy. It had been a harsh action though it had no doubt shortened the war.

He presented his papers to the guard who passed them to someone in the gatehouse. There was a long pause and he was admitted.

It was a long walk from the gate to the consulate building itself. Beyond a stand of trees there were hidden fortifications. There was even a moat, though it was disguised as an ornamental lake. He understood a Faraday grid had been put underneath the moat because it would upset the aim of anyone trying to shoot across it— and even artillery—as well as disorient anyone trying to cross it.

He was not challenged at the doors to the consulate and went through to the clerk in the lobby. He showed his papers once more and asked to speak with Mr Leamington. The clerk smiled enigmatically and asked him to wait.

Valentine took one of the comfortable leather armchairs scattered in friendly groups around the foyer. A waiter appeared and offered him a drink; he declined as it was still only morning. The place had always reminded him of a gentlemen's club.

After ten minutes he was invited to follow the clerk who took him up the majestically curved stairs and along a corridor of deep tufted carpet that absorbed every sound. He knocked at an unnamed and unnumbered door.

"Come."

The clerk held the door open as Valentine entered and closed it after him.

"Sir Bertram?" He said in surprise. There was no mistaking the perfect suit and impressive moustache. The man had not changed.

"Bill, bit of a surprise you turning up here."

"I could say the same, sir."

The last time they had spoken was when Valentine had quit the service in Sir Bertram Kingsley's lavish office in the Fortress.

"Take a seat, Bill. Drink?"

"No, thank you," he hesitated and then said. "I use Valentine now."

Sir Bertram sat down opposite him, behind the solid oak desk. Behind him wide windows looked out on to the lawns and trees. "Valentine?"

"My fiancée prefers it."

"Miss Anderson," the older man said, carefully enunciating each syllable. "So you're planning to marry her despite everything."

"I'm not sure I follow you, sir."

Sir Bertram looked as if he were on the verge of saying something then he smiled and waved his hand as if shooing away an irritating fly.

"Daresay it's none of my business."

"No."

"She's a clever little thing though," he continued. "Still no chance of recruiting her? Reliable females are very hard to come by."

"I didn't think you considered her reliable."

"Touché."

"Are you familiar with the mission I was on, sir?"

"Before you got distracted in Pondicherry?"

Valentine sighed inwardly. "Yes, sir."

"Are you sure there's a problem with Timmons?"

"There's no question of it."

"In your opinion."

"The evidence is in my reports."

"Errors in record-keeping?"

Valentine stood up. "If you don't wish me to pursue it then I won't. We'll call it even and I will be on my way."

"Sit down, Bill—Valentine."

Instead Valentine went to the window and looked out. "I travelled in their crews for a while after I filed my final report."

"And found nothing."

"Nothing solid. But there were rumours."

"Dammit, Bill, I can't arrest a man of Timmons' standing on a rumour. He's a leading industrialist for heaven's sake. He's been to the Palace and is probably due for a knighthood." Sir Bertram got to his feet and came to stand beside Valentine. We need hard facts and if you can't find those facts then, quite frankly, there's no point you being on the payroll."

"I'll find something."

"No hearsay. *Solid facts.*"

"Solid facts."

v

Maliha kissed little Barbara on the forehead. The baby giggled. Maliha found that she could not help but smile. She knew people did not consider her to be a very happy person, and it was true she found that most things angered her in one fashion or another. Except for Baba. Even when the child was unhappy Maliha could stop her crying and make her laugh. Maliha felt as if it broke something inside of her, yet she was happier when it happened.

"How are you going to find Riette's parents?" asked Barbara.

"I don't think I will," said Maliha. "The Frenchman who examined her said that, although she had been well fed after she'd been imprisoned by my uncle, she had starved before that."

"When she was with the slavers?"

"Well they probably didn't feed her well, but that would only have been for a short time," said Maliha. "No, she was on the streets or at least very poor. But she spoke a form of English and Dutch, not one of the native languages so she was from the city."

"Johannesburg?"

"As best we can determine from the slavers' records. If she had been from a city in the south she would probably have spoken just English."

"So you're just going to look for the father's parents?"

Maliha sighed. "I'm no longer sure," she said. "After the reaction of that man on the door and what Valentine said about the people in this place."

Barbara was silent for a moment. "If nothing else, my dear, you have knowledge of their son. I think if a child of mine disappeared I would want to know what happened."

"Isn't ignorance better?"

"Never."

* * *

Amita followed Maliha from the room and they made their way down via the lift. Being a completely modern hotel the lift had a Faraday device built into it which cushioned the ride. The device was ubiquitous. It infiltrated every aspect of their lives in one way or another. Maliha wondered what life would be like if Faraday had not discovered it—or if it did not work at all. She smiled to herself; that would need the work of a vibrant imagination. Perhaps one of the scientific romances of Mr Wells.

She pulled on her gloves as they left the confines of the building. She allowed the new doorman to call a cab for them. There was the possibility the previous fellow had been released from his employment for the trouble he caused. Perhaps he had just been moved. Either way she could not find it in her heart to be concerned; she did not care for bigots. She had had enough of them in her life. Her scarred thigh chose that moment to ache.

The doorman was holding the door for them but as Maliha stepped down to the cab she paused.

"If one wanted to make enquiries after a particular child who lived on the streets, where would you suggest one went?"

He looked at her as if he did not understand her question.

"Do you speak English?"

"I speak English, Miss."

"Well?"

He looked blank. She repeated her original question then added. "We are hoping to perform charitable acts."

That seemed to do the trick. Apparently the first request on its own was like a bent control card in a Babbage, clogging up the works and causing all calculations to cease. Besides what she said was not a lie; she did not lie. She had, however, learnt a few tricks from her association with Françoise Greaux for whom truth was a variable quantity.

She had provided him with a statement that was open to misinterpretation. He thought she meant general charitable works— the sort of thing English ladies loved to get up to—whereas she had a more specific situation in mind.

"You'll be wanting the market streets around the cathedral. That's where most of the beggars work the streets."

Maliha smiled. "Thank you for your assistance. Would you be so kind as to direct the driver? I wouldn't want to get it wrong."

She climbed in and sat in the worn seats. The cab smelled of something rotting. In this heat anything dropped and organic would go off quickly. Amita sat beside her.

The doorman and the driver exchanged words. And they set off at a casual pace.

At first they travelled along the same streets as the ones by which they had arrived then the cab took a turn into an area with more shops. There were markets in the open down every side street. The crowds that filled the streets were white. The ones she glimpsed in the side streets were black and Indian.

It had been bad enough being in a school filled with prejudice. She tried to make sense of her thoughts, after all everyone in India had a caste marked, more often than not, by their skin colour. Her own caste, the Brahmin, were almost as white as the British.

So why did she find the prejudice here so abominable? She thought about the way the original doorman had spoken. There had been hate in his tone. She had experienced that in school. There were some girls that hated her for being different. Not all, it was true, and that would no doubt be true here. But even so, to hate someone based on such a thing. She sighed.

She paid the driver with British coinage and he gave her change in the local currency. She had no idea whether she had been cheated. She must check the exchange rates or simply find a bank where she could exchange some money.

They were in a wide square bordered on three sides by a variety of shops. The people here were more mixed—whites, Indians and even a few blacks. It was only a moment before they were surrounded by beggar children. As tourists they were bound to be a soft touch, though Amita was intimidating. She was taller than Maliha and could loom menacingly when she chose.

Since the day Amita had been kissed by Valentine and he had divined her true nature, Maliha noticed Amita was more careful about keeping her face smooth. But she could do little about her somewhat manly features and composition, which served well when she wanted to be intimidating.

Maliha looked at the children surrounding her. She was not especially moved by their plight. Beggars were just as common in India; they worked hard and made the money to live. This was as it should be. However on this occasion she needed information.

"Who speaks English?"

The boy's name was Izak and he was mixed race; his skin tone favoured the white side of his parentage while his bone structure was native African. He accepted their coin and they got some food for him from a street vendor selling something like a potato with a meat filling mixed in. Maliha decided to have one as well; she was hungry and she thought it might help in putting Izak at his ease. Amita found them a seat under a tree and produced a little case of eating utensils for travellers from her bag.

Maliha let him eat his way through half of the potato—he used his fingers—before she began her interrogation.

"Have you always lived here?"

"Suppose."

"Around Johannesburg."

He nodded.

"I'm looking for a girl." He glanced up at her and then back at his food. She knew what had gone through his mind.

"You know the street kids?"

"I'm their leader."

As they were talking the kids who had not been invited moved in, trying to hear what was being said.

"Really? How does that work?"

"I'm biggest and the strongest. They do what I say." Some of the crowd nodded. Others laughed, though quietly.

"Good. So do you know Riette?"

"No. There's no Riette here."

"The Riette I'm looking for isn't here."

"If you know she's not here why you asking?"

"She's dead."

He stopped eating and looked worried. He glanced around. The crowd moved back.

"Don't be foolish, Izak. We did not kill her."

Amita interrupted. "This is Maliha Anderson; she is the avatar of *Durga Maa*. She brings justice and revenge to murderers."

"I don't know what that means."

Some of the street kids were Indian in origin and at least one of them picked up the words *Durga Maa* and whispered it to the others.

"Hush, Amita," said Maliha. "I found the people who killed Riette and they have suffered for their crimes."

"So what you here for?"

"Do you know about the slavers?"

He shrugged and squashed the last of the potato into his mouth.

"Kids come and go," he said.

"Some get stolen away," said one of the bolder children. "They steal the young ones."

Maliha did not contradict. Considering what happened to Riette she could imagine that slavers would be interested in children of any age. However it was getting off the point.

She pulled out another coin and held it up. Izak's eyes followed it.

"Riette?"

"There was a Riette lived under the church," shouted the bold child, it was a girl of about eight. Izak frowned at her. "Am I talking to the wrong person, Izak?"

"No, I knew Riette." He snatched the coin.

"So tell me."

"What's to say?" He shrugged again. "She lived under the church. She was a good pickpocket and she never sold herself."

"She had a man!"

"Shut up, Lilith."

Maliha smiled inside, so much for being the leader, but she did not react and kept her eyes on Izak.

"A farmer. He came in to the city to buy supplies. She met him and helped him get good prices. Then she was gone. Never saw her again."

Maliha dug out another coin. She held it up.

"Can you speak Afrikaans, Izak?"

"Yes."

"All right. I need a guide and I might need a translator. Do you want the job?"

"I'll do it," shouted Lilith.

Izak stood up and frowned at Lilith. "I will do it."

Maliha smiled at him. "Very good."

She stood up. "We'll begin immediately. I need to buy a baby's rattle, where can I get one?"

* * *

They went to a tea room and while Izak waited, she and Amita went inside to have a more satisfactory lunch. Once they were refreshed, about an hour later, they returned to the street.

They found Izak a little further along the road. He was eating a vegetable she did not recognise, as was Lilith next to him. She appeared to be pure African, a little like a young Riette. She wore a plain wrap-around cloth that was very tattered and almost worn through.

"What we do now, goddess?" said Lilith.

"Don't call me that."

"Madhuri said *Durga Maa* is a goddess and you look like Madhuri. And she—" she glanced at Amita "—said you were that."

Maliha frowned at Amita. "I'm not. Call me Miss Maliha."

To forestall any further discussion Maliha opened her reticule and pulled out the single thing that Riette had owned; a wraparound like Lilith's. Only dyed in many colours.

"Is that your *kanga*? It's lovely," said Lilith.

"*Kanga*? Is that what it's called?"

Lilith nodded and finished off her food. For all his sternness it seemed Izak did care. About Lilith anyway. Perhaps they were related.

"Is this expensive?" Maliha asked.

Izak turned his nose up. "Just cotton, not expensive."

"We can't afford it," said Lilith looking down at her rag.

"Is there any way of knowing where it came from?"

"Shop," said Izak. Maliha sighed; perhaps Izak had not been such a good choice of guide.

"Mama Kosi will know," said Lilith. On the other hand his assistant was very useful.

"Can we find Mama Kosi?"

Izak looked at Lilith and then at Maliha. "It will cost."

"It always does."

The two children led the way through the afternoon streets. They left the crowds in the centre of the city behind, heading north with the sun in their eyes. Maliha was disoriented. They were south of the equator now and the sun was tilted slightly to the north in the middle of the day. It made her feel as if east and west had become swapped.

"Don't mention being a goddess, Amita."

"I am sorry, *sahiba*. I thought it would impress them."

"That's the problem."

The houses went from good quality brick and stone to ones constructed from corrugated iron, both walls and ceiling. It was like the shanty town beyond the walls of the Fortress, though not as crowded.

If there was an impression she got here, even though they had been in the country less than a day, it was that there was infinite space.

They finally reached a house made of wood coated with mud though it too had a corrugated iron roof. There was a white painted fence surrounding it. Chickens pecked at the ground and there were several goats tearing up what little grass remained.

They stopped at the gate. There was a battered cowbell nailed to the gate post and a piece of string dangling from it. Maliha leaned over the gate; there was a length of rusty metal lying on the ground on the inside. It had the remains of the twine looped and tied through one end. She surmised the goats had got at it.

The lack of a corset meant she was able to lean over the gate and pick up the metal stick. She passed it to Lilith who made a racket on the cow bell. Maliha placed her hand over Lilith's hand to stop her.

A young woman wearing only a *kanga* emerged from the opening that served as a front door and looked at them impassively for a few moments then gestured for them to enter.

"You go," said Izak. "You only."

vii

Valentine found a cab and headed back to the hotel. He had made no arrangements to meet up with Maliha but he was not concerned for her safety. This was not a murder investigation; she was just trying to find the child's grandparents.

He changed into rougher clothes, filled an overnight bag and then dropped in to see Barbara. She was sitting in an armchair by the window, an open book in her lap. She did not get up.

"Baby's asleep," she said. She saw the bag and gave him an appraising look. "Should I ask what you're planning to do?"

"Just trying to finish the job I started."

"Hmm," she said, not sounding very convinced. "Does Maliha know?"

"We discussed it."

"She would be upset if you got yourself hurt."

"It's difficult to tell sometimes."

Barbara looked at him askance. "When was the last time she kissed you, Mr Crier?"

He could feel the embarrassment climbing his cheeks. "This morning."

"Indeed. I don't think you have anything to worry about in regard to Maliha. I observed it was quite – how shall I put it? – enthusiastic?"

"You saw?" He was mortified. Maliha kept her distance most of the time but every now and then she would leap on him, as she had this morning, and her kisses were extremely passionate.

Barbara nodded in the direction of the mirror on the wall hanging from the picture rail by its chain.

"Oh."

"You should be more careful," she said then added with a stern look. "I never asked her how she came by her injuries in Pondicherry."

The change of tack caught him by surprise. He knew what she was talking about but feigned ignorance. "Injuries?"

"Her back."

Valentine froze with the guilt that washed through him. Every time they embraced he felt the ridged scars on her back. The scars he had put there. He still wasn't sure why she had demanded he do it. "Experience" was her only explanation. He had stopped having bad dreams.

"She hasn't told you?" It was a pointless question since the answer was obvious. "I am not sure she would want me to say."

"But you know?"

"I … yes, I do know."

Barbara pursed her lips. She was annoyed at being thwarted. "Very well, I shall ask her."

Valentine cringed inside. If she asked Maliha was sure to tell her the truth and then what would Barbara think of him? He remembered the promise she had forced from him about never hurting Maliha. He would not be entirely surprised if Barbara blew his brains out with her shotgun.

As if he didn't have enough to worry about.

He went to the crib to see the baby, then took his leave picking up his bag on the way out.

He took a taxi most of the way back to the air-dock but got out a quarter of a mile from it. Unlike Pondicherry, Johannesburg was a major port because of both its mineral and agricultural wealth so ships were coming in and out all of the time. As he approached the perimeter fence the *RMS Macedonia* lifted from the ground with a roar of its six huge rotors. Smoke poured from its twin stacks and steam leaked around the turbines.

It went straight up but after it reached a couple of hundred feet the front rotors swivelled a few degrees and it moved forward. It thundered overhead gathering speed. Despite its altitude he felt the wind of its passing.

There was no pause as a Zeppelin, probably from the German-controlled states in West Africa, floated in and cut power in selected parts of its Faraday grid, bringing it down steadily.

Valentine wished briefly that he had the *Alice* back. She had been difficult to fly but he loved it—and so did Maliha. However his fixed-wing diesel air-plane belonged to the person he had been in Ceylon, before he resigned. Perhaps if he earned enough he could buy another one. Maliha would like that.

He wiped the smile from his face as he approached the fence. The inside was patrolled by guards. He did not go to the main entrance. Instead he made his way around the fence to a much smaller crew gate.

He presented his air-sailor passport, licence and log book. They were genuine and declared him to be a licensed and trained crewman by the name of Jonathan Dyer. No special skills, just a deckhand experienced with a variety of vessels and their manifests.

After his name had been logged he went to the crew hotel that bordered the fence. It was a four-storey building within easy distance of the various company hangars. He signed in and paid a week in advance for a room then went up and deposited his gear. He spent some time giving the small room a lived-in look, and dumped some dirty clothes in a corner.

Back in the lobby he checked the employment board. It showed the expected incoming ships and those that would be heading out. It was arranged by day and each vessel had a card pinned in the appropriate slot.

One of Timmons' fleet had made port yesterday and was due out in two days. He had been over the manifests of all forty-three ships at one time or another, but he had not been aboard. These ships were of standard design—though a mix of sizes and types— none of them matched the one he had seen in India.

He made his way up to the roof. This was a common gathering place for crew, watching the ships go in and out because it gave an excellent view of the whole landing field.

There were half a dozen men there: two talking together, a group of three playing cards and Keighley sitting in his usual armchair, brought up for his use only, facing across the field.

Walking casually so as not to give the impression he specifically wanted to talk to Keighley, Valentine strolled across and stood a short distance from the old man. As far as Valentine knew Keighley had been flying almost from the start. He had even been into the

Void and told tales of the blue sprites and red mushrooms—great electrical storms in the upper atmosphere.

"People travel too fast now, they don't see the marvels."

Valentine looked across at the old man. Had he thought those words or had the old man said them out loud? Valentine wasn't sure. Keighley didn't look round so Valentine guessed he must have just thought it.

Keighley was missing his right leg from the knee down and three fingers of his right hand. He would tell you the story of how he came to lose them to pirates in the Asteroid Belt for a drink and a smoke. He was lying, of course; there might be pirates between Mars, Earth and Venus but since there were no ships further out, what would they prey on? And more importantly, how would they find them in the vastness of the Void?

"Haven't seen you in a while, Dyer," said Keighley.

"Hired aboard the *Macedonia*," replied Valentine.

"I heard there was trouble."

Valentine affected an air of embarrassment. "Yeah, not my fault." The *Macedonia*'s captain and senior staff were only too willing to assist in spreading the rumour of a deckhand who had tried to sell off cargo.

"Word's got about."

Valentine went to the rail and looked out across the sun-drenched air-dock. A big cargo Zeppelin was readying for take-off.

"Got a new position?" asked Keighley.

"Not yet."

"Going to be hard finding any regular line that'll take you."

"There'll be something," said Valentine unconvincingly.

"Want me to ask around?"

"If you like."

Maliha went through the gate and up the path. She kept an eye out for animal dung but the path was clean. As she approached the girl glanced into the shack and held her hand up for Maliha to stop. She came to a halt.

Moments later another black woman came out. She was crying and fled past them both and out through the gate. Maliha turned to watch her go.

"Come inside," ordered the girl and Maliha entered.

It was difficult to tell how old Mama Kosi was. The *kanga* she wore left her arms and shoulders bare and the skin of her face and neck was very wrinkled. Her skin was black as night which accentuated the whites of her eyes. Her hair was threaded with beads, as was that of the young girl who seemed to be her maid, or perhaps apprentice.

"Sit," said the girl. Maliha placed herself in the cushions opposite the old woman, facing her across a woven mat.

Mama Kosi looked at her, reached out and touched her face, ran her hand down her neck and felt her shoulder then down along her arm and took hold of her hand. Maliha was not upset or put off; there was plenty of magic in India, at least many who claimed it.

The old woman said something and the girl translated. "Do you know what I am?"

"Sangoma," said Maliha. The old woman grinned, she lacked teeth.

"And you are the goddess of India."

Maliha closed her eyes. One joke and now this.

"I am not a goddess. I am not the avatar of a goddess. I just want some help finding someone."

She waited while the girl translated and wondered whether she would know what an avatar was. The girl didn't ask so Maliha let it go. The old woman patted her hand.

"Mama Kosi will ask the ancestors to guide your future."

"Thank you."

She waited patiently while the old woman chanted and shook some bones. It was hot under the iron roof. The shack smelled of herbs and hot metal. The girl went to the side of the room and Maliha heard her pouring a liquid.

The girl returned with a wooden cup which she passed to Maliha. "Drink."

Maliha gave it a sniff; there were herbs that had quite a sharp tang in her nose and something else underlying it. She decided it would probably be better to drink it down in one go so took a deep breath and let it go down without tasting it.

"Good."

"What was in it?"

"This and that."

The old woman had ceased chanting and grinned again. "Throw the bones."

A bone divination, thought Maliha. Something for the tourists. The small bones were worn smooth with age. She cupped them in both hands and rattled them around then cast them into the space between them.

Mama Kosi leaned over them. She poked one with a stick as if she were trying to make it roll over but it seemed content enough in its current position. Mama Kosi grunted.

She jabbered in a very animated fashion; her assistant listened carefully and waited until she was finished. "Mama Kosi says you are blessed by the ancestors. She says they will give you the strength to bear the weight of the world. She says you must honour your husband. She says you must find the lost."

"Thank you," Maliha said directly to Mama Kosi. It was the usual meaningless nonsense. The fact that she was going to be married was obvious from the ring on her finger. If the old woman knew who she was she would know that bearing the weight of the world was something Maliha did every day. And finding lost things is what she was doing. It appeared to have great meaning, but it was sound that signified nothing.

Maliha stood up. She opened her reticule and pulled out the *kanga*. "I'm trying to find who made this. Can you help?"

Mama Kosi snatched it from her. She rubbed it against her face. Then threw it back at Maliha with a scream and spoke very fast. The girl looked concerned and ushered Maliha from the shack.

"Mama Kosi felt the pain in the *kanga*," she said by way of explanation.

"But who made it?" asked Maliha again. "Do you know?"

The girl hesitated then took the cloth. She opened it out. "From the pattern and colours I think it would be Lema Owusu."

"Where would I find them?"

The girl shrugged. "In the south of the city."

Maliha gave up. She had a name and that would have to do for now. She was about to go but she remembered the woman who had been in the shack before her.

"That woman who was here, what did she want?"

"Her baby was stolen in the night."

Maliha did not know how to respond to that. She said goodbye and headed out to where Amita waited with the children.

"Do you know where to go?" said Lilith brightly.

Maliha looked at her watch. It was mid-afternoon, she was tired, hot and dusty.

"Yes, I need to find Lema Owusu who probably made this *kanga*," she said heavily. "But not today. I'm going back to the hotel."

Amita looked relieved. They walked back towards the centre of town and eventually managed to locate a horse-drawn hansom. Maliha paid Izak and Lilith for their assistance and told them to come back to the hotel at ten o'clock the following morning.

It was around four o'clock when they got back. Maliha checked in on Barbara and the baby while Amita drew a bath for her. She held the baby for a little while. Little Baba looked at her with serious eyes and did not laugh until Maliha forced herself to smile. The baby responded with a great beaming grin that made Maliha laugh. And the baby giggled.

"She is good for you," observed Barbara. "You were always too serious."

Maliha sighed. "I know."

"You can't carry the weight of the world alone."

Maliha looked up at her trying to see what Barbara was trying to say, but the older woman was just looking at the baby.

Half an hour later Maliha sank herself into the bath while Amita bustled around the room and laid out clothes for the evening.

Maliha absently rubbed the scar tissue on her leg. Izak had said something about children disappearing. But then they were street kids, so that could not be unusual. It would happen all the time.

And then the woman whose child had been stolen away. That was not unheard of either. She might even have been lying, or deluding herself. She might have killed the child herself accidentally and then blocked the memory. Such things happened.

Or perhaps someone in Johannesburg was abducting children.

Could it be the slavers? That did not make much sense since children did not make good slaves. Except for abuse, of course. Then they were ideal because they could not fight back.

Maliha cursed herself. It was easy to think of things like that when you had no direct experience, but she had known what Riette had been through and she now had Riette's baby. Such thoughts had a terrible reality that brought genuine pain with them.

But that was what made her the person she was. She could see things and imagine things that other people could not—or would not.

She let her head sink beneath the water but the silence and calm did not aid her. There was no two ways about it. She must determine if these incidents were related, and whether they were part of a pattern.

She rose from the water just as she had from the cleansing river when the priest had called her the avatar of *Durga Maa*.

CHAPTER 2

i

Early the following morning the baby had woken Maliha and Amita. Although it was Amita who dealt with the necessary, and used the hotel telephone device to order some fresh milk. Once she was awake Maliha could not go back to sleep.

She held the unhappy Baba for a few minutes while Amita dressed. Baba required constant bouncing and being talked at otherwise she cried. A baby has very simple needs, thought Maliha, but they are also very single-minded. If something is wrong they won't stop telling you about it until it is dealt with.

Maliha was grateful when Amita had finished dressing and took the baby from her. Maliha collected her dressing gown, put it on and tied the sash around her. She went to the French window, drew back the curtain and opened it. She stepped out on to the metal balcony. They were six flights up but the height did not concern her.

She leaned on the rail and looked down into the street. It was not even six o'clock and the streets were already bustling. Mostly with black people carrying goods from one place to another. There had not been that number on the streets during the main part of the day.

The balcony stretched along the length of the building with gates between the rooms, but they were not locked. Maliha looked in the direction of Valentine's room. It did not take her more than a moment to make up her mind.

* * *

Valentine came awake to a light tapping that increased in volume to a solid thumping. He sat up and saw a shadow at the window to his bedroom. He slid open the drawer of the bedside table and took out his revolver. Automatically he checked it was loaded. He got out of bed and went carefully to the noisy person at the window.

It was not that he thought he was being burglarised—most burglars did not advertise their presence—but he had learnt to be careful. With the gun at the ready he moved the curtain a fraction and saw the top of Maliha's head. What could possibly have happened?

He went through into his lounge and opened the door to the balcony. Maliha hurried through.

"What's wrong?" he said, putting his head out to see if there was anyone else with her. When he turned back she was undoing the belt of her dressing gown. It was a pretty thing which had an interesting sheen in the dim light. It showed off her curves.

"Nothing is wrong."

She shrugged it off and let it fall to the floor. She stood before him, in the half-light, wearing nothing but a cotton nightgown that revealed her shoulders then hung loose to her ankles. Now that she no longer wore a belt her curves lacked any definition.

He had seen her naked before. On the first occasion he had been busy killing the man that had touched her. On the second she had insisted he whip her until she bled. Neither could be considered a pleasant memory. But in the days that had followed that event, while her back mended, she had worn nothing above her waist much of the time. He had remained a gentleman at all times—save for a few surreptitious glances.

"Perhaps you should put that down; we wouldn't want it to go off."

"What?"

"The gun."

He placed it on the table by the window. When he turned back the nightgown was going over her head. She struggled for a moment and he could see her body naked from the waist down. Then her chest was revealed but nothing more—though he was reasonably happy with just that view. She seemed to be having trouble.

"Damn," she said.

"Can I help?"

"I forgot about the bow at the back of the neck, Amita usually does that for me." Her voice emerged from the folds of cloth that hung round her head. Valentine felt his body take control of him. He didn't resist. He stepped up to her and placed his arms around her naked body.

"For heaven's sake, Valentine."

"Hush, you'll wake Barbara."

He ran his hands down her sides feeling her cool skin. For some reason simply touching her released tensions in him.

"I am stuck."

"I know."

"Oh, I see, now that I'm powerless you want to take advantage of me?"

He slid his arms round her. He tried not to think about the scars as he slid his hands up her back. He pressed himself close.

"I believe I will make you regret this," she said and flailed her trapped arms ineffectually.

He would have liked to bury his face in her neck but the nightgown was in the way. Instead he moved his hands up to the back of her neck and located the knot. He pulled back slightly and looked at her breasts. The gentleman in him considered that they were, in her present state, out of bounds. It really would be taking advantage. But he did kiss her skin where they began to rise from her ribcage.

"Stop it," she said quietly.

"Is that what you really want?"

She tutted. "I have come into your room and removed my clothing, Valentine. What do you think?"

He kissed her a little lower and she pushed herself towards him. Then pulled back. "But I really would like to be able to join in."

He had not been concentrating on his attempts to undo the bow and had succeeded in pulling it into a knot. "I don't think I can undo it from here," he said.

Maliha sighed. She wriggled again and the nightgown came down over her arms. He helped her put it back on properly. Her body was hidden again.

"This wasn't quite the way I planned it," she said. She put her hands behind her neck and fiddled with the knot. "I can't do it."

She turned round and presented her back to him. He admired the curve of her behind. She noticed the delay. "Could you try properly, please?"

He tried. It was pulled tight. "I'll get my penknife." He headed off into the bedroom.

"Then Amita will know," she called after him.

"Does that matter?"

He jumped when her arms snaked around his middle—she must have followed—and held him as he rummaged in a bag. "Now who's making things difficult?"

Then she giggled. Valentine was astonished. He had heard her laugh before, yes, once or twice. She never giggled. It made her sound as if she were a young girl. But then she was barely twenty. She *was* a young girl.

"Found it," he said and turned on the spot so that she would not need to let go of him.

She rested her head against his chest. He opened the pen-knife behind her back and sliced through the tie next to the impossible knot. He could feel her breasts pressed against him and he knew his lust was obvious. A strange idea took him and he cut through the seam in the neckline of the nightgown.

He dropped the knife, gripped the cloth and ripped it apart. It tore at least as far as her thighs. She drew her arms up to his chest pushing herself away.

"What have you done, you idiot!"

"Shhhhh."

She sighed heavily and allowed the torn nightgown to fall. She did not cover herself as every other woman he had known had done.

She put her head on one side and looked at him. "Do you want to hurt me again?"

He went cold inside. "I didn't want to hurt you the first time."

"That's not an answer, though, is it?"

She turned from him and walked slowly to the bed, inviting him to look at the whipping scars across her back. And her beautiful posterior.

She drew back the sheet of the bed and climbed in. Her feet were under the sheet but it hid no other part of her. The light through the curtains highlighted her curves.

"Do you want me to?" he asked.

"Now you're avoiding the question."

"So are you."

"What I want, Valentine, is for you to stop talking, remove your nightclothes and come into this bed with me."

"Are you sure?"

"Yes, I am," she said. "Quite sure."

"Why?"

"Experience."

She lay back. She put her arms around his neck as he bent over her and kissed her on her lips. She pulled him down until he was pressed against her. His back was bent and it felt very awkward.

"Just a moment," he said as pushed back against her arms. "I can't stay like that very long."

"Romance books have a lot to answer for," she said and giggled again. On second hearing he realised it wasn't so much the giggle of a girl, more one of a woman.

He settled himself on his side, pressed up against her. They both ignored the way his manliness lay between them, demanding attention. She leaned up and kissed him on the nose and then placed her hand on his chest. She played with the hairs and ran her nail across his nipple. He shivered

She smiled. "Is that pleasant?"

He nodded. She seemed so relaxed and he felt as if he were a furnace about to explode. The times he had played the fantasy of this moment through his mind. The reality did not resemble his dreams—except for the way her body looked. In his imaginings they had writhed in passion as he penetrated her. They did not talk.

"You haven't read any texts on sexual activity, have you?" she asked.

He did not trust himself to speak, so shook his head.

She stared into his eyes and the hint of a smile ghosted across her lips. "You shouldn't lie to me, Valentine."

"I have not read the sort of thing I imagine you're talking about." Then he added. "But you have?"

She nodded. "Sir Richard Burton's translations of the Song of Scheherazade, the works of Count De Sade, there was a French translation of the Kama Sutra, not to mention the mundane and utterly false texts by British doctors."

"I've seen some gentlemen's magazines, and there was a moving picture of a man and woman."

"Moving pornography? That's inventive." She got up on her elbow. "What was it like?"

He could feel the flush of embarrassment wash over him. He remembered how he had been transfixed at the sight. "Strange. I don't really think it's a sport for spectators."

She snorted. "Now you're being disingenuous. There are lewd shows in every city. And, I have no doubt, even worse ones in exclusive men's clubs."

"You're right."

"Have you ever seen a show like that with real people?"

For a second his mind flicked to what the guru had been doing with her, and what he had done to her with both Amita and Françoise present.

"No."

His ardour was gone. She had talked it out of him. He felt terrible and guilty, as if he had lured her to his bed for his own nefarious purposes.

She lay back on the bed and stared up at the ceiling. He looked at her body. There was a crease of a scar an inch long directly beneath her right breast. He had not noticed it before; even when she had been undressed. He reached out and ran his finger along it.

"When were you shot?"

She grabbed his hand. "Don't."

"Sorry."

"I don't want to talk about it."

He lay on his back next to her, their arms touching.

"I'm sorry," she said.

"What for?"

"Spoiling it."

"I don't mind."

"I'm nervous," she said.

"I find that hard to believe."

"Well, I am. This is not something a woman chooses to do lightly."

She rolled over towards him and propped up her head on her hand. She was touching him along the length of his body, from her toes against his lower leg to where her right breast rested on his chest and her thick black hair fell around his head. She ran her other hand across his chest.

He thought about how she had willingly given her body to the guru.

"It was different with the guru," she said as if she had been reading his mind. "That was an investigation. It was the only way I could get him to talk. He had to think I was in his power."

"You were."

"I knew you and the others were coming to my aid."

She didn't use the word "rescue" he noted. "What about Françoise?"

She sighed. "I don't know, I was lonely—I wanted you, Valentine."

"Having relations with another woman is a curious way of showing your desire for me."

"You weren't there."

"I'm here now."

She leaned over and kissed him. Then in a sudden movement rolled on top of him with her left leg between his knees. Her thigh pressed between his legs, awakening him, and he could feel her warmth on his thigh.

The passion that had drained from him came flooding back. He pulled her tight to him and kissed her with abandonment. Her tongue forced its way between his lips. He ran his hand down her back—no longer caring about the scars—and squeezed her behind.

His other hand pushed between their bodies and found her breast. He pressed his fingers into her. "Harder," she whispered into his mouth. He dug the nails of both hands into her skin. She uttered a quiet groan as she rubbed her hips against him, again and again—developing a slow powerful rhythm.

He couldn't take the passivity any longer, pushed her over on to her back and climbed between her legs. He concentrated on trying to locate himself to penetrate her then looked at her face. She had stopped moving and her eyes were wide. It took an effort of will not to thrust himself into her.

They stared into each other's eyes for a long moment.

"Do it," she whispered.

He wanted to. Every part of his body and mind was focused on that single act. But her words about not making the choice lightly came back to him. If he was wrong about this he would never be able to look her in the eye again.

"Are you sure?" he said in a voice taut as a steel wire.

"I want you to," she said. "I need you to."

He nodded. She smiled for him but he could still see the fear. It was as if there was something inside her screaming *don't hurt me*. But his lust was willing to take her at her word. Taking his time, he pressed into her. He felt her hot sheath encompass him; he went deeper until he was fully inside her.

She closed her eyes and breathed out. A tear formed in the corner of her right eye.

"Are you all right?" he asked.

She looked at him and smiled. She pulled up her legs and wrapped them around his back. "More please."

Maliha tied her dressing gown then picked up the tattered remains of her nightgown. She glanced through into the bedroom; Valentine was lying in bed watching her. He was smiling, but then so was she.

"I'm going to make you pay for this," she said brandishing the torn cloth at him.

"I look forward to it."

She tutted and went out through the French window and on to the balcony. The street below was much busier now. She had only intended to stay with Valentine an hour at most but it had ended up being thirty minutes longer.

She would have to teach him how to bring a woman to paroxysm. It wasn't that she had not enjoyed the experience. She had been nervous but once past that stage it had been very pleasant. The guru may have been a con-man and a criminal but he had also been extremely skilled in pleasuring women. Of course he had had considerable experience.

Maliha thought she would very happily teach Valentine those particular skills.

The curtain across Barbara's balcony door was pulled back and the door was open. Maliha hesitated and then walked boldly past in the hope that Barbara would not notice.

"Maliha, would you come in here please?"

It was like the worst possible farce. Maliha came back and went into Barbara's room.

Barbara glanced at her attire and the screwed up nightgown in her hand.

"Tea or coffee?"

"Coffee."

"Sit down, dear."

Maliha sat in one of the armchairs while Barbara poured the coffee and brought over a cup. Maliha took a sip and felt the invigorating effect course through her.

Barbara sat in the chair opposite.

"I am not a hypocrite, Maliha. I am not going to tell you not to do something that I did myself when I was young."

Maliha was aware of Barbara's early love affair, however she was surprised at how candid she was being: admitting to sexual congress out of wedlock.

"I just want to be sure it's what you want."

Maliha took another sip before responding. "I appreciate your concern. And I think that you would be the only person in the world I would obey if you told me I should desist."

Barbara acknowledged the compliment with a nod.

"I love Valentine," —though I know I have treated him very badly— "and this is through my own choice."

"Very well, my dear, if you say so," she hesitated. "But it would become very awkward if he got a child on you."

"I am taking appropriate precautions to prevent conception," said Maliha.

Barbara smiled. "Of course you are."

* * *

When Maliha had returned to her rooms Amita had not said anything about her being missing for over an hour, or her nightgown being ripped almost in two. She helped Maliha wash and dress. Maliha carried the baby through to Barbara's room for the family breakfast. Little Baba was fascinated by her new wooden rattle made of animal shapes on a ring which she alternately held up, and then chewed.

Breakfast was awkward. Valentine kept smiling at her. And Barbara was clearly suppressing her amusement.

"I was wondering if you would perform an errand for me," said Maliha to Barbara.

"As long as it does not involve a great deal of walking."

"Just sitting and reading."

"And what would I be reading?"

"Old newspapers," Maliha said carefully. "There is something I have heard about and I wanted to know whether it deserves further investigation."

Barbara buttered a slice of toast and added a thin layer of marmalade. "Would I be at the library or the newspaper office?"

"I think the library would be best."

"What am I looking for?"

"Missing children."

"I'm not sure I want to read about children being killed." Barbara glanced in the direction of Baba, lying on the floor surround by cushions.

"Not dead. Missing. Disappeared."

"And that is supposed to be better, Maliha?"

Maliha gave a wry smile. "Well, at least there won't be lurid descriptions of corpses."

Barbara sighed. "I'll see whether the hotel can procure us a perambulator."

Valentine frowned at Maliha. "You think children are being taken as slaves?" The tone of his voice suggested he thought it unlikely.

Maliha shook her head. "I don't know yet; I don't even know if it's really happening. It might just be a coincidence. Anyway I think these would be quite young, perhaps under eight? I'm not sure," she said. "That's why I want it looked into."

It was ten o'clock when Maliha and Valentine made their way downstairs to the lobby and stepped out into the open with the sun beating down and dust rising from the street. Amita had equipped

Maliha with a parasol that complemented her peach-coloured dress. She put it up as they stepped outside. Valentine had a hat to go with his suit.

"Do you think we'll be here long?" asked Valentine. "In Johannesburg, I mean."

"Difficult to say, why?"

"I was thinking of hiring a car. I quite fancy one of the Daimlers. What do you think?"

But Maliha wasn't listening; her attention was caught first by Izak and Lilith who must have been in an alleyway across the road waiting for Maliha to appear. But behind them, following them, was a black woman. She had a pronounced limp caused by her left foot being turned in, though she did not use a stick and she had no trouble keeping up with the children.

"Let's move from the front of the hotel," said Maliha. She went down the steps and along the road to meet the group of three.

She stopped with Valentine behind and the three approached. Lilith had the grin that apparently never left her face but Izak did not look pleased. The woman behind looked old at first glance but Maliha realised that her apparent age was a product of her unkempt appearance. The *kanga* wrapped around her body was bleached almost colourless by years of sunshine. It did not leave much of the woman's body to the imagination.

Maliha glanced at Valentine; he was not looking in the woman's direction. She turned her attention back to the African.

"You must be Riette's mother," said Maliha. The cold edge of her tone would have cut steel.

iv

"*You know my little Riette?*" She spoke in a wheedling and ingratiating mixture of English and what Maliha supposed was Afrikaans, which was originally Dutch and similar to German which at least made it vaguely familiar.

Maliha turned to Valentine. "Take the children up the road, will you?" He raised his eyebrows. "Get them something to eat and drink. I need to speak to this woman alone."

"Are you sure?"

She turned and looked him in the eye. "Trust me."

He nodded and stepped behind her letting his hand brush against her back. She appreciated it.

"Come along then," he said in a forced friendly tone. "Where can we get you some breakfast?"

Maliha watched them walk away, then turned her attention to this woman who claimed to be Riette's mother. She was not sure why she was devoting any time to her; it was irrelevant whether she was or wasn't.

"Come with me," commanded Maliha and led the way back to the alleyway the woman had emerged from. Maliha took a couple of steps inside so they had at least a modicum of privacy.

"You found my little girl?"

"Shut up."

The woman clamped her mouth shut as if she had been slapped and stared at Maliha with wide eyes. Maliha looked her up and down, knowing that there was a sneer on her face.

"What's your name?" Maliha demanded.

"Akua."

"What do you do, Akua?"

"Do? I am a poor woman, lady." Her tone was ingratiating. "I do what I can to make ends meet."

"Like give yourself to men for money."

"Oh no, I would never do that."

Maliha could feel the rage inside her and did not truly understand where it came from. "Don't lie to me. You're a prostitute."

A look of fear crossed the woman's face then the smile again.

"I do what I can, missy. A body has to live."

Maliha felt some of the anger dissipate. It was not untrue. Sell yourself or die? Would she do it? The answer came back without delay. No, she would not. She would find another solution.

"What can you tell me about Riette?"

"Such a lovely girl, so sweet. She looked just like me as she was growing up. I was heartbroken when she went away."

"You're lying again," said Maliha. "This is a waste of time. Riette wasn't living with you when she left. You kicked her out or she ran away."

"I didn't kick her out!" The woman was suddenly vehement—enough for Maliha to believe her.

"In which case, she ran away from you. Why would that be?"

The question made the woman hesitate and look away.

The anger in Maliha rekindled. "How young was she the first time you sold her to a man?"

"I never—" Her lie was interrupted by Maliha slapping her across the face.

"You can't do that. I'll get the crushers on you."

"You disgust me."

"I loved my little Riette."

"How old was she when she ran away?"

"Ten."

Maliha closed her eyes. To be touched by a man at such an age. It had been bad enough for her with the guru when she understood what she was doing. She remembered how lost she had been when she had been sent away to school.

"Did you ever speak to her again?"

Akua shook her head.

"You're a monster," said Maliha. "Why should I not simply have you arrested?"

"No one cares what happens to the blacks, missy."

Maliha sighed, it was probably true. If they had been in South Africa proper with British laws and justice it would matter. But not here.

"Riette is dead," Maliha said simply.

"Dead?" Akua sounded disbelieving. "My little Riette. My sweet little baby?"

Maliha found it hard to reconcile how the woman expressed her love for Riette as a baby and yet had permitted her to be so abused.

"Why do you care?"

"Tell me she did not suffer, missy. Tell me my baby died quick."

Maliha hesitated, she wanted to punish Akua and tell her how Riette had suffered months of torture before being tricked into committing suicide. And yet, what good would it do?

"She did suffer for a time," Maliha said finally. "She died in my arms."

"Was her last words of her mother?"

"No," Maliha said. There was a limit to how much she would pander to the woman's illusions. She considered asking about Marten, but she could expect nothing but lies on that subject.

"Do you know who Riette's father was?"

The woman brightened up. "He was a good man. He was a soldier and he loved me. He gave me my beautiful Riette."

"A soldier? So he was white?"

Akua was crying and made no attempt to wipe away the tears. "He was my love. He said he would marry me."

Maliha shook her head. Akua was not entirely right in the head. Maliha found she could not be angry any longer. Perhaps there had been a boy who claimed to love her, perhaps he had left her broken and with child. It did not matter.

There was nothing here that would help. She needed to track down Marten. She turned away, towards the street. Pedestrians and vehicles passed back and forth less than two yards away. It was like a different world to this woman and this alleyway.

"Did she leave anything for me?"

Maliha stopped and turned back. "What do you mean?"

"Did my baby leave me anything?"

"She had nothing."

"Izak said you had her *kanga*."

Maliha could see the avarice in the woman's eyes. The avarice that had driven her to sell her own daughter for sex, condemning her to a life of horrors.

The anger was back. Maliha wanted to beat Akua's head against the wall until she was senseless. "Riette owed you nothing."

She stormed away before she did something she would regret. No. There was nothing that she could have done that she would have regretted. But that would not make such actions right.

Maliha fumed as she stormed along the side of the street full of anger. She kept replaying the things that she had not done to Akua in her mind as if she could get some satisfaction from such imaginings.

She glanced up as she came to a road crossing and saw Valentine on the other side outside a shop; he seemed to be enjoying a pie along with Izak and Lilith.

Then she stopped and stared at him.

This was the man who had committed murder in his outraged anger at the abuse she had suffered. Maliha was not afraid of the truth. And in the moment of seeing him she realised the anger she had felt towards Akua was the same as his. She had been able to resist because Akua's crimes were past and gone.

For Valentine it had been different. The guru had been there, in the middle of his crime against her. Would she have acted any different if she had been there when Akua had prostituted her daughter?

The truth still flowed as anger in her veins.

v

Valentine glanced up and saw Maliha on the other side of the road staring at him. The expression on her face was not one with which he was familiar. He did not try to analyse it; he just smiled and waved.

She seemed to snap out of whatever reverie she had been in. She checked the traffic and crossed at the first opportunity.

Valentine swallowed the remains of the pie and brushed off his fingers.

He gave her a querying look. She shook her head.

"Did you learn anything useful?"

She frowned, which he thought odd since it did not seem a particularly difficult question. Then she smiled. "Yes and no."

"Which means what?"

"I learnt something, but it was not related to our current task," she said.

"Are you getting married?" asked Lilith to Maliha.

"Why do you ask?"

"You got a ring."

"Well, yes, I am."

"To *him*," said Izak, he seemed shocked.

"Yes, to Mr Crier."

"You can't."

"And why can I not marry Miss Anderson?" said Valentine.

"She's coloured and you're white."

"Well," said Valentine. "That will not be something to stop us."

"You better not tell anyone."

Maliha sighed. "Never mind that. If you are all fed let's be getting on. We have to find the maker of the *kanga*."

"Why?"

"To find out who he sold it to," said Maliha, "to find Riette's lover."

"Why don't we just go to the shop?" asked Izak, genuinely confused.

"By all means," said Maliha. "Let us go to a shop."

*   *   *

The shopkeeper had recognised the *kanga* and kept good records. They now knew that Marten's family name was Ouderkirk and he lived on a farm to the south of Johannesburg.

Valentine and Maliha arrived back at the hotel at half-past twelve. Barbara, Amita and the baby were not back. To preserve proprieties they ordered food in their rooms separately and then Valentine carried his along the balcony to Maliha's room and they ate together.

He sat back in his chair and sipped the wine. It was South African but certainly the equal of some of the French wines he had tasted. Maliha drank only water.

He noticed that she was not saying very much and was picking at her food.

"Is there something wrong?"

She did not respond.

"Maliha?"

When she looked up and into his eyes he could see her thoughts were distant.

"Riette's mother."

"What about her?"

Maliha paused again and looked down at her plate. She prodded the remains of a half-eaten Battenburg cake with her dessert fork. Valentine waited for her, though this was a Maliha he had never encountered before.

"I wanted to kill her." She looked back at him suddenly animated as if a dam had broken. "I wanted to dash her head against the wall, Valentine. She let men *touch* Riette when she was as young as Lilith. I don't understand it and I wanted to kill her."

"There are bad people in the world, my love."

"That's trite and meaningless, Valentine," she said. "She's not evil, she's broken and desperate."

She went back to breaking the cake into smaller and smaller pieces.

"Is there something else?"

"I…" she trailed off, took a deep breath and started again. "I owe you an apology."

He would have laughed; he could think of a dozen things she had said or done that demanded an apology—in his opinion. Which was this?

"What for?"

"My reaction when you killed the guru."

When you threw me out of your life for daring to protect your honour.

"I did not understand," she said.

"And now you do?"

"The way I felt towards Riette's mother, I understand that's what you felt about that man."

"Much worse."

"Yes." She nodded but still had not looked at him. "I imagine you felt much worse."

"But you had more self-control than I."

"What would have been the point? Riette is dead. Her mother is broken."

"And you would have got into trouble for killing someone in broad daylight, in a public place, for no apparent reason."

Keeping her head down she looked up at him. Coy. "It did cross my mind."

"Whereas I just dived straight in and killed a man." It felt like he was telling a joke but neither of them laughed.

Instead she reached across the table and took his hand. "Thank you."

"Thank you?"

She gave him her smile. "Thank you for caring enough."

Maliha frowned at a knock on the door. "I didn't order anything else."

Valentine jumped up and began to gather the parts of the meal that had come from his room.

"Stop it," said Maliha. "What are we? Children caught out of bounds?"

"The assumption will be that something we were doing involved being out of bounds."

She glared at him. "Just be out of sight over there."

He did as she asked and went to stand so he would be hidden when the door was opened. There was another knock; it possessed less conviction than the previous one and Maliha paused mid-stride.

Valentine started towards her but she held up her hand to stop him.

They waited and there was no further knock, but Maliha could see a shadow moving on the outside. The door handle turned and the door pushed open slowly as if it were pouring honey.

Maliha moved swiftly to the side and stood in front of Valentine. He put his hand on her shoulder. She shrugged it off.

The sound of distant laughing drifted through the open door from further down the corridor and a man dashed in. He turned to close the door and froze at the sight of them looking at him.

"Ray Jennings," hissed Maliha. She and Valentine stepped forward as one. Maliha pushed the door shut as Valentine once again slammed the rodent of a man against the wall, pressing his forearm into the man's neck.

Maliha stood with her back against the door.

"I'll shout for help, so help me I will," Ray almost choked.

"How angry are you feeling, Mr Crier?"

"Angry enough, Miss Anderson."

"Did you know, Ray?" Maliha said casually. "The last person who made Mr Crier angry died painfully."

Ray coughed. "Really?"

"Oh yes. You really wouldn't like Mr Crier when he's angry." She moved in on the two of them until she was close to his weasel face which was going red. "Nor me, and I'm not feeling very friendly at the moment either."

Ray did not seem to have anything further to say and, now that she thought about it, she couldn't recall the last time he took a proper breath. His eyes were beginning to glaze over. She looked at Valentine and came to the conclusion that he really was very angry and unlikely to let up the pressure on Jennings' neck in the near future.

A dead body in the hotel room, even that of a low-life like Ray Jennings, would be an inconvenience. She put her hand on Valentine's arm. "That's probably enough, Mr Crier. I believe Mr Jennings has got the point."

Valentine let him go and Jennings slumped to the floor.

"I hope you haven't killed him."

Jennings groaned.

"He's not dead," said Valentine in disgust.

"Put him on the sofa." Maliha went to the table and poured a glass of water. She turned back to see Valentine tossing Jennings into the cushions where he bounced once. He stared at Valentine in terror. Maliha handed Jennings the glass. Pain lanced across his face as he swallowed a mouthful. He sipped instead.

Valentine confronted her. "And you said we should leave him alone."

"I didn't expect him to start breaking and entering."

"I'll contact the British Consulate and have him shipped back to England. I know some people that can get him locked up permanently."

"That's not legal," croaked Jennings.

Valentine turned on him. "Oh no, Mr Jennings. It will be completely legal. A traitor like you can be locked up indefinitely or just hung."

"I'm not a traitor."

"You are if I say you are."

Jennings opened his mouth to utter some further bravado but no sound came out.

Maliha shook her head at Valentine then turned to Jennings. "Now you understand the potential risks perhaps you'd like to explain why you broke into my room."

vi

The perambulator supplied by the hotel was brand-new. Amita could smell the freshness of the wood and the mattress material. They had also supplied sheets and a pillow to go with it.

It had been delivered by one of the desk staff with a chambermaid pushing the pram itself. The design provided a rain and sun hood that concertinaed from the head end, and a rain sheet that clipped over the body.

Amita changed the baby's nappy and dressed her in a light dress. Too much heat was not good for babies. She prepared several bottles of water. Setting out with a baby was like organising army manoeuvres.

When Barbara had finished dealing with the staff and signing a note saying she was happy for the cost of the pram to be added to their bill, they set off. Amita felt like a nanny—then again that's effectively what she was. She spent more time looking after the baby than she did dealing with Maliha's needs, but then her mistress was significantly less demanding. And considerably more considerate. Amita quickly learnt that young babies are very selfish creatures.

But that was all right because little Baba was the sweetest thing she had ever met and when the baby smiled for Amita it made her melt with happiness. Their baby might need a lot of attention but she gave back so much.

They exited the hotel and the doorman assisted in getting the pram down the stairs. Baba was completely hidden from view so no doubt he could pretend to himself that she wasn't black.

Barbara had acquired instructions to the library from the desk.

"I really don't wish to spend hours reading old newspapers," said Barbara. She was using her stick and they progressed quite slowly. Amita was aware how much Barbara's health had degenerated in the time she had known her, and she was surprised Maliha had not commented on it. It was not like her to miss something like that.

"Do you?"

"No, *mem sahib*."

Barbara stopped in the street forcing other pedestrians to go around them. "Oh don't 'mem sahib' me, Amita," she said. "You have opinions, tell me what you think."

Amita briefly looked at Barbara before casting her eyes down again. "I think they will not let me or Baba into library." If Mrs Makepeace-Flynn did not want to be called *mem sahib* it was difficult to know what to call her.

"Which means it has to be me."

"Perhaps I find someone who will know?"

"I don't want to be walking around all day either."

"I understand library is often very cool, perhaps you could go inside and wait? You could ask people there and they may help you?"

"And you'll have the baby?"

"If that is acceptable."

"Don't see much of a choice." Barbara set off again at a slightly faster pace. "Maliha is a good girl but she can be so single-minded she forgets to take others into consideration."

"Yes, *mem sahib.*"

Barbara grunted.

Amita watched as Barbara climbed the library steps. Each one was clearly an effort after walking for nearly half an hour. She never complained about her physical condition, but perhaps that was because Amita was only a servant.

They had agreed to meet in two hours and Barbara had said that if she could not find anyone to talk to she would do as Maliha had asked and read some newspapers.

They had passed a sign for a park a short distance back, so Maliha turned the pram around after checking to make sure little Baba was all right. Her skin was cool enough and she was fast asleep.

The park looked pleasant with lots of trees and paths running between tall bushes with elegant flowerbeds scattered among them. It looked so artistic that it was clearly artificial. There was also a sign forbidding entry to blacks. If Barbara or Maliha had been there they would have insisted on her accompanying them. But by herself it was not worth the risk.

Instead she pushed the pram along the road that ran around the park's perimeter. The buildings were all new and built in an unfamiliar style. It was European of course, but not the British she was familiar with; they looked somehow wrong.

As the road rounded the far end of the park she saw a black woman pushing another pram and heading into the park. A segregated area no doubt. Amita followed and indeed there was a sign indicating that indentured blacks were allowed in this area.

Which meant that there were several women with their mistresses' children. Some pushing prams and others sitting rocking them with their hands or feet. Amita choose a younger looking girl sitting on her own in the shade of a huge tree with multiple trunks. It looked as if it had been there a long time and Amita guessed the park had been built around it.

The two of them sat side by side in silence for a while. Amita got out a bag of fruit. "Would you like apple?"

"No, thank you."

As they were in the shade Amita put down the hood of the pram. Baba was still fast asleep. The girl peered into the pram.

"I don't know if you can bring a black baby in here."

Amita laughed. "Sign said blacks allowed."

The girl smiled. "Where are you from?"

"Ceylon."

"Where's that?"

"India."

"Oh," the girl looked at Baba again. "Why have you got a black baby in such an expensive pram?"

"My mistress found her," said Amita then realised how bad that sounded. "By accident. Child's mother died. We find child's family." And in saying those words Amita felt a pang of sadness.

"Oh," said the girl. "I'm Zakiya."

"Amita."

"Who's your mistress?"

"Do you know Maliha Anderson?"

The girl shook her head.

"She is great investigator. When someone is murdered she will find killer and bring them to justice."

"Like police."

"Cleverer than police."

The baby in the girl's pram made little crying sounds. Not continuously but now and again as if trying to attract attention.

"Peter does that when he's bored." She leaned across and lifted the boy onto her knee. He was older than Baba and seemed very aware of his surroundings. When Zakiya smiled at him he giggled.

"He seems good child," said Amita. The girl nodded. "My mistress went to see Mama Kosi."

That got a reaction. The girl looked horrified and crossed herself. She looked as if she was going to leave.

"My mistress heard children are going missing."

The girl's fear intensified. "Why talk to me about it? I have done nothing."

"No," said Amita. "No one says you did anything. But you know about it?"

Peter cried and the girl bounced him on her knee until he laughed.

"Can you tell me anything about it?" asked Amita again.

"They say an evil animal spirit walks in the city. It is angry and at night it takes children away. No one knows what happens to them; they are just gone."

"How many?"

Zakiya shook her head. "No one knows. Always it is the poor families and no one knows. The police they do not care because it is the children of the poor blacks."

Amita stood up; she did not want to be late meeting Barbara back at the library.

"Can your mistress stop it happening?" asked Zakiya.

Amita took the brake off the pram and turned it. It bounced on its springs.

"My mistress is goddess of vengeance. She will stop it."

vii

Maliha stood over the little man. Back in England he had seemed bigger, and more dangerous. There he had been in his element with allies and the ability to run back to London if things got too hot for him. Here he was on his own.

Valentine had relieved him of his camera and placed it on the table.

"So, Ray, do you mind if I call you Ray?" she said.

He shook his head.

"What are you doing here?"

"Getting a story," he said.

"What story?"

"I reckon following you will always lead to a story."

"And did it?"

He glanced at his camera but said nothing. Valentine had been lounging against the wall in a way that implied he was not threatening but somehow managed to convey the precise opposite. Now he stood up straight.

"I really think you should answer my questions—truthfully."

"Yeah, I got some interesting pictures of you going along the balcony to his room and not coming back for over an hour."

"And where were you when that happened, Ray?"

"You're not denying it then!"

"Ray, where were you when you took those pictures? On the ground on the road opposite?"

He nodded.

"Six flights down," she said. "That's a long way for a little camera like that."

"If I say it was you doing the dirty with him," he nodded in Valentine's direction, "then that's what people will believe."

Maliha held up her hand to stop Valentine from hitting him.

"And is that what you want to be remembered for, Ray?"

He frowned. "What do you mean?"

"Wouldn't you prefer people to compare you with Winifred Churchill?"

"That cow? I don't think so."

"That cow who gets front page coverage, articles in *The Times*, and knows several members of the Royal family personally."

"Nothing special about that, she's got connections. She's a toff herself."

Maliha stood back, closed her eyes and sighed. How was it possible that someone could be so … stupid.

"Which would you prefer, Ray, a sleazy scandal story for some rag that everyone will forget and will do nothing for your future career, or something so big it'll make all of Winifred Churchill's stories look like reports about the village fete?"

She went to the window while her words sank in. No doubt it would take a while; he had probably never even considered the possibility that he might actually get to report on something significant.

Of course that did require this to be a major case. It was not certain how the British public might respond to another story about the Transvaal. The second Boer War was still fresh in everyone's mind, and Kitchener had done some very bad things to win. The British were still paying to get the Boer farmers back on their feet.

On the other hand, if she was right, this would be a story about women and children. That would always work.

"What story?"

She smiled.

* * *

Barbara pushed her way through the doors from the cool of the library's interior into the hot air and sunshine. It was as hot here as it could be at the Fortress, but the humidity was always high there. The heat here was a lot drier which made it more tolerable. Perhaps she should retire to Johannesburg.

She shook her head. She was already retired and all her friends were in Ceylon. She was too old to change now.

Amita was waiting at the side of the road with the baby. She saw Barbara coming out and hurried up the steps to assist her.

"Would you like me to get you a taxi, *mem sahib?*"

Barbara wanted to say no, it was such a short way to the hotel, less than half a mile. But the walk here had exhausted her and even with the rest she had had in the library she still felt weak. She nodded.

Amita looked at her with concern. "Are you well, *mem sahib?*"

"I'll be fine."

The first taxi driver had argued about taking the pram but Amita had simply hailed a second one while the first was still there on the kerb. The second driver was more amenable.

Amita helped Barbara inside, and took little Baba from the pram while the driver strapped it on the top of the steam-powered vehicle. The first man stood and watched. Barbara tried to moved forward to help Amita climb in but found her body was unresponsive. She felt as if she could not breathe; as if someone were sitting on her chest.

Pain shot through her back. "Amita…" she breathed making almost no sound. She felt pins and needles crawling up from her fingers digging into the muscles of her arm. Numbness seeped through her from her extremities to her heart and she could not move.

She heard Amita shouting at the driver through what seemed to be layers of cloth. She had the sensation that they were moving fast; she could not see properly and her eyes did not want to obey her. She worried about the baby and whether the pram would fall off the roof.

Then she got angry with herself; she couldn't afford to be ill.

They stopped and there was a bustle around her. She found herself being carried on a stretcher. She was not sure where they were. The lift was a blessed relief for a short time; something about being in the lift relieved her of some of the pressure. Though she still felt numb.

She could see Amita's dress and wondered why any man would want to be a woman. She had always found being a woman so very hard.

She was brought from the lift and the pressure returned. She got the impression they were in the hotel and not a hospital by the colours of the walls.

Maliha's voice drifted through the baffles in her ears. She sounded like she was crying. Barbara wanted to tell her to stop, that she would be right as rain in a day or two, but her mouth would not obey her.

She felt herself being manhandled again, and she was in a bed. Maliha sat beside her and had taken her hand. Barbara could barely feel it. She tried to say how much she loved Maliha but the words would not come.

The movement in the room ceased.

viii

"Can we afford all this?" asked Valentine.

He and Maliha stood at the side of the room watching the engineers connecting up the Faraday boards that had been placed under Barbara's bed. She had fallen asleep again after a few minutes of lucid wakefulness but she did not seem to be able to speak.

Valentine found it unnerving. He was sympathetic, of course; he liked Mrs Makepeace-Flynn very much. She had been a complete ogress when he first met her, but her months with Maliha had changed her. And now this. It was so difficult being around someone so ill they were completely incapacitated. It was hard to know what to do.

Now it had happened—a heart attack, the doctor had said, but not a serious one—it was easy to recall, with perfect hindsight, how she had been losing her strength over the past few months. But she always put on a brave face and kept going regardless. It was the British way.

Everything had turned backwards.

Amita had banged on Maliha's door and then walked in without any invitation, told them what was happening with a force he had never seen in her before.

Maliha had gone to pieces and looked as if she was going to collapse then dashed out into the hall to find Barbara. He had half-expected Amita to push little Baba into his arms and chase after her but instead she wanted to know who Ray was and then told him in no uncertain terms to get out and when Amita leaned over him, he did.

Then she turned on Valentine. "Go to Maliha, Valentine, she needs you. I take care of other things."

She used their Christian names, and somehow he did not mind. The world had gone topsy-turvy.

He had arrived as they were putting Barbara into her bed. She looked awful, like a ghost of herself. No longer the strong woman she had been but thin and drawn. Maliha sat holding her hand and crying.

Valentine stood by the window until the doctor arrived. He went outside during the examination but Maliha refused to leave. She wanted to know everything. Valentine thought that she probably knew it all already but, he was beginning understand, while Maliha knew more facts than he would ever know, she had no experience to hang them on.

That was why she did what she did. Why she put herself through things that no one else would even consider. She had to understand the reality.

He sighed and put his arm around her shoulders. The hotel was fully equipped with electric in every room but a Faraday required more power than was normally supplied. They were running a line all the way down to the generator room in the cellar.

The Faraday would reduce the strain on Barbara's body and aid the healing. So the doctor said.

"How can you ask if I can afford it?" she snapped. "It's Barbara."

"Because, my love, there will come a time when we have to pay the bill."

"I can afford it," she hissed.

She had spent the night with him. They had not made love. He held her and she cried a lot of the time.

It took another hour before they got everything hooked up and functioning. The men wouldn't switch the machine on until the doctor returned, which ended up being lunchtime.

The Faraday was engaged and Valentine saw an immediate improvement in Barbara's breathing. Or perhaps he was imagining it. The doctor had been monitoring her pulse during the switch on and after a short time he nodded to himself. He checked Barbara's breathing and frowned.

"Clear the room please."

Valentine gave Maliha a comforting hug. She probably regretted sniping at him because she reached up and squeezed his hand. He released her and followed the engineers from the room.

One of them gave him his business card. "Should be all right, but just in case."

Amita came out of Maliha's room with little Baba in her arms. "Mr Crier, we must discuss matters."

It seemed the new dominant Amita was not going away. He went after her and they sat at the table.

"I will discuss staff," she said without preamble.

"Staff?"

"The maid of Mrs Makepeace-Flynn not needed but nurse needed."

"That makes sense."

She nodded. "Little Baba also need a nurse now."

"What about you?"

"I am Miss Maliha's maid. She need me."

"Yes, all right. I suppose."

He was concerned that it would be a lot of messing about managing the staff.

"I manage staff," she said decisively.

He acquiesced. It seemed like a good plan.

"Very well," he said. "Anything else?"

She shook her head. "Not now. I will deal with these matters."

For which he was grateful; he had no experience with running any kind of household.

He knocked on the door to Barbara's room, taking care not to trip on the cable that snaked under the door and along the corridor to the stairwell.

Maliha opened the door. Her face was wet from crying again. Valentine went in and closed it behind him. She went back to the bed and sat. Barbara was asleep. Valentine didn't know what to say. He got a chair from the other room and sat near the window so he could look at Maliha.

"Amita says that black children from the poorest families are going missing regularly," she said.

"Do you really want to talk about this now?"

"What else is there to do?"

He had no answer. "Any idea who's doing it?"

"An evil spirit, apparently."

"I see."

She glanced over at him. "But I don't think it's slavers—although it wasn't clear the implication is that they disappear one at a time with a gap between."

He suddenly had a morbid thought which made him feel as if he had been around Maliha too long. "They are getting used up and replaced."

"Yes."

CHAPTER 3

i

Maliha had refused to leave Barbara's side. Valentine wondered whether it had something to do with her not being there when her parents died in the fire. Though if she had been she would be dead too. Everything about this place seemed depressing.

He had hired a horse-drawn cart, and not a machine, and was making his way to the Ouderkirk farm south of Johannesburg. He was under strict instructions not to mention the baby.

"These are Boer farmers, Valentine. They don't marry blacks and a child born out of wedlock—well, it just doesn't happen. Officially."

"I thought that was why we came here?"

She had sighed. "Yes, it was. And I thought that it would be a simple matter. Then we had trouble getting a baby into a hotel just because of its inheritance."

"So why am I going?"

"Completeness. And I thought you wanted to track down Timmons and Marten Ouderkirk is a possible lead. You need to follow it."

So here he was. Chasing down a possible lead, driving through the open countryside of the Transvaal. Cultivated grassland with cows and sheep roaming across. It could almost be England except for the trees. And the sun so high in the sky.

He had asked the last person he had met on the road: a man of about forty which meant he had probably fought against the British during the war. And been on the losing side. He had not been very forthcoming but said the Ouderkirk farm was about a mile further on. And that had been twenty minutes ago.

He reached an unmarked but well-used track lined by fencing in good repair. Why would you bother signposting a farm when everyone hereabouts knew who was who and where they lived?

He brought the cart round and followed the track through an orchard of mixed fruit trees and round a rise to the farm. There was a pack of sandy coloured dogs lying out under a tree in the middle of the loop for carts to turn at the front of the stone-and-brick built hut with the ubiquitous corrugated iron roof.

Parts of the building looked recent while the main chimney stack seemed older and had burn marks up the outside. Valentine sighed. The work of Kitchener and his scorched earth policy. The British had burnt everything to prevent the farms supplying the Boers with food.

He somehow doubted he would be very welcome but perhaps his news, such as it was, it would improve his welcome.

He climbed down from the cart. A few of the dogs glanced up at him but did not come to investigate. They were bigger than a Labrador but much leaner. One of them got to its feet and stretched; it was proportioned like a greyhound but with a lot more muscle. Fast and powerful. They must be hunting dogs of some sort. He noticed they each had a dark strip along the spine.

"If you don't bother them, they won't bother you."

Valentine turned. The man, somewhere in his late 40s, wore a sturdy leather coat over a checkered shirt and grey trousers tucked into solid boots. He had pushed back his coat to make it clear he had a gun.

"What breed are they?"

"Breed? Not a breed, they hunt lions."

Valentine glanced at them again, he could believe it. He turned back to the man; the way he stood made Valentine sure that walking up to him with his hand outstretched was not going to work. There was a movement at the window; they were being watched from inside as well.

"My name is Valentine Crier."

"Valentine Crier, is it? Interesting name."

"Are you Mr Ouderkirk?"

"I am Dirck Ouderkirk, Mr Crier," he said. "What does the British Government want this time?"

Valentine didn't bother denying it. "Do you have a son called Marten?"

There was a cry from inside the house. A woman in dowdy dress and a headscarf burst from the door. "Where is he? Where is Marten?"

The man put out his arm and she came to a stop at the bottom of the steps up to the front door. The look on her face was a combination of hope and fear. Valentine knew he was not going to satisfy either.

"That would be an answer for you, Mr Crier," said the farmer. "Yes, we have a son called Marten. What have you to tell us of him?"

"I will tell you all I know, which is not much," said Valentine. "But I would be grateful for some water perhaps."

The farmer seemed to deflate as if his bravado and strength were leached away. "Very well, Mr Crier. Marjit, prepare some tea for our guest."

Within a few minutes they were seated in a big kitchen. A picture of the Madonna and Child sat on one wall. There was a big cooking range and a huge table with ten chairs around it.

"You have other children?"

"Marten had four brothers before the war, Mr Crier, and four sisters. After the war he had three of each."

"I'm sorry."

"Everyone is sorry, Mr Crier," he said. "But sorry doesn't bring them back."

"No."

"Have you ever lost anyone, Mr Crier, anyone close?"

He thought of how Maliha had thrown him out, and Barbara lying like death. He knew what that felt like. "Yes." He wasn't going to give the man the righteous satisfaction he wanted.

From where she worked at the cooking range Marjit said quietly. "The loss of people we love is not a game to be won or lost."

She walked across the room and set a cup down in front of Valentine and one for her husband. Then she took a seat beside him, but stayed back as if she were only an observer.

The farmer glared at him. "Tell me what you know of my son, Mr Crier."

ii

"As I said, I don't know a great deal."

"Is he dead?" The words fell out of Marjit Ouderkirk as if she could not prevent them.

"I don't know," Valentine said. "It's difficult to explain."

"Be still, Marjit. Let him tell his tale."

Valentine took a deep breath. "Your son used to go into Johannesburg, is that right?"

"I knew it was a mistake, but he insisted," said the farmer. "It's a place of deep sin."

"He did meet a woman. As far as we can tell they were in love."

"Love is a word they use to hide the sin of lust."

"Yes, well," said Valentine. He could imagine how the man would view his relationship with Maliha. "And he just disappeared one night."

"He left a note saying he had gone to Australia with a woman," said the farmer.

"Australia?"

Marjit got up and went to a drawer. She took out a piece of paper, brought it back and handed it to Valentine. He tried to read it but it wasn't in English, but the word Australia was clear enough, as was the name Riette.

"Yes, the woman's name was Riette."

"Did they go to Australia?" asked Marjit.

Valentine shook his head. "No, I don't think so. The story about Australia was a lie created to trap people. Riette turned up in India as a slave and was murdered."

Marjit crossed herself to ward off the horror. Dirck's face was hard and fixed.

"And Marten?"

"We don't know," Valentine held his hand up to the question Marjit was about to ask. "I am certain he did not get taken to India. We were able to capture the slavers in India, and their records did not have Marten's name."

"So he may not be dead," said Marjit, her face lighting up with the hope he had seen earlier. Dirck's face remained expressionless.

"I am trying to track down who took them and perhaps where they were taken. Can you help?"

Dirck looked thoughtful then nodded. "I believe there is someone who may be able to help you."

Marjit looked at her husband in horror. "You knew something and you did not tell me?"

"Enough, woman, I did not tell you because I did not think it had value," he said. "But now it may."

"Anything you know could help."

"There is a man, lives in the town, he is a drunk. Before Marten disappeared this man claimed he would be taken to a far-off land where he would be king. Afterwards he spoke less and drank more."

"You think he might have been planning to take that trip and missed it?" said Valentine. "Can you tell me where I might find him?"

"I will take you, Mr Crier," said the farmer. "You will need me for translation and also protection. There is little love for you British in these parts."

* * *

Valentine drove the cart while Ouderkirk rode beside him.

"You fought in the war," said Valentine.

"You did not, or I think you would not ask."

"I have never been a soldier."

Ouderkirk looked out across the undulating landscape. "I fought in the war along with my three older sons."

"The Boers fought bravely."

"The soldiers are always brave," said the farmer. "It is the generals that keep themselves away from danger. And your generals that burned our lands and homes, and killed our wives and children."

Valentine knew he was referring to the concentration camps. The men were taken off to India, Australia and other places and most had a reasonably decent life of it. The women were put into camps in South Africa subject to disease and starvation. Thousands died. The only point in Britain's favour was the effort put into changing the situation when it was discovered. It had been Winifred Churchill who had written the news article that shocked Britain into action. But it had been too late for so many.

"If I could take back what happened," said Valentine.

"Everyone has regrets, Mr Crier, but judgement is for the Lord."

They went on in silence, passing farms and pastures. After fording a wide but shallow river they came up into a small town. Unlike the farm it did not look to have been burned down, but there were still scars from bullets and artillery in the wood and stone. Some had been painted over but their nature could not be hidden.

They passed through a block of residential buildings, mostly stone built with corrugated iron roofs. People stared at them as they passed, some nodded to Ouderkirk.

The market square was lined with shops—bakers, butchers, cobblers and more. Even a shop for women's clothes though Valentine was sure Marjit Ouderkirk, like most, had been wearing clothes she made herself.

They tied up the horses outside a public house and went inside. It smelled of tobacco and stale beer. It was clean but years of occasional spillages had seeped into the wood. It was a comforting smell as if every pub was, in some way, a reminder of home.

There were a few men drinking—a group of two, another of three—all talking in low voices. One man slumped at a corner table with a half-empty glass in front of him.

The smiling barman said something in Afrikaans. Ouderkirk responded in barely more than a growl and jerked his thumb at Valentine. The barman's face dropped and he stared at Valentine for a moment before finding a glass that needed cleaning.

The other men glanced up at Ouderkirk's words, watched Valentine for a moment then continued their conversations.

"Hey, Ten." Ouderkirk approached the man sitting on his own and swatted him around the head. The man groaned and said something in Afrikaans. It did not sound friendly. His face had the red and bloated look of someone who had long ago stopped worrying whether they drank too much.

"My friend here only speaks English, so you speak English." Ouderkirk turned to Valentine. "This is Ten Eyck Noecker. Ten Eyck this is Mr Valentine Crier."

"English? I'll kill the English."

"He can hear what you're saying, Ten. He wants to hear your story about being a king."

Ten Eyck Noecker looked up at Valentine and sneered. He picked up the half pint of beer in front of him and drank it down.

"Would you like a drink, Mr Noecker?" said Valentine.

"I will accept a drink from an Englishman."

Ouderkirk took the glass from his hand. "I will fetch the drink, but you are paying Mr Englishman. Why don't you and Ten get to know each other?"

Valentine sat down on a chair on the other side of the table and looked across at Noecker. His eyes focused then wandered vaguely before refocusing.

At one of the focused moments Valentine said. "Mr Ouderkirk said you were going to go away."

"The lies of Englishmen."

"What man?"

"Roberts. Captain Roberts he said his name was." Noecker leaned forward conspiratorially. "He didn't want to tell me about the colony, but I made him tell me."

"Colony?"

Noecker looked around then hissed "Australia" so loud that everyone in the bar could hear him. Valentine pretended he had whispered it.

"Australia?"

Noecker nodded. "Going to take me and some others."

"I thought you had missed it."

Noecker's face fell. "Missed it?" He seemed to be examining himself, his memories. "Missed it. I missed the boat."

Ouderkirk returned with a pint for Noecker. He hadn't bought anything for himself or Valentine. Noecker grabbed up the drink and swallowed noisily. Some of the beer escaped his mouth and wetted him down the front of his shirt.

"Why did they want you, Mr Noecker?"

"Always room for good men and women he said." Noecker had both fists wrapped around the glass and he clung to it. "Missed it. Couldn't find the place. Saw it go up though."

"What did it look like?" Valentine tried to hold back his excitement; if he was right he knew exactly what it would look like.

Noecker seemed to fade out.

"He's gone," said Ouderkirk.

"Like timber," said Noecker.

Valentine frowned. "Timber? What do you mean?"

"Like wood, square chopped short."

"I wasted your time, Mr Crier," said Ouderkirk. "Let's go."

"No, he's right, I've seen one as well. That's exactly what they look like." Valentine was delighted. There was one last thing. "Where did you have to go to take the ship?"

Noecker looked surprised, as if no one had asked before. "Eikenhof."

Valentine looked at Ouderkirk, he nodded. "Hill with trees, not many people."

iii

"Amita, I need you to find Ray Jennings."

Maliha sat at the table in the sitting room of Barbara's suite. The door to the bedroom was open and Maliha had moved the table so she could see Barbara on the bed. Lunch had come and gone. Valentine wouldn't be back until the evening at the earliest. It was possible he would be gone all night. She shivered at the thought. She did not want to spend the night alone.

Amita had not responded but nor had she moved. She looked as if she wanted to protest.

"Say what's on your mind."

"You do not like Jennings, *sahiba*."

Maliha could be wrong but there seemed a subtle change in Amita's demeanour. Though she was strong and had more than once used that strength to defend Maliha, she had always been almost mouse-like in temperament. Uncertain. She did not like to draw attention to herself because of what she was. But now she seemed to express more confidence, and a readiness to argue was apparently a symptom.

"No," said Maliha. "He is an appalling little man."

"And you want me to fetch him."

"I don't mind whether you bring him here or I can give you a message for him. There is something he can do; it will confirm my promise to make him part of something bigger if he doesn't use those pictures he has."

"I will take message. He should not be here with *mem sahib* so ill."

Maliha glanced in at Barbara. She barely moved but the doctor insisted she was mending. He had listened to her heart and was sure there was no permanent damage. Maliha knew how uncertain such a diagnosis was, but did not mention it.

"Very well, let me write a letter for you to take."

She spent twenty minutes composing her instructions. She appealed to his better side and asked for his help in determining when and where the black babies had disappeared. She explained that the locals thought it was an evil spirit. She contemplated mentioning her goddess aspect, he might get better information if he was working for a goddess, but decided not to. It would be something more he might use against her in the future. She did not trust him any further than she could throw him—under normal gravity—but he would act in his own self-interest so ensuring that his desires aligned with hers was all she needed.

Finally she gave Amita the address of Ray's hotel. It could be a bit awkward Amita turning up at a hotel to talk to a man but Ray was not likely to be in a very respectable place anyway. She trusted that Amita would be able to deal with any problems.

Amita had only been gone a few minutes when the telephone rang.

The bell made a considerable racket and she was concerned it might disturb Barbara. She jumped to her feet, crossed the floor and pulled open the twin doors. She lifted the earpiece from its mount which cut off the ringing. The mouthpiece horn protruded a little too high for her, and she had to stand on tip-toe. She located the earpiece correctly and said "Hullo".

"Miss Anderson?" The voice of the female operator had almost no trace of accent and was very clear if tinny, like on a phonograph.

"Yes, this is Miss Anderson." Maliha made sure she spoke clearly.

"There is a woman in the lobby who would like to speak with you."

"What is her name?"

"She says her name is Ulrika Putnam."

"I don't know her. Did she say what it was about?"

"She said it was about a baby."

"Send her up. I am in Barbara Makepeace-Flynn's room."

Maliha put the earpiece back without a goodbye. Then realised they already knew which room she was in from the telephone call. No matter.

She found herself quite excited; Ulrika Putnam must be white otherwise she would not be in the hotel. And about a baby.

She glanced around the room, it was all in good order, good enough to receive a visitor. The power cable across the floor looked odd but never mind. Maliha went into the bedroom and checked that Barbara was still breathing. She pulled the door to her room a little more closed when she came out.

The expected knock on the door came a few minutes later.

"Come in."

Ulrika Putnam was barely five feet high and at first glance looked no older than perhaps fifteen. But she carried herself with such an air of tiredness and despondency she seemed much older. She had pale skin and blond hair. Though small she walked with her shoulders hunched as if trying to hide her generous endowment. She had no wedding ring and was alone. Her clothes were of good quality and clean but had seen better days.

Maliha smiled. "Please take a seat, Miss Putnam."

The woman sat on the sofa indicated. Maliha took her seat at the table and glanced in to Barbara who had not moved.

"You are Miss Anderson?"

"I am."

"The investigator?"

Maliha would have become annoyed if she were not used to it. "Yes, I am she and I am barely twenty years old if that matters to you."

"Oh, no," she said quickly. "No, I was…"

"Expecting someone older. A spinster of a certain age."

The girl looked embarrassed and nodded.

"Miss Putnam. Your father is Afrikaans, and your mother is, what, Swedish?"

The woman looked wide-eyed and nodded again.

"You, however, are not married yet and found yourself with child. For which your father threw you out of the house. You have somewhere to stay but no money.

"You were told that if you got rid of the child you would be allowed back into the family and so you gave your child to someone who promised to look after it for a sum of, what, the equivalent of say ten pounds sterling per month, with some extra at the start. Which your mother has probably paid without your father's knowledge.

"You have provided the money in good faith but the promise of being able to see your child again has been denied you and now the person looking after your child has vanished. You have heard the great detective Maliha Anderson is in Johannesburg and you have come to ask me to find your child."

The girl burst into tears.

Maliha stole another glance into Barbara's bedroom. Her arm had moved, Maliha was certain of it. The delight of that was tempered by the certainty that Ulrika Putnam's child was probably dead; while some people did provide proper adoption the fact Ulrika had been denied access did not bode well. Still, it did provide an interesting possibility that had not occurred to her before.

The girl got control of herself. "How…?"

"You look like a Viking, have a Scandinavian Christian name but have a Dutch family name. You wear no wedding band but your breasts are heavy with milk and are, I imagine, causing you some discomfort."

"But how do you know about my family?"

"No magic. You have decent clothes but you've been wearing them for several months. So, no money and no home. The Dutch are sticklers for propriety and would not want the slightest shame attached to them so out you go. But your mother was not brought up in their tradition so she would not abandon you."

"But how did you know I was unable to see him?"

A boy. "Because you're here."

"No magic, then," Ulrika said. "Can you find my baby boy?"

Maliha sighed. "Are you sure you want me to?"

"Please."

"You might not want to know the truth."

"You are saying he might be dead."

"Yes."

"I want to know, and if he is then I will light a candle and mourn him."

"Very well."

Despite the obvious padding at the front of Ulrika's bodice Maliha saw a slight darkening where it was becoming wet.

"I may also be able to do something about your other problem."

"My other…oh." The poor girl looked mortified when she realised what was happening.

Maliha looked through to the bed again. Barbara's arm had definitely moved. She turned back to Ulrika who was heading for the door. "Wait, don't go that way."

The girl stopped, confused.

Maliha went to the door that led through to her suite. "Come along," she said.

Timid as a mouse Ulrika followed. The nurse was sitting on a straight-backed chair reading a book.

"This is Ulrika," Maliha said to her. "She will act as wet-nurse for the time being."

"The baby does not need a woman's milk, madam."

"No indeed, but I doubt she will object. More importantly, Ulrika has lost her baby and needs help."

The nurse understood and went into the bedroom to wake the baby. Maliha turned to Ulrika. The stains were bigger but there was one more matter to deal with. "Miss Putnam, I am sure you are a sensible young woman but I should probably tell you that Baba is not a white baby."

"She's yours?"

"Well, as to whether she is mine is perhaps a philosophical question, but no, I did not give birth to her. Little Barbara is black."

Ulrika hesitated. "Black?"

"Is that a problem for you?"

There was a pitiable cry from the other room. Maliha could almost see the natural reaction of a mother to rush to a child in need. Though even Maliha knew that was just a niggly little cry. No real upset.

Ulrika's nature was at war with her nurture. Nature won and she went through into the bedroom without another word as she fumbled with the cords that held her bodice.

iv

Amita found the hotel without any difficulty. It was towards the west, in the direction of the Klipspruit. The hotel's exterior looked as if it had once been ornate but it had taken a great deal of damage from guns and bullets.

There was no doorman. There was a clean and pressed suit behind the counter, unfortunately the man inside it was dirty and looked as if his thinning and greying hair had never been washed. He scratched himself.

"Ray Jennings," she said.

"Room three-ten."

"I know."

"You can go up."

"Send someone to fetch him."

There was a moment of reassessment: clean skin and hair, beautiful sari, perfect manicure. Not a prostitute, at least not one anyone staying here could afford. Amita loomed.

"I'll send someone to fetch him."

The someone was a cook who argued but was eventually persuaded. Amita stepped away from the counter and took in the dreary interior of the hotel lobby. Wood stained dark, black tiles, cream painted walls which seemed to be turning yellow. The intense smell of stale tobacco and other smells that Amita was familiar with from her previous existence.

This was the sort of place she had frequented in those days.

She heard the two men come stumbling out of the stairwell. There was a lift but it looked as if it was never used.

She turned to face Ray Jennings and was surprised to realise that even he looked better than this place. She held out the letter from Maliha which he took and read. Twice.

"She thinks she can figure something out from that?"

"My mistress is cleverer than everyone."

"And you're coming with me?"

"She thinks women make people talk more."

"Yeah," he said and glanced around at the clerk at the desk. Ray got closer to her. "But you ain't a woman, are ya?"

Without a moment's hesitation Amita punched him in the solar plexus. Ray dropped to the floor wheezing to catch his breath. The clerk stared.

"No insult … intended," squeaked Ray with his face in the dust.

* * *

Amita stood outside in the sun. It was the hottest part of the day and she found some shade against the wall of the building opposite. She disturbed a box and half a dozen rats ran for safer cover.

Ray finally emerged from the hotel with his camera and other gear. He squinted but apparently did not see her in the shade. She stepped forward into the light. He jumped then made his way across the road avoiding a bicycle that shot past.

Amita smiled pleasantly. "You are not better than me, Ray Jennings. But Miss Anderson is better than you or me."

Ray frowned then shrugged. "Whatever you say."

"Listen to me, Ray Jennings," she said, still smiling. "Miss Anderson is good person. She thinks if she help you then you leave her alone."

"Yeah, I know." He shifted the weight of the bag on his shoulder.

"But I know you, Ray Jennings. I know men like you. If you hurt my mistress I kill you."

"Kill me?"

"Dead." Amita put her head on one side. "You think I not do it?"

He appeared to be giving her comment serious consideration. "Yeah, all right. If I hurt her, you'll kill me."

Amita nodded and changed the subject. "Where do we go?"

"Well we need someone who actually knows something about the black kids going missing."

"Mama Kosi."

"Yeah? Who's she then?" Ray rummaged in his bag and pulled out a straw hat with a wide brim. It was crushed from being in the bag but he straightened it out until only parts of the brim drooped and then crammed it onto his head.

"She is Africa witch," said Amita and pulled a loop of her sari over her head.

"Great," said Ray. "You know which way to go?"

"This way," she said pointing down the street. "It is not far from here."

Amita set off with long strides that had Ray almost running to keep up. It amused her that the man was following the woman.

"So…" said Ray when he eventually caught up with her and came alongside. "Can I ask about you without you hitting me?"

"You ask, I decide."

"I mean, don't get me wrong, you make a good-looking woman but big," he said it cagily and kept his eyes on her as if he were ready to dodge if one of her arms came swinging out at him.

Amita said nothing. She had never been questioned like this before. Ray seemed genuinely curious and not disgusted. The people who did not know what she was treated her like a woman which was what she wanted. Those who found out fell into two groups. Those who accepted her, mostly the other *hijra*, but sometimes people like Maliha. Barbara and Valentine were aware but Amita knew they only tolerated her for Maliha's sake.

And there were the others who would stone her to death given the chance. Men, women, British or Indian it did not matter, they hated her for what she was. The women were the worst.

Now there was Ray. "You have question?"

"I dunno really, just interested," he said. "When did you realise you wanted to be a woman?"

"I do not know. Never asked."

Ray was quiet for a while as they laboured through the roasting streets. The buildings had shrunk into the small one and two room residencies Amita had seen before. The number of trees increased. She stopped under one of them. Ray was panting and sweating.

"I am sorry to go so fast."

Ray brought out a bottle of water from his bag, unscrewed the lid and drank. "Can't decide whether India is worse than here or the other way round." He paused gathering his breath. "Either way I'd be happier back in London."

"Your home is in London?"

Ray nodded. "Yeah, Limehouse. It's not a quality place but it's where I was born. Where I grew up."

"Where you want to die?"

Ray looked at her. "Something like that."

"I'll remember."

He took another drink. The door to the house opposite was open; most of the doors were open. These people had nothing to steal. There was a child of perhaps three years old standing in the doorway staring at them and sucking his thumb.

"So when did you know you wanted to be a woman?" he asked again.

She thought for a while. "I wanted to wear what my older sister wore. I wanted to be beautiful like her. I was six or seven years. I was beaten for putting on her sari."

"Well, you look all right." The compliment came out as an awkward grunt and he rushed the words but it sounded real.

"Thank you."

He jumped to his feet. "Better be getting on, this case won't solve itself and your Maliha's relying on us, right?"

"She is Miss Anderson to you," Amita said then looked up the street. "Mama Kosi is close."

v

Valentine and Ouderkirk reached a place where a gate led through a fence.

"This is the place," said the farmer.

It had been at least eight months since the ship had been here so they were not looking for any recent track marks.

They went through the gate and shut it behind them then continued on foot. There was no sign this area was being used for livestock but you could never be too sure. A short distance away there was a stand of trees.

They found a patch where the grass had not grown back fully and the ground was covered with the remains of ash and charred sticks.

"Watch out for snakes," said Ouderkirk as Valentine used his hands to push back the grass. "Some like the shade and others will bathe in the sun in the top of the long grass."

Valentine cast around until he found a fallen branch that was a good size and used that instead. Ouderkirk wandered further.

"Here's another, Crier," he shouted. Valentine followed him. Another fire as overgrown as the first; that might make them the same age.

They kept looking and located a further seven charred patches. At one they found a pewter spoon. Ouderkirk examined it; Valentine thought the handle was unnaturally splayed. "Local make," said the farmer.

"This is the place then," said Valentine to no one in particular.

The trees made a natural curve around the hill and the two together would ensure a large vessel could land and still be well hidden.

Valentine set off across the open space beyond the trees and up the hill using the branch he'd found as a walking stick. The slope was gentle and it was easy going but took him a good five minutes. Ouderkirk did not accompany him.

He reached the top of the hill. To the east was the road they had come along which continued north and crossed the river that was the northern border of this pasture. To the west the field went off into the distance until it was cut off by a fence. It was the same in the south. There were clumps of trees but no animals that he could see anywhere. Just some birds circling overhead.

He looked at the space between the hill and the river. If he was flying a ship as large as the one he had seen in India that's where they would land.

Was that a rectangular indentation? He wasn't sure. He was so eager to see some evidence that he was just as likely to imagine it. Ouderkirk did not know exactly what Valentine was looking for, perhaps if he could see it too, without being told what he was looking for.

Ouderkirk had been bent over and examining something in the long grass.

Valentine waved his stick and shouted. "Hey!"

The farmer glanced up and then stood up straight; he took a few halting steps in Valentine's direction and then pointed at him. He shouted and started running up the slope as if the hounds of hell were after him.

Behind Valentine something made a grunting noise in its throat. The direction seemed to come from somewhere near the ground. Valentine tensed and tightened his grip on the branch.

He heard fast padding of paws on the ground and threw himself to the side, rolling so he could see what was attacking him.

An animal shaped like a dog with short legs flew through the space where he had been. Its form was silhouetted against the sky so he could not make out any details but there was a hint of both stripes along its body and spots on the hindquarters.

Whatever it was had not considered the drop-off down the slope. It flew out and down hitting the ground hard and tumbling. Valentine scrambled to his feet still clinging to the branch. The animal was already moving towards him. The sound of a shot echoed across the hill.

Valentine hoped Ouderkirk was a good shot. The animal did not even flinch but accelerated fast and launched itself at him again. He swung the branch and caught it on the side of its body as he dodged again. It tried to turn in mid-air and snap at him. He felt the air move as it passed and its wiry fur brushed across the back of his hand.

If only it would give him enough time to get his gun. The creature stumbled on landing again, as if it were not entirely coordinated. It paused, panting. Valentine took the opportunity to reach for his holster and as he did so he saw the glint of sunlight reflecting off the barrel. It lay two yards away.

The creature slammed into his side knocking him down. He cursed his stupidity for getting distracted by the gun. He rolled away down the hill in the direction of his weapon. Pain shot through his ribs as he rolled over the gun and left it behind.

He caught a glimpse of Ouderkirk. He was not far now.

The animal was leaping again. Valentine rolled back and towards it, shortening the distance. As it went over him its paws brushed his arm. He grabbed up his gun, aimed and fired. There was a double report. The creature hit the ground and slumped into a pile of fur.

Valentine got up on his knees. The animal was pushing itself up again. It turned and started back at him again. Valentine fired second time, third, fourth. He could see it jerking as each bullet hit home. The blood splashed from it. It jerked as Ouderkirk's shots went into its body from the side.

Click. Click. Click.

Valentine stopped pulling the trigger of his empty gun. The strange animal staggered twice and finally collapsed to the ground. Its ragged breathing sounded twice more and then it went silent.

Before he got to his feet Valentine reloaded. He kept his gun trained on the animal as he climbed to his feet and brushed some of the dirt from his clothes. Ouderkirk approached, he was panting hard.

They approached the animal lying there. Blood leaked slowly from the ten wounds that Valentine could count. Its eyes were still wide open, and they were uniform black.

"Hyena," said Ouderkirk. "Probably rabid." He looked with concern at Valentine. "He did not bite you?"

"I don't think so, no, I'm sure it didn't." He poked it with the branch. "Really didn't want to die."

"It was sick, dying, maddened with the rabies." Ouderkirk shook his head. "Good thing it didn't bite you or I'd shoot you now."

"It definitely didn't bite me," said Valentine. "You can check."

Ouderkirk did. And declared him free of rabid hyena bites.

"So have you seen enough, Mr Crier?"

"Just one thing more," said Valentine. "Look at the space between the river and where the hill starts. Can you see anything?"

"What am I looking for?"

"No clues. I want to know that I'm not imagining it."

Ouderkirk shaded his eyes against the sun and stared down into the valley. He turned his head from side to side looking up and down the length. Then paused. "I see a rectangle in the grass."

"How big?"

"Bigger than a church."

Valentine smiled and set off down the hill towards the river.

"Is that what you wanted me to say?"

vi

Maliha came back into Barbara's rooms and went through into the bedroom. Barbara's arm was back where it started: lying flat beside her. Maliha wondered for a moment whether she had imagined it, but no, she recalled the previous positions with complete clarity.

There was a curious effect when one approached an active Faraday device: the sensation of one's skin being brushed lightly. She imagined it was the transition into lower gravity crossing the nerves.

She sat on the edge of the bed. Her body and head received the full effect of lightness while her legs extended out of the field and had their true weight. She wrapped Barbara's left hand in hers. It felt cold but not overly so. It was strange how affected she was by the woman's illness. The possibility that she might lose her solid friendship had torn at her heart the same way the death of her parents had.

"I believe I have made you into my mother." She spoke the words out loud and as she did so Barbara's eyelids fluttered.

A surge of hope and excitement went through Maliha. "Barbara? Can you hear me?"

There was a long moment during which nothing happened, then Barbara's eyes opened. "Thank god," breathed Maliha.

But her hope was strained. Barbara's eyes were open but she did not focus nor look in Maliha's direction, but her eyes did not close. The words of two dozen medical texts were poised in Maliha's mind crammed with words that did not describe what she was seeing. Save one: the one that described the paralysis that could follow a heart attack.

Maliha squeezed Barbara's hand. "Can you hear me?"
Nothing.
"Can you close your eyes?"

There was a pause and Barbara's eyelids slid down and covered her eyes. Then, almost as if it was an effort akin to lifting a bucket of water, they opened again. Maliha felt as if she were breaking with the twin forces of joy and despair. Joy because Barbara was conscious; despair because all she could do was blink.

But it was communication and it was a beginning. Maliha thought quickly what would be the best way to utilise this limited system.

"Barbara, I understand that you can hear and understand what I am saying. I will speak to you and ask questions. If the answer is yes, or you agree, I want you to close your eyes and open them. If not, just do nothing. I will wait a short time to allow you to blink if you want to," she spoke clearly and slowly so that there would be no misunderstanding. "Do you understand?"

Again the pause, then Barbara blinked. Maliha wanted to laugh, shout and even perhaps dance. Instead she found her eyes filling with tears.

She realised she needed to continue the conversation.

"Good. I am so happy you are awake. I'm crying." She lifted Barbara's hand and touched it to her the wetness on her cheek. "Can you feel it?"

Yes.

"Are you hungry?"

Yes.

"I don't know what would be appropriate for you to eat. I will have to send for the doctor."

Barbara's hand jerked. Maliha stared at it and then at Barbara's half-shut eyes still staring at the ceiling.

"Did you move your arm intentionally?"

Yes.

"You want me to stay."

Yes.

"Can you see?"

Yes.

"And you're just looking at the ceiling. That must be very boring."

Maliha stood up. The gravity change made movement very awkward and caused strange sensations in her insides. She ignored it. Carefully she lifted Barbara into a sitting position—the Faraday device made that quite easy—then arranged the pillow in such a way as to support Barbara's back. Finally she lifted the older woman back into the pillows.

Barbara's head kept falling forwards and Maliha was concerned she would overbalance and fall. In the end she re-organised the pillows so Barbara was lying back but propped up. Finally she fetched a cushion from the lounge and put it behind Barbara's head, then sat beside her again, holding her hand.

"Is that better?"

Yes.

"You didn't want me to go."

No response.

"You want me to stay?"

Yes.

Maliha had been deliberately ignoring the investigation even though she wanted desperately to know whether Barbara had discovered anything. But it could take such a long time learning anything of value if all they had was a silly guessing game. There had to be something better.

There was.

"I am going to fetch some things that will help you communicate," then as an afterthought, "and someone who can work with you."

Yes.

"I'll be back soon."

Maliha flew from the room as if there was a devil on her tail and rushed back to her rooms. Ulrika was in the bedroom holding the baby with the nurse beside her. Little Baba looked as if she was going to explode. Eruptions from either end were always quite unpleasant.

"I have another task for you, Ulrika. Can you read and write?"

"Yes, Miss Anderson."

"Good. Come with me."

Ulrika stood and lifted the baby on to her hip.

"Leave the baby."

They went through into the sitting area and Maliha utilised the telephone. It was not so difficult if one imagined the person at the other end was beside you. She spent several minutes explaining what she wanted, having to repeat herself twice to be sure the operator understood the message to pass on.

Then she led the perplexed Ulrika to Barbara's bedroom.

Ulrika stared at the helpless woman.

"Stand where she can see you." Ulrika moved to the end of the bed. She was not tall and was easily in Barbara's field of view.

"This is Ulrika. She is helping with little Barbara for now and she is going to help you talk to us."

There was a knock at the outer door. Maliha glanced at Ulrika as if she were about to order her to go to the door but then seemed to think better of it.

"Come and sit here." Maliha stood up and moved through the Faraday field. "No, on second thoughts, come with me."

It was one of the male staff laden with an easel, board, some twine and chalks in a tin. Maliha took the chalks and board, leaving the easel to Ulrika.

A few minutes later they had the blackboard on the easel at the end of the bed.

"Write the letters of the alphabet in a grid six along and four down with the last two making a final line on their own. Make sure the lines and columns are neat and large so they can be read easily. Use the twine to make straight lines across and down the board."

Leaving Ulrika to the task she went back to Barbara. "With this you will be able to say what you want."

Barbara's arm twitched and her eyes closed. *Yes.*

Maliha smiled. Ulrika seemed competent though very sad. At least she no longer seemed to be in pain.

For someone who dislikes people so much, you do seem to collect them. The voice in her head was Barbara's. Maliha squeezed Barbara's hand as if she really had spoken. "It's not that I dislike people," she said. "It's just that they can be so terribly dense."

There was nothing to see when he reached the rectangular depression in the ground. The terrain was dry but the edges of the hole had weathered. Even so the depth of the indentation was a good six inches. He could barely comprehend the weight of the vehicle that could do that. Even with the Faraday device, designers of flying vessels tried to keep them as light as possible.

That's not to say that a vessel like the *RMS Macedonia* was not heavy; it was thirty-five thousand tons, but compared the power of its rotors it was comparatively light. But he had seen one of these machines floating silently across the sky in India with no apparent means of achieving buoyancy or propulsion.

He could not accept the possibility that slavers had achieved the complete nullification of gravity. Only the British had that technology. Though it was only a matter of time before it was stolen or duplicated, of course, but Rutherford and Tesla's inventions were the property of the Crown and no one else.

But what did that leave? A more powerful form of the Faraday device? Scientists and inventors had been refining it for all the years since its discovery. The maximum had been reached twenty years ago; no one had been able to better it in all that time.

But the truth stared him in the face. The slavers had either complete nullification or something close to it. He should report it but, for some reason, he was reluctant to do so. At least not yet, he told himself, he needed proof.

"Tell me about hyenas," he said abruptly to Ouderkirk.

"They hunt in packs like dogs," said the farmer. "And they are very dangerous."

"They attack men?"

Ouderkirk shrugged. "They stay clear of men but there are stories of them taking children. Maybe a man if there is a drought and their prey is scarce."

"And one on its own?"

"They only hunt together. One on its own must be diseased. As I said, rabid." Ouderkirk paused, then: "Why?"

"Nothing really," said Valentine. "It just seems like a strange coincidence that it should be here where the ship landed."

Ouderkirk gave a snort of derision. "How can it be a coincidence if they are months apart?"

"You're right." Valentine sighed. "Would that be the farm that this land belongs to?" he pointed at the buildings in the distance.

"I expect so; I don't know the families in this area."

"I'd like to talk to them."

Ouderkirk looked for a moment as if he would refuse. "Will it help you find Marten?"

"I don't know," said Valentine. "But it might."

"We should get the horses."

* * *

The ride to the farm took them across the river and then along its banks until they reached another bridge back across it.

Ouderkirk brought his horse to a standstill before crossing the bridge. Valentine came up behind him in the cart and stopped. In the middle of the track leading up to the farm buildings was a pile of clothes with bleached-white bones protruding from them.

Without a word passing between them both men checked their guns. Ouderkirk stood up in his stirrups and scanned the area. Valentine brought the cart round, got down and tied the horse. Ouderkirk stayed in the saddle. Valentine glanced up at Ouderkirk, who nodded.

Valentine moved across the flat bridge. It was a primitive affair of planks without any rail. The farmer kept pace a short distance behind; Valentine trusted he would provide warning of any attack.

He approached the bones and their shape became clearer. "Lord above," he muttered. The bones comprised a human skull and a hand reaching forward. It was a child—a boy from the clothes—who could only have been nine or ten.

"Was it animal or man?" asked Ouderkirk. His voice sounded hard.

Valentine bent down to examine the bones and the clothes. He did not want to touch them; it felt like sacrilege. One of the arms was completely missing with a leg and foot a short distance away. What remained the clothing looked ripped in places. He did not want to touch it but, with his gloved hand, he turned the skull gently. It was complete.

"Animal, I think."

"That is a blessing."

"Is it better to be shot than mauled to death in terror?" said Valentine.

Ouderkirk grunted. "Animals are honest, Mr Crier. Men are devious. If we found the man that did this we might hesitate and be corrupted by their speech."

"I somehow doubt you would, Mr Ouderkirk."

"My son is probably dead for a dream that failed."

Valentine stood up and turned to him. "Is that a reason not to dream?"

"I do not think the world has benefited from the dreams of men," he said. "I prefer to live by the dreams of God."

Valentine changed the subject. "Do you think the rabid hyena did this?"

Ouderkirk dismounted and, keeping hold of the reins, knelt down beside the skeleton to examine the marks. "Looks like teeth marks, could be the right size. But hyenas will eat carrion before they'll hunt. Something else might have brought him down."

"How long would it take for a skeleton to get picked clean like this?"

"Perhaps two months."

"How long could an animal be rabid before it died?"

"A few days, maybe." They both stood up and scanned the area again. Nothing moved.

"It can't have anything to do with the slavers then." Valentine looked ahead towards the farm. "I suppose we should check the rest of the buildings."

Ouderkirk tied up his horse with the cart and they went ahead on foot. Without speaking of it they chose to check the barn and stables first. They crept forward, weapons ready, a short distance from one another. The stable doors were wide and they checked each one.

The long-dead remains for four horses were reduced to bare bone. Not even the flies and insects had any further interest. In the main barn there was what had probably been a milk cow.

That left the farm building itself.

The main door was wide. The interior dark.

Valentine was fairly sure that whatever had done this was long gone. But there was still the nagging fear that something nasty would leap out at him from the shadows.

He and Ouderkirk stood at the steps leading up to the door. All was quiet except for the constant buzz of insects.

"You first, Mr Crier."

Valentine got a firm grip on his gun, climbed the steps—cringing when one of them creaked—and passed through to the black interior.

Light filtered through dusty and curtained windows. His eyes adjusted to the lower light levels and he frowned at a tangled pile in the middle of the main room. It slowly differentiated into bodies, animal and human.

"Hyenas?" said Ouderkirk at his shoulder. "How can it be?"

Six of them. Two directly in front of them, their fur still intact but drawn tight across their bones. There were four more further into the room, lying amid a confusion of human clothes. He could see three detached and eyeless skulls around the room.

A search of the rest of the house found women in an upstairs bedroom. The door had been barricaded but broken in. They too were now nothing more than clothes and bone.

Ouderkirk crossed himself again.

Valentine suddenly felt sick. He ran from the room and down the stairs. He managed to get outside before his stomach emptied its contents on to the ground.

When Ouderkirk emerged moments later Valentine could see he was not unaffected; his face was pale and his hands trembled on the gun.

They did not speak as they headed back past the child that had escaped only to be chased down. They said nothing to one another during the entire journey back to Ouderkirk's farm, arriving as the sun went down.

viii

"This is how it will work," said Maliha to Barbara and Ulrika. "Ulrika, you will take your chalk and move it from one row of letters to the next. You wait at each one and look at Barbara, if she does not blink after a short time, move to the next row. Do you understand?"

Ulrika nodded.

"When you know what row to use you will move your chalk from one letter to the next pausing after each one waiting for Barbara to blink again. Which she will do when you reach the letter she wants.”

Maliha paused, it was hard to contain herself. She had so many questions she wanted to ask Barbara but she had to start from the beginning and take it slowly. She settled herself. Little Baba was asleep, while Amita and Valentine were making their enquiries. Everything that could be done was being done.

She turned to Barbara and held her hand. “Did you discover anything of interest at the library?”

There was a long pause then a blink. Maliha’s heart leapt but she schooled herself to calm. “Good.” Then she hesitated; she knew she could walk all over other people’s feelings and concerns. Barbara could have died and now all Maliha wanted to know was what she had discovered. “Do you want to rest?”

There was no blink.

“Are you sure you want to do this now?”

Yes.

“All right,” Maliha took a deep breath to control herself. “I will leave you and Ulrika alone. You tell her what you discovered but if you get tired you must rest.”

No response.

Maliha lifted Barbara’s hand and held it to her cheek. “Barbara, I don’t want to lose you. If you get tired, you must rest.”

Yes.

Maliha gave her hand a final squeeze and kissed the old woman on her cheek. She stood and went to the door. She looked back at Ulrika whose eyes were full of fear.

“You’ll be fine, just write down what she says,” said Maliha. “I’ll be back in an hour or so.”

* * *

The lift operator pulled shut the metal concertina doors and pressed the button for the ground floor. Maliha watched the floors drift upwards past them and felt guilty. She should not have left Barbara alone with Ulrika; after all what did she know about the girl?

That she was hurt and lost. That she was abandoned and hopeless. That she would cling to anything that gave her hope of seeing her child again.

And leaving Barbara? Maliha had not realised what a strain it was dealing with someone who was so limited in their ability to communicate. What would it be like if her reason had gone as well? Maliha shook her head; there was no merit in thinking about it. As far as could be determined Barbara's mental state was not impaired, only her physical ability.

According to everything Maliha had read it should be possible for Barbara to recover that ability, or at least most of it. She could easily live for another ten or twenty years. Especially if Maliha saw to it that she was in a Faraday for all that time.

Everything would be all right.

The lift operator pulled back the gates with a crash and Maliha stepped out almost automatically, adjusting to the increased gravity outside the lift space.

She crossed the foyer towards the exit and unfurled her parasol ready to erect it outside.

"Miss Anderson?"

She turned at the call. Rising from one of the armchairs was a man with an untidy mop of thick blond hair and similarly coloured facial hair cut into a Van Dyke. He was not tall but well built and not unpleasing to look at.

"What can I do for you, detective?"

He did not deny it and if he was surprised at her identification of his profession he did not show it.

"Miss Anderson, I would like a private discussion if possible?"

"You have the advantage of me, detective…"

"Chief Detective Karel Vandenhoek."

"I was about to take a walk, Chief Detective Vandenhoek. You may accompany me, if you wish."

He acknowledged with a nod of his head and followed her out through the front doors. The doorman closed it behind them. Maliha snapped the parasol into position.

Across the road she noticed Izak and Lilith. They had started to move forward when she came out but retreated when they saw the man with her. Maliha angled the parasol so that he could not see her head and brought her finger to her lips. Izak grabbed Lilith by the shoulders and walked away.

"What do you think of our city, Miss Anderson?"

"It certainly has the character of the Dutch."

"And what character is that, do you think?"

"Dedicated, pious and dogged."

"You are saying that the buildings are uninspiring."

"That would be impolite."

"I'm afraid it would be the truth," he said. "We have been here a long time and are not part of the Dutch empire. Most of the original settlers wanted nothing more to do with them."

"I am familiar with persecution," she said.

She had no particular goal in mind so headed towards the market in the centre of the city. They reached a main road and she allowed him to take her elbow and guide her across safely.

The streets were filled with vehicles and pedestrians but it was almost as if they had a personal escort clearing the way because no one ever seemed to obstruct them. Maliha could see the sidelong glances and recognised the prejudice in them.

"What did you want to talk to me about?"

"It is a delicate matter."

"Too delicate for you to come right out and say it? Must I guess?"

They turned into the main square and crossed the tram lines to the tree under which she had stood yesterday with the beggar children.

"You have a black baby in the hotel."

"Yes, I do. She is my ward."

"Is that correct?"

Maliha felt herself grow hot with anger. She did not need this to add to her difficulties. "Yes, Chief Detective Vandenhoek, I delivered her from her mother's womb with my own hands and the mother died. I am responsible for her."

"But she's black."

"Would you allow an innocent to die just because it had a different skin colour?"

He said nothing. There was a space around them that no one entered. She glanced around, not a single one of the beggars was visible across the square. Did they really fear the police that much? It seemed that perhaps they did.

"Is that all?" she said. "Or are you going to order me to throw her out of the window?"

"There has been a complaint."

"From whom?"

"One of the other residents of the hotel," he said. "The hotel management do not feel they are able to deal with the situation."

Maliha wanted to scream at him—and then realised it was unlike herself, why was she like this?

"So," she said acidly. "Let me see if I understand this correctly: there is some bigoted fool staying in the hotel who feels that the mere presence of a *baby* in the hotel in some fashion taints them and they cannot bear it? And as a result a complaint has been made to the *police?*"

She looked at him but he was scanning the market, as if seeking out crime, so she changed the subject to the one she had an interest in. "Are you aware that babies are being kidnapped?"

He laughed. "You heard about the devil stealing babies? The blacks are very superstitious, like children, Miss Anderson. Most likely the babies are dying or being killed by their own parents or kin and they cover it up by claiming an evil spirit stole them away."

"So you've never investigated?"

"No, Miss Anderson, we don't chase fairy tales."

"And if it was happening to white babies?"

He became serious and looked her in the eye. "Nothing like that is happening to white children. Nothing."

"Would you mind escorting me back to the hotel, Chief Detective?"

She did not wait for his reply but left the shade of the tree and headed back out of the market. She had crossed the tram lines and was on the other side of the road before he caught up.

"You people don't understand what it's like here, Miss Anderson," he said in a tone tinged with anger.

"What people am I? Do you mean coloured people like me?"

"Foreigners," he said. "You did not have to live through the oppression of the British."

She turned on him, ignoring the fact they were in public. "I have had to live with the bigotry of the British all my life. Have you noticed the colour of my skin? Of course you have. Well, I have had to deal with the same kind of prejudice from the British that you dole out to the native Africans. So do not for one second try to elicit any sympathy from me for the *plight* of your complainant because," she took a breath, "I have none whatsoever."

She turned and left him behind.

CHAPTER 4

i

Amita thought it looked like a field of tents. They had driven to Klipspruit in a horse-drawn cab. None of the white owners of steam taxicabs would bring them.

"Place stinks," said Ray.

The main road west out of Johannesburg had brought them to this settlement for blacks. According to Nkechi, Mama Kosi's assistant, they had been moved out of the city over the past five years. Neither Amita nor Ray had asked why because the answer was already clear.

The new homes looked like triangular army tents but constructed of brick and the ever-present corrugated iron. There was a door at each end and one window in each side. Hundreds of them stood in regimented rows, looking as if they went on forever.

"What is that bloody smell?" said Ray again as he jumped from the carriage to the dusty road.

Nkechi turned to him. "Sewage."

"Don't your lot know how to stay clean?" said Ray.

Amita thought that if he had addressed her in such a way she would have flattened him again. But if he had learnt his lesson with her, it was not something he felt the need to apply to anyone else.

Nkechi, however, did not rise to his obnoxious behaviour. "It is not our sewage, Mr Jennings. It is the white sewage of Johannesburg."

"They stuck you next to their shit-hole?" he said.

"Yes."

"Don't know how you stood for it. And these places, Christ, London slums are better than this."

"Is that the truth?" Amita asked with genuine curiosity.

Ray paused. "Well, some of them."

Nkechi led the way down one of the paths between the brick tents. Women and children watched them pass. It was as if they moved in a bubble of silence. Amita could hear talking and children playing in the distance, beyond their sight, but wherever they moved the residents were silent and watchful. Even Nkechi did not acknowledge anyone.

"I don't think they like us much here," said Ray. He was walking at the rear behind Amita who followed Nkechi.

Amita smiled at him and, knowing what she wanted to say, made an effort with her English. "You are as popular here as you are anywhere."

"Oh, very funny, yeah? Ha-ha."

"Do you have family, Ray?"

"Not really, no."

"Either you have family or not."

"Yeah, well, got a couple of aunts and uncles. No one close."

"No wife?"

"No." Then he sneered. "You?"

Amita smiled. "I have Miss Anderson, Mr Crier, the *mem sahib*, and little Baba."

"You're just a servant."

"Yes," she said. "But I have home."

"Yeah, all right, got your point." Ray stopped talking.

For all that Nkechi had said the smell was from the sewage farm—she could see some taller buildings a few hundred yards away to the east, back towards the city—parts of the path were raised on planks above pools of human waste. The streams were not flowing in the direction of the sewage farm. They were not flowing at all. The air was thick with flies.

Fifteen minutes later they emerged on the other side of the field of homes. It was slightly up hill which meant that these houses—if you could use the term—were in an advantageous position.

They moved along the line of front doors until Nkechi stopped in front of one and knocked against the door frame. Ray got out his camera and took three photographs, checking the little window that showed the counter every time he wound on the film.

There was a fast and incomprehensible exchange between Nkechi and what sounded like a woman inside. Finally Nkechi turned to them. "We are invited inside."

Amita had to duck as she went through. The interior was very dark and it took a few moments for her eyes to adjust. There was no furniture, just bare earth and a curtain made of a threadbare carpet. A woman sat on the floor opposite. She wore an old but colourful *kanga* but was otherwise bare. She looked to be in her forties.

"Can I take a picture of her?" Ray asked Nkechi. "She's not going to think I'm stealing her soul and try to kill me?"

Nkechi turned her gaze on him and did not even smile. "No, Mr Jennings, she knows what a camera is." She nodded at a line of photographs attached to the underside of the ceiling-wall.

"All right," he said. "Smile." The woman did not but he snapped anyway. "Probably not enough light," he muttered.

Nkechi and Amita sat down, cross-legged. Ray followed them to the ground but sat half sideways with his legs out. He pulled out a note pad.

"What questions do you want to ask?" said Nkechi. "I will translate."

"Biographical details first," he said. "Name, age, that sort of thing."

Amita only half-listened as Ray asked his questions and they went to and fro between Nkechi, the woman—who was the grandmother of the missing child—and Ray. He seemed to know his business once he was doing it. Although he lacked the insight of her mistress.

The story was that, during the night a few weeks before, the child had simply disappeared from the house. There had been no alarm, no one had woken when the child had been taken from their midst, although in the morning they had all felt sick and had fevered heads. No one in any neighbouring house had heard anything. This meant it had to be an evil spirit.

Once they had finished Ray had offered some money which the woman had refused. Once they were outside Nkechi took the money instead. "I will ensure the family receive benefit from it. They will not accept it from you."

Amita was surprised when Ray looked at her for confirmation. She nodded so he handed it over.

The next house was one row in from the front. The story was the same. Every story was the same. And every house that had lost a child was located near the northern border of the camp.

After interviewing the fourth Ray called a halt. "Nothing new coming up here; they've had so long to talk about it, if there was anything important they've forgotten it."

Amita found herself surprised again. "How do you know?"

Ray shrugged and looked across the open land towards great mechanical cranes steaming away in the distance, marking one of the mines. "Always the same. It's why the police like to keep witnesses apart; if they talk to each other they end up saying the same thing even if it's not true."

They headed back to where the cab waited for them across the mire of the black town as the sun tilted towards the horizon.

"Christ, I'm hungry," said Ray.

Maliha leaned over the end of the cot. Baba lay asleep on her back. Her spindly limbs splayed out awkwardly and her head on the side. It was too hot for a cover, even a sheet, so she lay there in nothing but her linen nappy.

The sun was going down. Maliha did not want to go back into Barbara's room because she was still angry with the stupid policeman. Were the hotel staff so afraid of her they were not willing to speak with her directly? Was it because she was Indian? It must be difficult for them to reconcile their attitudes when she travelled with so many white people. Good.

Little Baba moved spasmodically and stirred in her sleep. She looked as if she might have woken herself up, as she sometimes did, but then settled again. Maliha breathed out long and hard. Watching the baby was therapeutic. It was not possible to remain angry looking at a sleeping child.

Baba put her thumb in her mouth and sucked. Maliha glanced across at her bed and wished Valentine had come back. If only it were that easy to find comfort for an adult. She needed Valentine to hold her. She wondered when she had become this insecure and uncertain, but knew immediately that she had been like this from the time her parents had sent her away to school. The only difference now was that she had someone to whom she could reveal her weakness in safety.

She went to the open French window. She did not step out on to the balcony but stayed in the shade and let the gentle breeze cool her skin. The nurse returned and sat with the child. Maliha went through the connecting passage and into Barbara's suite.

"She is asleep, Miss Anderson," said Ulrika who stood as Maliha entered the bedroom. "Some men came to check the machine."

Maliha panicked and dashed to the bed. She waved her hand over the bed and felt the comforting weightlessness.

"Did I do something wrong?" Ulrika asked in a worried tone, taking a few steps towards Maliha with her hands clasped in front of her.

"No," Maliha said sharply. The girl flinched. "No, nothing wrong at all. I am overwrought." *Which is a first*, she thought. "I think you should sleep in my bed tonight."

"I would be all right on sofa or even the floor."

Maliha shook her head. "No, Mr Crier probably won't be returning tonight. I will sleep in his bed. It's better if you're near the baby in case she gets hungry."

"Thank you."

And it means I can pretend I am close to him. Maliha shook herself. What's wrong with me? I'm behaving like … ordinary people.

She recognised the irony of such a statement. "Did Mrs Makepeace-Flynn manage to tell you anything before she became too tired?"

Ulrika perked up. "Yes, I wrote it down." She went to the end of the bed and produced a note pad.

"The system worked then."

"It was slow, but we managed. She can move her arm as well."

Maliha nodded absently as she took the pad; it was not one she recognised. "Where did this come from?"

"I asked the nurse to find it so I could write everything down. She said it would be charged to your account."

"Yes that's fine."

The letters had been written out in capitals as they were spelt out. Some of them seemed blurred as if they had been wet.

WHITE MOTHER KILLED CHILD GONE HUSBAND GAOL TWO WEEKS

A smile crossed Maliha's face. She knew the detective had lied when he said nothing was happening to the children of white families.

"Do you know anything about this story?"

Ulrika shook her head and wiped the back of her hand across her eyes as if she was going to cry. Maliha was about to plunge on and then realised.

"I'm sorry," she said, frustrated at not being able to ask her questions; everything here was so awkward. "Have you had anything to eat?"

She shook her head again as if she did not trust herself to speak.

Maliha went to the telephone and ordered food for six. She turned back to Ulrika who stood in the middle of the room with one arm wrapped across the front of her body, her hand grasping the elbow of her other arm.

"When will you look for my Henry?" she said quietly.

Maliha closed her eyes. "Sit down, Ulrika." When she opened her eyes the girl was still standing. "There." Maliha pointed to the sofa near the main door. "Sit there." She did as she was instructed.

Maliha went to the table and turned one of the hard-backed chairs to face her.

Ulrika rubbed her hands together and did not look at Maliha. "Henry is dead, isn't he? That's why you're not looking for him."

Yes, I would be very surprised if he were not dead, Maliha thought to herself but instead she said. "It doesn't work like that, Ulrika. I have to have information which will give me clues as to where to look."

"You haven't asked me anything."

Maliha sighed. "No."

"You want to know about dead black babies and dead white babies but you don't want to know about my Henry!" She sobbed, at first trying to hold it in and suppress it, then she could not hold it in any longer. The crying poured from her as if her heart was being slowly torn in two.

When little Baba cried Maliha could barely prevent herself from running to comfort her. Ulrika was no different now. Maliha crossed the room and sat down with her arm around her, wondering when she had become someone who cared how other people were feeling.

The girl was still crying when there was a firm knock on the door. There was a polite pause and the door handle turned. Maliha hoped it was Valentine but she knew he would never have attempted to enter without an invitation.

Amita poked her head around the door. She took in the scene and stepped in but kept a firm hold of the door.

"You will wait outside," she said through the doorway.

"Why?" came Ray's plaintive voice.

Amita shut the door without responding. "I do not like that man very much," she said to no one in particular. She pulled the hood of sari cloth from her hair and sat down on the other side of the girl and gave Maliha a questioning glance.

"This is Ulrika," Maliha said over Ulrika's bowed head. "She has asked me to find her baby son."

Amita nodded.

"And she will be staying with us."

"Where will she sleep?" asked Amita.

"In my bed tonight."

Amita frowned.

"I will be sleeping in Valentine's bed."

Amita's frown lightened only slightly.

"He hasn't returned."

Amita nodded. "Ray says he is very hungry."

"He can wait," Maliha said without emotion. "Was your trip successful?"

"I do not know," said Amita. "We spoke to women who have had their children stolen but Ray says their words cannot be trusted."

She looked up as the faint cry of an awakening baby filtered through from the neighbouring bedroom.

"All right, I'll talk to him later."

Ulrika lifted her head, her eyes were red from crying. "She wants feeding."

Maliha stood up and held Ulrika's hand to help her up, Amita stood as well. "Amita will you take Ulrika through to Baba? She is feeding her."

Maliha was not sure whether Amita fully understood her meaning but it did not matter. She would soon enough.

Maliha sighed. There were so many things going on at once, it was almost like being caught in a whirlwind as she tried to grasp at wind-blown straws. She glanced in at Barbara—she was still asleep—then went to the door and flung it open. There were two trolleys of food outside and no serving staff. Ray was helping himself to some cold chicken.

"Bring those in," she said and went back inside making no move to assist.

iii

When Amita returned Maliha had her take food through to the nurse and Ulrika before serving the rest.

They sat around the table eating the impromptu meal. Ray's manners could do with improving; she was not impressed with the way he reached across the table and took sips of water to wash down his half-masticated mouthfuls.

Maliha noticed how he and Amita kept up a dance of glances: Amita would look at him then his eyes would turn towards her and she would look away. Then after a while he would direct his attention to the food and she would look back at him. Or the other way around. All the while the aura of animosity between them was almost palpable.

Not her problem. At least it was not a problem she wanted. They could sort it out between them whatever it was.

They cleared the plates. Ray had certainly had the lion's share and he finally sat back satiated.

"Thanks for that, missus," he said. "Really hit the spot."

His London accent meant that the final hard consonants of his words were so quiet they were mutated into some sort of vowel sound.

"Very timely 'n all."

"Shall we get down to business, Mr Jennings?"

Ray reached into his jacket pocket. "Mind if I smoke."

"Yes."

Ray continued to pull out his cigarette case and clicked it open.

"Yes, I mind."

He gave her a sideways look then slid it back into his pocket and sighed.

"Did you find out anything useful?"

"Nothing I can put in a newspaper," he said. "What if I go and smoke at the window? Would that suit, your majesty?"

"Yes, Mr Jennings, if you really must have a cigarette you can do it at the window."

He touched his forehead in mocking acknowledgement, then stood and went to the window. He pulled out the stainless steel case a second time and extracted a cigarette. With a match from a box he took from another pocket, he lit up, shook the match so it went out and tossed it over the balcony. He took a long drag on the cigarette, held the smoke in his lungs for a long time and then blew the smoke into the open air.

"Better now?" asked Maliha not hiding the antagonism in her voice.

"Yeah, much better."

"What did you discover about the missing children?"

He gave a smile. "An evil spirit comes in the night, casts a spell over the whole house and takes the kid."

"What form does this spell take?"

He grinned and pointed at her with his cigarette. "I knew you was clever."

She waited while he took another drag on the cigarette. The end glowed bright as the air was drawn across the burning embers. He had already consumed half its length.

"Yes, Mr Jennings, many people know that I am clever. I can't say it's much of a revelation." His grin was quite infuriating.

"You tell me," he said.

"What?"

"You tell me, do your party trick."

She glowered at him. Why not. He had said what she needed to hear. "The family know nothing and wake up in the morning feeling ill."

"Ha!" he shouted.

"Quiet, you idiot," she hissed. Ray put his hand over his mouth as if stifling any further noise. He was laughing. She glanced into Barbara's room. The light was fading but Maliha could see her well enough. Her eyes were closed.

"Come on," he said. "What else?"

"All the buildings from which the children had been taken were close to the edge of whatever encampment you were in."

"You're a right bloody genius, that's what you are." He took a final pull on his cigarette and tossed it over the side. "Dunno what ya needed me for."

"Details," she said. "I need a map of the area with the stolen children marked. If you managed to find out when the children went missing that would be useful."

He came back to the table and glanced into the bedroom.

"What's wrong wiv her?" he asked.

"She's old."

"That's the one that was married to the General, ain't she? Him that killed himself on the liner—the shirt-lifter."

She slapped him. And then looked at her hand and at his face as if she could not quite believe she had done it. The response had surprised her as much as it had him.

"Christ," he said, rubbing his cheek. "What is it about you bloody women? First Meeta then you."

"Amita hit you?"

"Bloody right she did, and she hits a lot bloody harder than you," he said. "But then he would, wouldn't he?"

Maliha found that she wanted to beat Ray Jennings to a bloody pulp. Her body became tense and strained with the effort of not doing so. The intent of murder must have been in her eyes because he took a step back and held up a hand defensively.

"Look, I don't bloody care, all right?" he said, now holding up both hands.

Which just made her suspicious but it was simpler to let it drop.

"Did you manage to elicit anything else useful from the families concerned?"

"They live in a shit-hole."

"Must you use that language?"

He shrugged. "I'm telling it like it is. It's next to a sewer works and got no sewers of its own." He took a breath. "What would you call it?"

She frowned. "A sewer works?"

"Yeah."

She paused. "All right, Mr Jennings. I think that will be all for today. Do you think you can arrange a map with dates and times by tomorrow morning?"

"Yeah, prob'ly."

"Ten o'clock?"

"Whatever you like." He hesitated as if he was not sure how to take his leave, then touched his forehead but this time without the supercilious attitude. She nodded back to him. He went past her to the door and opened it.

"Look, Miss Anderson," he said. She waited expectantly. "Just wanted to say thanks for letting me do stuff for you."

He rushed out and slammed the door before she could respond.

She went in to the bedroom and checked that Barbara was properly covered by the sheet then shut the windows, closing out the sounds of evening and the light from the full moon. When she returned to the lounge Amita and Ulrika had returned. They stood waiting for her.

She waved them into seats and sat down herself. Ulrika seemed to have recovered from her earlier tears though her eyes were still red. She had a lighter complexion than most due to her Scandinavian forebears no doubt.

"I am sorry, Ulrika," said Maliha. "You were right to chastise me. I had done nothing though I wanted to fill in details on the other missing children."

"But I gave Henry away, he wasn't stolen from me—I mean, not like that."

"Amita, would you call down for some tea?"

Amita went to the phone and opened the box.

Maliha returned her attention the Ulrika. "I was asking whether you knew anything about the woman who had been killed and her child stolen."

"The one in the newspaper?"

Maliha nodded.

Ulrika looked like she might cry again but seemed to get some control of herself. "I don't know much but it was a few weeks ago. A poor family who lived in the west of the city. The husband woke up in the morning to find his wife stabbed and their baby gone."

"And the police think he did it."

She nodded. "They arrested him."

Maliha looked over at Amita who was talking into the mouthpiece with the other part pressed against her ear. She turned back to Ulrika.

"Do you know what baby farming is?"

Ulrika shook her head. Maliha sighed; she was not looking forward to this and hoped the tea would arrive soon.

"Do you think it is uncommon for young ladies like you to succumb to the temptations of the flesh and get with child?"

She looked hunted. "I don't know."

"It's not uncommon," said Maliha. "It is very common indeed, despite it being possible to prevent pregnancy with proper procedures and timing."

Ulrika looked interested but then lapsed into her previous state. "It is too late for me."

"The frequency of such pregnancies led to the trade in children. You give someone money and they promise to look after them."

"Yes."

"What was the name of this woman you found who promised to care for your child?"

"Auntie Flo."

"And what did you think of her, Ulrika?"

The girl looked up at the question. "What did I think?"

"Did she inspire confidence in you? Did she seem a woman that truly loved children?"

Ulrika squirmed in the seat as if the very question made her uncomfortable. "I … I think … she said she loved children."

Maliha grew angry at the girl's obstinate avoidance of the truth. "And did the nature you saw in her match the words?"

Ulrika shook her head.

"Did you trust this woman?"

"I had to!" Ulrika shouted and stood up. Maliha looked pointedly in the direction of the bedroom door. Ulrika sat down. "I had no choice."

"We always have a choice."

Amita had finished with the telephone and now stood next to Ulrika's chair. She handed Ulrika a kerchief as she wept once more. Amita caught Maliha's eye and gave her mistress an admonishing look.

"Some of these are not bad women," said Maliha. "But there are those who have no heart. They realise that if they do not need to spend the money they receive on the child they will have more for themselves. There have been cases of women who killed the children they took in."

"Why are you saying this to me?" demanded Ulrika between sobs. "Do you hate me so much?"

Maliha closed her eyes and felt her own tears burning behind the lids.

"I don't hate you but I need you to understand what may be the truth here."

"The most likely truth?" asked the girl.

"Yes."

iv

The sun lit up the room and filled her closed eyes with sourceless light. She buried her head further into the pillow. She could smell the left-over scent of his shaving lotion then smiled as she thought of holding him close and breathing in the scent of his body.

A shadow passed across the sun. The mattress squeaked and someone pushed her plait back from where it lay across her face and lips pressed against her cheek. Bristles scratched her face. She was not sure whether she was still dreaming.

"Good morning, sleepy head." A calloused hand came down on her bare shoulder and squeezed gently.

She rolled on to her back and opened her eyes. Her cheek had not lied, he needed a shave.

"Did you miss me?" he said. She reached out, grasped him by the shoulders and pulled him down to her. She kissed him for a long time, holding him as tight as she could as if she were a drowning woman clinging to a log.

"Seems that you did," he said when she finally released his lips. He rolled off her and she followed with her arms still round him. She rested her head on his chest and was calmed by his firm heartbeat.

"What's wrong, my love?"

"I don't know," she said into his shirt which was still dusty from his journey. "I am scared, Valentine."

He gave a laugh that was almost a snort. "You?"

"It's not a joke," she said. "Something about this makes me very afraid."

"About what?"

"Someone stealing children."

"It's really happening?"

She nodded, scraping her cheek on his buttons. She got up and knelt by his side. She was aware that her nightgown did not hide her body very well, but this was Valentine; she liked the way he admired her.

She studied him in his travelling clothes and frowned. They really would have to have the sheets changed; the dirt from the road was falling off him into the bed. She glanced at the clock on the mantel, it was only seven o'clock. He must have started very early.

He looked thoughtful.

"What did you discover?"

"I found Marten Ouderkirk's family. I don't know whether my information helped them or not, but they let me stay the night at least. It was as well we didn't tell them about Baba. They are as bigoted as any in this place. I imagine it would have done more harm than good; they certainly would not have wanted to keep her. Except perhaps to punish her in her mother's stead."

Maliha nodded. "But you found the place where they boarded the vessel?"

He smiled and nodded. "There was a drunk who was recruited but missed the boat." His face fell.

"What is it?"

He raised his hand and ran it down her arm making it tingle. "I adore the colour of your skin."

"What did you discover?"

"I don't know, Maliha," he said. "Mr Ouderkirk accompanied me, and that turned out to be a great blessing. We found the place the ship had landed. It was of the same type that I saw over Pondicherry, perhaps even the very same one." He trailed off.

"But…?"

"We were attacked."

"By men?"

"No, by a hyena."

"A pack."

"Just one."

"They eat carrion and only hunt when they must, in packs."

Valentine shrugged. "It would seem that this one had not read the rulebook."

"Was it rabid?" she said, suddenly worried, she glanced across his clothes looking for a tear.

"I'm all right," he said. "You and Ouderkirk both! If you like I will strip naked for you to check."

She gave a coy smile and he tutted.

"We went to a farm nearby. Everybody was dead and had been for a long time. And there were dead hyenas mixed up with them."

"You're saying a pack of hyenas attacked a farm?"

He nodded, pulled himself up and went towards his bathroom. "That's impossible."

"Tell the hyenas. And what's more," he said. "The one we killed? Its eyes were pitch black. No pupils at all."

She frowned. "How could that be?"

"I'll leave the clever stuff to your intellect, my dear." He stood up and stretched, working the kinks out of his back. "I need to get clean."

Every penthouse bathroom had hot and cold running water and she soon heard the water thundering into the bath. She brushed the dirt out of the bed as best she could. She was tempted to go out on to the balcony but after Ray Jennings had taken those pictures, no matter how poor they might be, she decided it might not be the best move. Instead she just threw the windows open to let fresh air in.

She busied herself tidying around the place until she heard him groan and splash into the bath. She could not prevent the smile that crept across her face.

It took a little courage, she was not like Françoise Greaux, but he had not locked the door to the bathroom. She went to the door that led through to Barbara's suite and locked it to avoid any awkward interruptions, then returned to the bathroom and pushed open the door.

The way the bath was arranged he lay facing the door. He had his eyes closed. The water was clear but the ripples and distortion obscured the view of his entire body. She pushed the shoulders of her nightgown to the side and wriggled so it fell to the floor.

In her bare feet she stepped up to the lip of the bath and stretched one leg over and in. The movement of the water disturbed him and he opened his eyes. He must be tired, she thought. She could see the thoughts running through his mind as he realised what was happening, then attempted to cover himself, then realised she was naked and finally simply made room for her.

Climbing into a bath was not a very elegant action but she managed without too much embarrassment and then sank down into it. They had to let some of the water out otherwise it would have splashed over the top. She sat awkwardly with her head among the taps, and her legs intertwined with his.

He seemed almost incapable of taking his eyes from her breasts. She decided it must be because he was so tired.

"I have not heard of sharing a bath," he said.

"It has a long tradition," she replied.

"Really?"

"The Romans did it all the time."

"The Romans were thoroughly debauched."

She smiled. "And we are not?"

"Not thoroughly," he said. "Not yet."

"Is that a promise or a threat?"

"Which would you prefer?"

She flicked her fingers into the water and splashed him. He plunged both hands in and thrust them at her, launching a wave that reached her chin and splashed on to the floor.

They burst out laughing.

"Always overdoing your retaliation, Mr Crier," she said.

He nodded. "That is the story of my life."

"Well," she said. "I believe I must check your body for rabid hyena bites."

"Really?" he said and then paused, apparently the prospect of what might be to come was overwhelming, then he recovered. "Yes, I expect you should. Where would you like to start?"

"Here!" she said, grabbed his foot and lifted it out of the water. His posterior slipped forward and his head sank backwards. He came up spluttering.

"You will pay for that, Miss Anderson."

v

The bath had been fun, Valentine thought as he pulled on his boots and laced them tight. They so seldom had any time for simple enjoyment. Usually they spent their hours dealing with violent death or dangerous murderers. She was driven to do it, and he did it because?

He was at a loss. Once upon a time he had done it for King and Country; it was his duty and he felt it had value. Now he did it because he wanted to please Maliha and, perhaps, part of him also objected to having an incomplete case. If he could find Timmons and bring him to justice then perhaps he could face her without the guilt that lurked at the back of his mind.

He glanced over at where Amita was assisting Maliha into another flowing dress he had not seen before. Amita had brought the clothes and items through into his rooms. This dress was an attractive pastel yellow. It had a decorous neckline and length— barely revealing her ankles or her breastbone—but left her arms bare.

Amita tightened the white belt that cinched Maliha's delicate waist. Valentine smiled to himself as he tied the laces on his other boot. He had told Maliha there would have to be changes with Amita now that he and Maliha were engaged. And there had been: he had changed. Somehow he no longer felt embarrassed knowing that

Amita was a woman in clothing and attitude alone. But that was apparently enough.

They took breakfast in Barbara's suite at nine o'clock and he was introduced to their new stray, Ulrika. He made no comment. Maliha seemed to collect random people but always she would put them to work in one way or another. She brought him up-to-date on the information supplied by Jennings—another stray, though in this case a most unwelcome one, like a dog with mange that insists on following you home.

The girl, Ulrika, looked tired as if she had not slept well. Maliha had not discussed why she was here but he gathered from the conversation that she was being a wet-nurse to Baba. He said nothing despite knowing that Baba had been taken off the breast back in India. He let it go; it was not a subject one discussed at the breakfast table.

"What are your plans, Valentine?"

He jumped at his name; he had been so engrossed in his own thoughts.

"I will be heading back to the air-dock to see if there's any news. What about you?"

"I need to talk to the man accused of killing his wife," she said. "If he's innocent he will know something."

"What about Barbara?"

Maliha sighed. "I would prefer to stay with her, of course. But Ulrika will be sufficient: someone Barbara can talk to. Anyway I can't trust Ray to investigate properly."

"You would trust him at all?"

Maliha shrugged. "He is a newspaper reporter. He can be trusted to do what a newspaper reporter would do."

"Lie?"

"Omit inconvenient facts."

She smiled at him across the breakfast table in full view of Amita and Ulrika. He smiled back. Unaccountably Ulrika grabbed up a napkin and dabbed her eyes before excusing herself and going back into Maliha's rooms.

Maliha stared after her. "I am not going to second-guess my every thought and action simply because it might make Ulrika cry," she said, quite huffily Valentine thought.

"Why did that make her cry?"

"I have no idea."

* * *

Valentine stepped out into the main street and put on his fedora to block the sun's glare. He had left Maliha with Ray Jennings. He had turned up at ten o'clock and eaten what was left on the breakfast table. It was astonishing watching him put away such a quantity.

He had looked up and grinned. "Stay stocked up as you never know where the next meal is coming from—an old infantry saying."

"I doubt you were ever in the army," Valentine had commented.

"Don't make it untrue."

Valentine forbore to agree with the nasty little man and left as soon as it was polite to do so. Maliha had come out into the hotel corridor with him and they kissed. Once again she became the woman he had found in bed that morning.

"Be careful," she had said holding him tight.

"Careful is my middle name."

"Valentine is your middle name."

"Only one of them."

"Be careful," she said again.

"I will."

Then she kissed him again and went back into the room without another word, shutting the door on him.

Across the road he saw the two street children that had been hanging around Maliha, what were their names? Izak and Lilith? They might be able to help him. He crossed the busy street dodging carriages, steamers, diesel machines and trams. Not to mention bicycles and other pedestrians.

"If you marry the goddess will you be a god?" said Izak without any preamble.

Valentine smiled then thought how angry Maliha would be at Izak's description. "She's not a goddess, that was just a misunderstanding." There, he had done his duty though he knew it would make no difference whatsoever.

"Is she gonna find the stolen children?" asked the little girl.

"If she can."

"She going to bring fire out of the sky and burn the bad people?"

"No, she's not going to do that. She's really not a goddess."

Lilith looked unconvinced and very unimpressed that he should lack faith. He decided he needed to take the upper hand as the conversation was careening out of control.

"I wondered if you would be able to help me."

"You working for the goddess?"

"Yes." After a fashion. "But she's really not a goddess."

"Your name is Crier."

"Yes."

"Do you cry a lot?"

Valentine sighed. How many times had he heard that joke in his life? But he looked down at the child. She was deadly serious. He was about to say no, because crying was not perceived as a manly trait, but what was the truth? He had cried many times since he had met Maliha.

"I cry as much as the next person, I suppose."

"But your name is *crier*," she insisted.

"And yours is Lilith," he said.

She looked at him as if he was crazy. It occurred to him that he wasn't going to explain to this child who Lilith was.

"What do you want to know?" asked Izak apparently deciding that his sister, or whatever she was, had been doing too much of the talking.

"I need to go to the air-dock and see if there's a message for me. If there isn't—" he paused wondering if he should ask but it was probably too late now. "Do you know the bad places where air-sailors go?"

"Are air-sailors stealing the children?"

"Shut up, Lilith," said Izak and hit her across the head. "I know some places. You want me to take you?"

Valentine wanted to say no, he certainly did not want Lilith near those places, but truth was he could do with a guide. It would make his job a lot easier.

"If there's no message, yes," he said. "But not Lilith."

"She'll be with me," said Izak.

Valentine did not bother arguing.

vi

Maliha with Amita and Jennings took the cab to the central police station. It was not far; nowhere in Johannesburg was any great distance. As the capital city of a country it was not very large. However Maliha did not want to walk and felt arriving in a cab would look better.

The policeman behind the desk glanced up as she entered then proceeded to ignore them. Maliha felt the anger building but she did not know how to deal with these people and entrenched prejudice.

"Oi, mate," said Ray, in a conversational way.

"Can I help you?" said the sergeant, looking only at Ray.

"Yeah, bet you can," he approached the desk and spoke more quietly, almost conspiratorially. "You know who this is, right?"

"Not sure I really care, mate."

"She's someone who can get your rear-end hauled across the nearest fire, and you broken back to copper. If not out all the way."

Maliha could not believe what she was hearing. She turned away from the desk to hide her face. It was not that she wanted to laugh but it was utterly outrageous. She forced herself to study the map of Johannesburg and its surrounds on the wall.

"Let me introduce meself," said Ray. "Ray Jennings, reporter for the Manchester Guardian—you heard of that, right?"

"Yes, of course."

"Remember in the war when that woman reporter, Churchill, she blew the whistle on the women's camps, got the Brits to fix it? And reported on the state of the farmers and got the Brits to give them money too? Well she's a mate of mine. Works on the same newspaper."

Maliha could not see the sergeant but as Ray's ridiculous story unfolded she could imagine him being taken in.

"But what's that got to do with this one?"

"She does investigating. You know those stories about Sherlock Holmes?"

"I've read some."

"This one is like a real Sherlock Holmes."

"But she's coloured."

Maliha's amusement turned to fury; she could feel herself go rigid with anger. Amita placed her hand gently on Maliha's shoulder.

"Don't let that fool you, she's solved loads of crimes and even had her aunt locked up for murder. She's got no soul that one."

"What's that got to do with me?"

There was a long pause. Maliha desperately wanted to turn round but forced herself to remain where she was. She realised they were still talking, but so quietly she could not hear the words.

The sergeant finally cleared his throat. "Miss Anderson."

She turned. The supercilious look on his face had been replaced by a nervous apprehension. She walked towards the desk and he leaned back in his chair. She glanced at Ray; it was now he who looked smug.

"What can we do to assist you today, Miss Anderson?"

"I would like to interview the man you arrested for killing his wife."

The sergeant gave Ray a sidelong look. "That's not usual. I would have to get permission."

Maliha was desperate to know what Ray had said to him but it had such an effect at this point that perhaps she could press the point. She placed her hands on the desk and leaned across. He drew back further; he definitely gave off the aura of fear. Not useful in the long term but perhaps for a quick success it could be utilised.

"I'm sure you are a good policeman, Sergeant," she began, his fear deepened to terror. Oh for heaven's sake! She smiled. "I would require no more than ten minutes with the man. Just me." She heard Ray grunt but she did not correct herself.

"I suppose for ten minutes…"

She smiled again. "Thank you very much," she said before he had a chance to change his mind.

* * *

Maliha had come to the conclusion that all police cells were the same. Especially when they were all designed and built by the British. Whether it was a lack of imagination or a desire for consistency. Or perhaps there was only one way to build a prison cell. There was a small window in the wall opposite the window.

Wit Nickells was a muscular man, with thin and tightly cropped hair. His meagre beard was blond. He might have been a strong man before but now he looked broken and stooped.

He stood when he realised it was a woman entering. There was no look of disdain in his insipid blue eyes; in fact there was no look of any emotion or life at all. Standing was an automatic response.

The door closed behind her with a solid thud and the scrape of metal as the bolts were drawn.

"Mr Nickells," she said. "I am Maliha Anderson."

There was not the slightest flicker of recognition from him; it was almost as if she hadn't spoken at all.

"I want to ask you some questions."

He sat down on his metal frame bed and leaned back against the wall.

"You are British?"

"Indian."

"They have women police in India?"

"I am not police."

She glanced around but there was nowhere to sit except beside him. She decided to remain standing.

"Are you a lawyer? I have a lawyer."

"No, nor am I with the newspapers." She sighed, there was a mould she was being forced into that she was entirely uncomfortable with, but in this case there was no option. "I am a private investigator."

"I cannot pay for an investigator."

"You don't have to." Maliha glanced at her watch, the minutes were ticking by. "I am working for someone else but I may be able to help you if you can give me some information."

"What makes you think you can help me?"

"I know you didn't kill your wife and child."

He looked at her properly for the first time. His eyes focused on her face and glanced across her body, making her wish Amita had chosen something a little less modern.

"How do you know?"

"Never mind that," she said, conscious of the time. "Tell me about when you woke up that morning."

"I got up and Suzanne was not in the bed. I thought she must be with Pauel."

His recitation of events was almost sing-song, as if he had replayed these words a hundred times. He probably had which meant there was nothing of value.

She interrupted him. "Was the window open?"

"The window?"

"Yes, the window, was it open?"

She could see the stuck mechanisms of his mind breaking free as he recalled. "No, the window was closed."

"Is it usually closed?"

"Yes, often it is closed."

"What about that night? Had you or your wife closed the window that night?"

She could see him working through the memories, then a light seemed to dawn. "No, we had left it open."

"Good," she said. "All right, tell me when you woke, how were you feeling?"

The discovery had injected life into him. This time he was eager to answer. "My head felt bad. My arms and legs did not want to move. I saw the clock and I was late for my shift."

Maliha nodded. "Thank you. Now let's talk about before that night. Was there anything unusual or did your wife tell you about anything strange happening?"

He thought for a while. Maliha resisted the temptation to look at her watch, not wanting to interrupt his train of thought.

Finally he shook his head. "Nothing strange." There were tears forming in his eyes. "Do you know where my boy is?"

"I don't know yet."

"Do you think he is alive?"

She hesitated. "I don't know."

"You think he is dead?"

She met his eye and nodded. "Yes, it is most likely but he has not been gone too long yet. There is a little hope."

Angry shouting penetrated the cell.

Maliha stepped away from the door. "If you think of anything else you can send for me; they may let me see you again."

He nodded and then jerked his head up. "There was a burn on the carpet."

The bolts slammed back with violent noise. "Which room and where in the room?"

The door crashed open revealing a red-faced Chief Detective Karel Vandenhoek. "Get out of there, Miss Anderson."

Maliha said nothing but stepped out promptly. Vandenhoek had to reach in to grab the door handle and before he could close it Wit Nickells' voice floated out. "The bedroom door."

vii

Maliha sat upright in the chair facing the chief detective's desk. The room was spotless. There was an electric desk lamp and a modern telephone sitting to one side of the clean blotter. She could imagine that the chief detective replaced it every day. Directly in front of her was his wood and brass name plate announcing his name and position. Beyond it, nearer to his chair, was a neat pile of card files. One file lay open on the blotter.

"It is not clear to me what I should charge you with, Miss Anderson."

"That is entirely up to you, Chief Detective."

He made a noise in his throat that sounded like a growl.

"I have been checking up on you."

"Oh, yes?" She allowed herself a private smile.

"I contacted the British Consulate. It seems they have a file on you."

She said nothing. The consulate would not reveal any of the more interesting events she had been connected with. She studied the open file; it was the report on the Nickells case.

"I went to the consulate and read it."

No response was required so she gave none.

"It seems you are regularly interfering in police business."

A knot of anger ignited in her stomach. Interfering? "You mean I have solved a number of cases. I imagine Inspector Forsyth was quite congratulatory."

It was Vandenhoek's turn to be silent. He took his seat opposite her. She could see the suppressed fury in him. There was going to be no easy way of dealing with this. Staying meek would only validate his outmoded concepts.

"You told me that there was nothing to investigate in relation to the missing children," she said. "And yet you have a man in your cells whose child is missing."

Vandenhoek laughed derisively. "Nickells killed his wife and boy. He's just a murderer, Miss Anderson."

"Where's the child's body?"

"He must have thrown it in the river, or burnt it, or just left it in the open for the animals."

Maliha kept her voice calm despite her anger. "Why didn't he do the same to his wife, Chief Detective Vandenhoek?"

"It doesn't matter. I don't need to know why a crazy man does crazy things; I just have to stop him."

"And the fact that the events of Nickells' child's disappearance are exactly the same as those for the disappearing black children means nothing to you?"

"What happens to the blacks is of no concern to me," he said though his voice was less certain. Perhaps there was a decent policeman in there somewhere.

"There are at least five instances where a black child, under the age of six, has disappeared from their camp. In every case the family woke up feeling ill, with headaches and muscular discomfort. The same thing that Nickells described to me."

"But there were no deaths," he protested.

Maliha noted that despite his claims he was familiar enough about the other missing children to know there were no deaths. She thought it best not to comment. "Because Suzanne Nickells got up at just the wrong moment to see to her son, or perhaps she could not sleep. She interrupted whoever came to take the child and they killed her."

Vandenhoek stared at her.

"Tell me, Chief Detective, what will you do when the next white child is stolen from their home? Will you arrest the parents for that as well?"

He stood up and went to the door. "Goodbye, Miss Anderson."

She followed him and he pulled open the door for her. She stopped directly in front of him, giving him nowhere to look but at her.

"How many children will have to go missing before you realise something very bad is happening in your city?"

* * *

Amita and Jennings were seated in the reception area of the police station. They both stood as Maliha entered from the corridor with the chief detective looming behind her.

Vandenhoek stopped beside the sergeant's desk, now occupied by a different man, while Maliha kept walking. Amita and Jennings fell in behind her as she headed for the exit.

She did not turn as she pushed her way out into the midday sunshine. She held out her hand and Amita gave her the parasol. Maliha released the catch and pushed the mechanism to open it. She headed down the street with Amita striding behind her and Ray scurrying after.

"Well?" said Ray as they turned a corner heading north through a business district. Almost every brass plaque on the wall announced the name of a company dealing in gold or diamonds with the occasional accountant and bank.

There was a vast amount of money in the Transvaal and all of it going into the pockets of foreign companies. Maliha could understand the frustration of the original inhabitants, particularly the blacks who were not even allowed to own land.

"It seems the chief detective had not considered the possibility that the missing children of the blacks could possibly be connected to the missing white child."

"You put 'im straight."

"Yes."

"What did he say?"

"That's when he asked me to leave."

"Afrikaans Government Hush up Missing Children," said Ray then shook his head. "Nah, not good enough. South Africa Police Kill Children. Better."

"Not true though."

"If they're not following up then they're killing children, ain't they?"

Maliha took a left turn, Amita followed but Ray stopped on the corner.

"Where you going?" he shouted. "The hotel's back this way."

Maliha ignored him and kept going. Ray chased after them. "Hotel's the other way."

"If I was going to the hotel that would be helpful, Mr Jennings," said Maliha. "We are, however, going to Wit Nickells' house."

"The police will have been all over it."

"Yes, they will probably have obscured any possible useful clues but perhaps we may find something since they assumed it was Mr Nickells from the outset."

She strode forward along streets that transformed from business to middle class residential, then lower middle class and finally cramped brick houses for the working classes. She took the turns at street corners confidently.

"How come you know where you're going?"

"I read the address from the file on Vandenhoek's desk."

"This place is a maze—I thought you'd never been here before?"

"I looked at the map."

She could feel Ray staring at her. "Right," there was a pause then "but—"

"Time to shut up, Ray," cut in Amita. Maliha held in her surprise.

"Yeah, all right, Meeta."

CHAPTER 5

i

In some ways Valentine was grateful that he had got a message. He really had not wanted to traipse around the seedy side of Johannesburg with two children. Even if they had seen a lot worse than he had. As it was, there was an unsigned message to meet with a Captain Blake this afternoon. He was running a little late.

The electric lights in the pub were so dirty with yellow cigarette residue that they cast a dim but livid hue through the place. It would not have taken much to clean them up, but the clumps of men hunched around tables in the dim light would probably have taken their business elsewhere if more light had been shone on it.

He crossed the sticky floor to the bar and ordered a beer.

"Lookin' for Captain Blake," he said to the barman as he pulled the pint. The man finished the pint and let the final brown drops land in the glass sending ripples back and forth through the thin foam.

"Tuppence, mate."

Valentine dug the coin out of his pocket and added a florin.

"If you know this captain…?"

"Take a seat, sailor. You never know what the afternoon might bring."

Valentine was on his second pint when Izak stuck his face through the door and was promptly chased away but not before he and Valentine had exchanged glances.

Other men came and went. Some sailors, some not. The groups of men shifted, combining, separating, some went out together, others waited and joined newly formed collections.

Valentine had rejected the attentions of a third prostitute—younger than Izak—when a man came and sat at his table depositing a third pint in front of Valentine. "Very kind, mate," said Valentine.

"Captain Blake."

Valentine straightened himself in the chair. "Sorry, Captain."

"Relax, sailor," the man leaned back in his seat and sipped his pint. He studied Valentine in the dim light. For his part Valentine chose to look awkward and did not meet the man's gaze. He clutched the pint with both hands as if it were a lifeline.

"What are your skills, Mr…?"

"Dyer. Jonathan Dyer. Able Seaman, cargo, Captain."

The captain nodded. "And what's your problem with getting work at the air-dock, Able Seaman Dyer?"

This was the first test. Valentine needed something that was a valid excuse for him not being able to use the legal routes but would not make him an unattractive choice.

"I borrowed some supplies, Captain."

"Borrowed?"

"There was an over-supply of cargo. No one would miss it, so I arranged to sell it."

The captain smiled. "I see, so it was all a mistake really?"

"Aye, sir."

"Until they checked your tally against the records and found that yours was where the mistake lay."

Valentine looked away and lifted his pint to his lips.

The captain pulled a leather-covered cigar case from an inner pocket and extracted one. He bit off the end. Valentine fumbled for matches and lit one for the man.

Captain Blake settled back and sucked in the pungent smoke. He breathed out. "What ship?"

"*RMS Macedonia*, captain."

He nodded. "Ever steal anything from the passengers?"

Valentine shook his head. "No, sir."

"All right, Dyer. I may have something for you. I'll be in touch."

The captain remained seated which meant the words were a dismissal. Valentine got to his feet and gave a half bow. "Thank you, Captain."

The man waved him away.

Valentine blinked in the sunshine as he stepped out into the open air. Izak headed towards him but turned away at the shake of Valentine's head. After checking his directions Valentine headed away from the pub. There was a man on the corner selling the latest edition of the Johannesburg Chronicle. He bought a copy and headed towards the air-dock. The perimeter fence was in sight when he went into a liquor shop and bought a bottle of their cheapest whiskey for a shilling.

He went to the crew hostel, got his key, then headed up the three flights to his room. Once inside he messed up the bed as if he had been sleeping in it then sprinkled a few drops of the booze on the sheets. He roughed up the newspaper and dropped it on the floor, then went out to the WC on the landing and poured half the bottle of whiskey down the bowl.

The case with his belongings sat in the bottom of the wardrobe; behind it, in the corner, was his supposed letter of dismissal. After what Maliha had done to protect the company's interests in the past, there was little they would not do to assist.

Finally he lay back on the bed, still wearing his boots. The bed was not very comfortable; the mattress padding had worn thin and the springs protruded in places. It was exactly the sort of bed that belonged in the type of room that disgraced Able Seaman Jonathan Dyer would use, until his money ran out and he ended up on the streets.

He closed his eyes and dozed.

If he had judged the situation correctly, Captain Blake would be using his contacts to check whether Valentine's story was true. There would not be much: the name of a sailor kicked off the ship without much fuss because the shipping line did not want any bad publicity.

They would search his room and find the letter. They would see a man who had turned to drink even though it would mean his money ran out faster. A desperate and broken man.

The only question was whether it would be enough to convince them.

And then what?

He and Maliha would be separated once more. They might never see one another again.

ii

Ray did not utter another word until they reached the house of Wit Nickells. The house was a detached two-up two-down of brick with the completely expected corrugated iron roof.

"They don't have much imagination when it comes to roofs, do they?" said Ray.

"It's cheap and easy to use," said Maliha. She headed for the front door.

"Only whites live round here, Maliha—ow."

Maliha glanced round. Ray had his hand to his head and was frowning at Amita. "You say *Miss Anderson*," said Amita.

Maliha turned back and tried the door. It was locked.

"'Ere, let me," said Ray. Maliha gave him some space and examined the window at the front. Ray dug around in his pockets and pulled out a key. He fitted it in the lock and turned it.

"What would you be doing with a key like that?" asked Maliha as she returned to where he waited.

"Do you really want to know?" he said.

"Perhaps not." She looked into the dark interior. "Try not to touch anything. Or disturb anything."

"Or walk on anything?"

"Exactly."

"We'll just wait out 'ere then, shall we?"

"No, come in or you'll attract attention."

Maliha stepped through. The door gave on to the main room at the front, a door led through into the kitchen/scullery and there was a staircase leading up to the next floor with a cupboard beneath it.

A dark wood table stood in the centre of the room. There was a plant pot in the middle. The plant itself was dried up and dead. Four plain straight-backed chairs stood around the table and there was an old armchair by the window.

It looked unlived-in. There was a thin layer of dust on everything but beneath it the table's surface looked polished.

The scullery was the same and a search of the cupboards and larder showed nothing of value. Everything had been cleared out and left clean. The only thing that was out of place was the dark patch in the sandstone floor. The place where Mrs Nickells had been found, stabbed to death. Maliha tutted.

She headed upstairs, the steps creaking as she went.

"All right if we 'ave a look round now?" asked Ray.

"Be my guest," Maliha said as she climbed.

The two rooms on this floor were the main bedroom and a smaller one containing a child's cot. The main bedroom was hidden in half-light. Maliha went to the window and drew back the curtains. The carpet was a dull red and what had probably been white but was now grey.

There was a mark on the carpet by the door.

She went over and crouched down with the light from the window on it. The carpet was simply woven, there was no pile, but there was a small patch that was burnt. She ran her gloved fingers over it, the tips were blackened. She brought her fingers to her nose. Charcoal.

The discolouration was a rectangle about six inches long and two wide. It faded towards the door and round the sides but the middle and end nearest the bed were solidly black. It suggested a tube that was hot at one end lying on the carpet.

She stood up again and looked at the walls. She recalled Wit Nickells' fingers; they were not discoloured by cigarettes, and his breath had not carried that distinct odour she had come to expect from smokers. He did not smoke and smoking among women was confined only to radical females. It was unlikely Suzanne Nickells was a smoker. There were no ashtrays but they might have been removed by whoever stripped the house.

She hurried downstairs. Halfway down the stairs she found Ray was examining the door to the scullery while, when she reached the bottom, she saw Amita staring out of the front window.

"Is there any cigarette residue on the walls, Ray?"

He looked at her then scraped his fingernail down the wallpaper beside him. He studied the result, sniffed it and rubbed it between his fingers. "Don't think so."

"Good," she replied, lifted her skirts and ran back upstairs.

She walked back into the main bedroom and stood on the burnt patch. She turned round slowly staring carefully at the bed, the walls, the window, the wardrobe and the door. Everything looked clean.

Why was everything clean? Who cleaned the house where a murder had taken place when the accused might be found not guilty and return? Unless they were sure he would be condemned. Why clean everything?

Because they had got it wrong. They had made a mistake and were worried they might have left evidence behind.

She continued turning on the spot. Steadily step by step.

They had a device, in a tube, activated by heat that generated a noxious gas. Those who inhaled the gas became unconscious.

Turn.

In the tiny homes of the black families they could release their gas and everyone would be rendered helpless. They could steal the child and take their tube with them. No one investigated because no one cared.

Then they thought they would take a white child—how did they identify which one? They arrived at the home but Suzanne Nickells surprised them, one of them grabbed up the nearest weapon and killed her. They continued their mission and put the tube in the bedroom to incapacitate the husband. Then they took the child. Even if the babe had cried out its father would not have heard.

The intruders had one clever person with them and he had brought the knife to the bedroom and put it in Wit Nickells' hand to condemn him. Thinking, rightly, that no one would investigate further even though the child was missing.

And it was all supposition. No court here would accept it.

For a moment, Maliha wavered. How could she possibly save Wit Nickells from the gallows? Only by finding the child and those who abducted them.

She stopped turning and stared at the door frame.

"Bring me a chair!" she shouted. There was an exclamation of surprise, possibly from Amita, and an indeterminate thud. The sound of people moving and then a chair scraping the floor. Followed by a short argument. And then a thumping on the stairs and a clattering as the chair rattled against the banister.

The chair appeared being carried by Amita. Maliha indicated a point just inside the bedroom door. With Amita's help she climbed on to it, bringing her eyes in line with the top of the frame.

She ran an unsoiled finger along the length of the top of the frame. It was slightly sticky. She looked at the faint yellow-green deposit with satisfaction. Holding Amita's hand she climbed down and sat on the chair. Then took a sniff.

The smudge on her glove smelled sweet, almost like honey, but caught in the throat like smelling salts—ammonia. She felt light-headed and the room swam.

And woke to Amita's concerned face, Ray just behind her. Maliha frowned. She had not heard him coming up the stairs. Then she realised she was lying on the bed.

"How long was I unconscious?"

"One or two minutes, *sahiba*."

"That is a very potent concoction."

It might have been the after-effects of the drug but she felt far more positive than she had up to then.

At last she was getting somewhere.

iii

When they chose to retire in the evening, Maliha decided there was no point in pretending that she was not sleeping in Valentine's bed.

After all, she reasoned, who was here? She had already discussed the matter with Barbara, Amita was not concerned and Ulrika had had carnal relations with her son's father, whoever he was. Maliha paused at the thought she had considered Amita as being someone whose opinion was relevant. Then smiled to herself; it was good manners to consider everyone's feelings regardless of their status.

In fact the only person she might have to persuade in the matter was Valentine himself who was far more likely to be concerned with appearances—yet only for Maliha's sake. She called Amita over after she had sent Ulrika to bed with the baby.

"I will be sleeping in that room," Maliha indicated Valentine's door, "so I won't need you tonight, Amita. But if you could come in around seven thirty that would be fine. I will be wanting a bath."

"Yes, *sahiba*," said Amita. "Do you wish nightdress tonight?"

"No, I won't be needing one."

Amita nodded. "Goodnight, *sahiba*." She closed the door behind her. Maliha turned to see Valentine shutting the adjoining door behind him. She heard the lock click and frowned.

She walked over and rapped on it. The lock clicked again and he pulled it open.

"Haven't you forgotten something?" she said.

His immediate reaction was to glance behind her to see if anyone was looking.

"They've gone to bed," she said.

He smiled and stepped through the door pulling her into his arms. The kiss was warm but did not last long enough. He did not pull away but held her in his arms; she could feel the pulse in his neck against her cheek. It was a trifle fast which could be due to arousal.

"Is something wrong?" she asked.

"No, of course not."

She pulled free of his embrace and took his hand. She led him through into his rooms, pausing only to let him shut the door.

"Leave it unlocked," she said, then at his questioning face. "So Amita can come through in the morning to run the bath."

He looked for a moment as if he would still lock the door, and then acquiesced. She drew him on, through the lounge, negotiating the furniture and into the bedroom. She pulled him to the bed and pushed him down on to it. Then stood back.

She always planned her life and actions so carefully but she found, in her relations with Valentine, it was always better to simply follow whatever thought or instinct was suggested in the instant.

She stood in front of him, hands at her sides. She found herself breathing heavily. She contemplated activating the phonograph but decided it would be more of a distraction. She was not *Salome*.

"What are you doing?" he asked with a slight smile on his face, though it did not vanquish the worry she could see infecting him. She smiled and placed her index finger against her lips.

She turned her back on him trying to remember where the fastenings were for the dress she was wearing. Recalling the map of Johannesburg was easy compared to this. She reached one arm over her shoulder and the other round her back to disengage the hooks from the top down, revealing her shoulders.

Before the first of the whip scars he had inflicted—under her instruction—came into view, she turned back towards him. She had half of the fastenings undone and pulled the bodice down, exposing herself, then pulled her arms free of the sleeves. She switched off the lights and paused while their eyes adjusted.

It reminded her of the time she had been forced to step onto the stage at school to recite a poem by Blake. The sheer embarrassment of being the subject of attention where every pair of eyes was criticising the colour of her skin.

She closed her eyes and snaked her hands above her head. The action lifted her breasts. He breathed in noisily and she smiled. She had seen dancers in a kinematograph and read descriptions of dance—she had even been taught before she was sent to Britain. The music need not be heard; it could be thought and felt. She needed only a rhythm in her mind. She rejected all the trite songs of Schubert. Then the intense rhythms of the *tabla* came to her and she heard the rhythm in her mind.

Her hips slid to the side and back again in time to the beat of her thoughts, slow and sedate. She remembered her training and moved her hands. She felt her body become the flickering flames of a fire.

She swayed and her body writhed to the inner rhythm. She focused only on herself. On her own movements. She turned on the spot. His breathing became harsher, catching in his throat as he watched. Her movements may have represented flame but now she burned. She ran her palms across her skin feeling the sheen of sweat.

The hair that Amita had meticulously pinned up in the beginning of the day fell down across her face, shoulders and back. She pressed her thumbs into the dress at her hips, catching the bloomers beneath as well. Smoothly, in time to the inner music, she pushed them down to her knees. She stood up straight; with one foot and then the other she stepped out of them, naked save for her sandals.

She did not cease to dance. Now she knew he was captivated she turned round revealing the scars he had made on her.

More than anything she wanted to push him back on the bed and force him into her. She knew he would not resist, though they had not been in that position before. But tonight was not the night for her to dominate him. He needed to be the strong one because he was the one that was lost.

She moved in front of him and knelt. Sitting back on her heels, her head down. Now that she stopped the air from the open window blew cold across her damp skin.

He did not move. She reached out and untied first one boot and then the other. He lifted his foot allowing her to remove it along with his sock. She did the same with the other. He stood up and she could hear the faint rustle as he unfastened his shirt buttons. It fell to the ground beside her. The slight clink of metal on metal indicated he was undoing his belt. One leg and then the other emerged. He wore short drawers for undergarments and they joined the other clothes.

She watched his feet as he headed to the bed and climbed in. She remained where she was. He must command her.

"Come to bed, Maliha."

In a fluid motion she leaned back so the soles of her feet were flat on the floor then stood up. She kept her head bowed. He had the sheet pulled back ready for her and she lay down on her back beside him with her hands at her sides, not stiffly but subservient to his desire.

He placed his hand flat on her belly then slid it gently up until he cupped her right breast. He leaned forward and placed a butterfly kiss on her left nipple, then bit gently. She shivered.

He moved closer. His body pressed against hers. He brought his hand to her cheek and turned her head towards him and kissed her. She mirrored his pressure and the intensity of his passion. She would give back whatever he gave to her.

For minutes they touched and kissed. Always he seemed to be on the verge of tears, and so she was too.

When he finally squeezed between her thighs and penetrated her, she felt nature's passion driving them higher, while the weight of humanity dragged them down. She failed to reach paroxysm though she drove him to his. But she did not mind, she had done this for him.

"I don't want to lose you again," he mumbled as he fell asleep.

iv

Amita opened her eyes to the dim grey of the bedroom at night. It wasn't unusual; little Baba often woke needing changing or feeding. But on this occasion there was no sound from the baby.

Someone was moving in the other room.

Perhaps Ulrika had got up to use the WC but Amita could hear Ulrika's breathing at the end of the bed. She looked around the greyness of the room. The door to the main room was shut but there was a light moving behind it.

Someone was in the mistress's suite. It would only be a matter of time before they opened the door to the bedroom. One woman had already been murdered. What if the child-stealers had been

watching her mistress and had come to silence them all? What if they
wanted to steal little Baba away?

The window opening on to the balcony was the only means of
escape but there were things to be done before they attempted it.

Amita pulled back the sheet and slipped out of bed. Her bare
feet made no sound on the carpet that covered the floorboards. She
paused, should she wake Ulrika first? No, the door must come first.
The light beneath the door had increased in intensity.

She covered the distance in four silent strides and leaned her
shoulder against it. She reached out to the key and saw the bar handle
dipping. She had arrived just in time. Pressure increased against her
shoulder, she caught hold of the key and turned it. The door opened
a fraction despite her efforts and the key would not engage.

Amita rammed her bare foot against the bottom of the door.
Whoever was on the other side of the door would know he was being
prevented. Subtlety was no longer required. She pulled away for a
second, the pressure on her foot increased then she slammed her full
weight against the door. It slammed noisily back against its frame.
Ulrika woke with a strangled half-cry and the key turned with a
satisfying click.

Amita threw herself away from the door as the air vibrated with
a deafening explosion. And a hole ripped through the door.
Something on the far side of the room shattered.

An angry voice shouted in the other room and another defensive
one shouted back. Ulrika was alternately squealing and breathing in
sharply. Then the air filled with the baby crying.

Amita dashed across the room to where Ulrika was lying. She
had not got up but was lying with a sheet over her head. Ripping the
sheet from her Amita grabbed her wrist and yanked her to her feet.
"Get out the window."

The room echoed to a great thump as the invisible assailants
threw themselves against the door. Amita did not think the door

would last long but someone must have been alerted by the gunshot. Ulrika had frozen in the middle of the room as they struck the door. Roughly Amita shoved her in the direction of the window then turned to the crying baby. She gathered up little Baba, wrapping her in the blanket.

She headed over to where Ulrika was struggling with the sash window, trying to force it upwards from its slightly open position. There was another solid thump from the door and the sound of cracking wood. Amita shouldered Ulrika aside and shoved the baby into her arms. She unlatched the window and slammed it upwards.

There was another thud. The frame splintered. The door crashed open. A shadow moved into the room preceded by a gun.

Amita screamed like a banshee, took two steps to get up speed and threw herself at the intruder.

The gun went off.

* * *

Climbing from the window looked impossible with the baby. Ulrika didn't know what had happened with Amita. She had to get out. She sat on the window frame. She did not dare look into the room: Amita might be lying dead; the man might be coming for her. *She had to get out.*

Holding the crying baby tight she pulled her legs up one at a time, ripping the thin cloth of the nightgown Amita had lent her. She fell through and landed heavily on her knees and elbows. She had her hand behind Baba's head and stopped her from striking the grid. The child was momentarily silent from the sensation of falling. The metal grid of the balcony cut into Ulrika's leg. The pain was motivating.

Releasing one arm from around the child she pushed herself to her feet.

She went to run but something tugged at her nightdress and then gripped her shoulder. She turned her head and stared into the eyes of white man with a thick beard. His fingers dug into her shoulder. She felt the energy go out of her—she could not fight.

The baby screamed.

Energised by her instinct to protect the child, Ulrika bit the fingers digging into her shoulder. Hard. She did not let go but clamped down harder and harder. He swore and tried to pull his fingers away. She was almost jerked from her feet but released him, tasting thick blood. She ducked as a shadow flew past her.

A fist struck the man across the jaw.

"Bastard!" shouted Valentine.

Ulrika wasn't sure whether he was insulting the man or crying out at the pain he had inflicted on his own fist which he shook for a moment.

Valentine grabbed her by the shoulders and shoved her away, in the direction of his room. She staggered a few steps and then stopped as Valentine swung at the dazed man again, this time striking him in the neck. It was then she realised Valentine was not wearing any clothes. She turned away trying to comfort the crying baby.

The French window of Barbara's suite opened and Maliha's head appeared. "Come inside quickly." She gestured vigorously and Ulrika stumbled towards her, the nightdress seemed sticky around her knees and the balcony had sharp protrusions that dug into her bare feet.

As she got to the French window Maliha reached out and took the child from her, which was a relief to the soles of her feet but within moments she was inside standing on the blessed carpet.

The light was still off in here as well but the illumination from the windows played across the room revealing that Maliha too had nothing on. She seemed to be examining the child in the dim light.

Before she had a chance to avert her eyes Maliha thrust the baby once more into her arms.

"Feed the baby in Barbara's bedroom. If Barbara wakes up, tell her there's been some trouble but we're dealing with it."

Ulrika just stared at her.

"Do you understand, Ulrika?"

She nodded.

"Then go!" Maliha gave her a shove and she staggered through into the bedroom. Closing the door behind her made her feel safer even if it would not stop anyone. As far as she could see Barbara was still asleep. She took the baby to the armchair in the corner and sat down. Little Baba was just whimpering now that the fuss had died down.

Ulrika pulled down the shoulder of the nightdress and put the baby to her breast. The sensation of suckling calmed them both.

v

Maliha shut the door behind Ulrika. The sound of Valentine swearing drifted through the open door on a breeze. There was no sound from beyond the door to her suite. She unlocked it as quietly as she could and pulled it open.

Nothing moved. She pulled the door wider and stepped back in case of attack.

"Maliha, call for a doctor, Amita's been shot."

"I am not hurt," came a plaintive voice from somewhere near the floor.

"Your arm is bleeding."

"It is not much."

There was a commotion of voices outside the room. Maliha dashed into the bedroom and grabbed her dressing gown. "Valentine you need to put something on. Right now."

She pulled open the telephone case and called down. News of the gunshot had apparently reached the ground floor. Perhaps others had rung down.

"This is Maliha Anderson; my maid has been shot by intruders. We need a doctor immediately."

"Yes, Miss Anderson."

"And the police. I want Chief Detective Karel Vandenhoek."

"The chief detective?"

There was an urgent and loud knocking on the door. Maliha glanced over at it. It was probably not locked since the intruders had gained entry that way. She turned her attention back to the call as there was more knocking.

"There has been a shooting of a foreign national in the most prestigious hotel in Johannesburg. I was speaking with him only today. I think he will want to know."

"I will tell them what you said."

Maliha put down the phone and went to where Amita was now sitting up against the wall, holding her right arm up against her chest with her left.

"It does hurt, *sahiba*," she said.

Maliha nodded. There was a lot of blood on Amita's clothes and the floor—they would have to replace the carpet completely—but both entry and exit wounds in her upper arm seemed to be only seeping blood.

Light in the suite increased as the door from the corridor opened. Maliha toyed with a couple of courses of action then decided that being a helpless victim would be the best approach.

"Who is it?" she called out in a quavering voice. "Please don't hurt us."

"Hotel porters, miss," came a gruffly South African accent which seemed familiar. "Are you all right?"

"No, my maid has been shot, she needs medical assistance."

Amita grabbed Maliha's wrist. "I cannot be examined," she said with genuine fear. Maliha put her hand over Amita's and squeezed it.

"I know, we'll keep you here. They will only look at your arm."

The porters entered in a rush. There were three of them, all white, the oldest was the one she had embarrassed when they first entered the hotel.

"I have called for a doctor and the police," Maliha said. "Please check to make sure they are gone."

The men spread out through the rooms but were back within seconds.

"No one, miss," said the older one. He looked through the doorway and down at where Amita sat on the floor in her blood. Almost hesitantly, almost as if he had to force himself, he said. "I served in the Anglo-Boer war, miss. I have some experience with bullet wounds. I can look. If you like."

She looked up into his moustachioed face and met his eye. She nodded and pulled back to give him room. One of the other, younger, porters slipped through and checked the room.

"The baby's gone!" he shouted. The other two froze. The older man moved first to examine Amita's arm.

"The baby is safe," said Maliha. "The wet nurse escaped through the window with the child."

Maliha noticed how the older man's eyes flicked to the door lock and frame taking in the bullet marks around the lock and the splintered wood. Maliha knew that he wanted to not believe her story.

"A lot of blood maybe," he said. "But a clean wound. This will heal nicely. Do you have something for a bandage?"

"The tablecloth," said Maliha. "Cut in strips."

He nodded and lifted his head. "Dirk, make bandage strips from the tablecloth."

"There are scissors in the third drawer down of the bureau," said Maliha.

The sound of Valentine rapping on the window attracted her attention; she pointed in the direction of the French window. He disappeared and then appeared at the bedroom door.

"How is she?"

"The bullet went through her upper arm," said Maliha.

The second porter pushed past Valentine and held out dangling strips of white cloth to the one on the floor. He glanced up and growled. "They need to be rolled up."

The youngster gathered up the ends and attempted to extract one. Maliha and Valentine simultaneously reached out and took an end each. They pulled and the strips separated.

They each rolled them up fast around their hands but Maliha was the first to hand one to the porter tending Amita. He took it and wound it tight about Amita's arm. She winced with her eyes squeezed shut but said nothing.

Maliha stood up as Valentine passed his rolled bandage to the second porter.

"Amita," said Maliha switching to Hindi. "You have to say that I was in the bedroom with you and Ulrika."

"Of course, mistress."

"Do you know what they were after?"

"No, mistress, but if they knew this was your bedroom, perhaps it was you."

Maliha nodded then turned to Valentine. "I need to check on Barbara," she said. "Will you stay here?"

"Of course."

Maliha went into Barbara's lounge through the connecting passage. She closed the door and leaned against it. Tears ran from her eyes. This was just too much. They could have killed Amita. They could have killed or taken the baby. She could have died herself. Or lost Valentine.

She shook herself. Why should dying be a problem? She had put herself into those situations more than once. But that was the point. On those occasions she had known what she was doing. This was like the time the rebels had attacked Barbara's house, but even then she had realised it was coming, if belatedly.

There were only two reasons they would want to attack: if she was closing in on the child-stealers, or if someone had decided to take a violent dislike to the presence of a black baby in the white-only hotel. Not impossible but far less likely.

She stood up straight and wiped the tears from her cheeks, then rubbed her eyes until they unblurred. This was not a time to become the victim of events.

vi

She knocked on the door of the bedroom. "Open the door, Ulrika."

There was a long pause. Maliha gave the girl time. Eventually she heard a soft padding across the carpet inside and the key turned in the lock.

Ulrika stood there in her nightgown, holding the baby, looking lost and scared. Maliha had a flashback to the boarding school except it had been her own image in the mirror she had seen, at age eleven, thousands of miles from home among people who despised her.

Maliha went in and shut the door.

She went over to Barbara to ensure the Faraday was still active. She paused to listen to the old woman's breathing; it was steady and firm.

"She has not woken," said Ulrika.

"Good," responded Maliha. "Let's sit down."

Ulrika went back to the armchair, where she could prop up her arms to support the sleeping child.

"Tell me what happened."

Ulrika related the events.

"They did not speak?"

"I could not hear their words."

"Pity. Very well," Maliha said. "You know that I was with Mr Crier."

Ulrika's face reddened and she could only nod.

"It is not something to be ashamed of; we are engaged." Then she wondered why she was justifying herself. "I do not wish others to be aware of our physical relationship. I'm sure you understand that?"

Ulrika nodded again.

"So we will say that I was also in the bedroom and helped you escape through the window with the baby."

A fear came into Ulrika's eyes. "Will there be police?"

"Yes."

"I cannot stay here."

Despite her words Ulrika seemed too terrified to move. Paralysed in the chair.

Maliha stared at her as connections clicked into place. "Hans Putnam is your father."

Hans Putnam, the Mayor of Johannesburg. Maliha closed her eyes. This night was getting better and better.

There was a knock on the door.

"Maliha, the chief detective has arrived," said Valentine as he came in.

"Thank you."

"He's in Barbara's lounge."

"I'll be there in a minute," she had a sudden thought, "would you mind waiting with Barbara in here?"

"Yes," he said though he seemed unsure. Maliha hurried to the door and let him in. She put her head out and saw the chief detective standing by the French windows. "I'll be with you in a moment."

She grabbed Valentine by the hand. "What have you told him?"

"Nothing," he said. "I said I was woken by the gunshot but by the time I arrived the birds had flown."

"Good," she said and glanced at the rabbit girl in the corner, still the expression of sheer terror on her face. "She's the daughter of the Mayor of Johannesburg."

"Shit."

Maliha gave him a stern look. "Yes, quite, but please don't use such language."

"What are we going to do?"

"We have done nothing wrong."

"No I know, but—"

"But nothing, Valentine," she said. "We'll stick close to the truth except where you and I were together."

"Because we've done nothing wrong."

"It's not wrong," she said. "It just won't be seen as appropriate."

She gave his hand a squeeze and went out into the lounge, acutely aware that the dressing gown did nothing to hide her shape. Well, that might help. She put on the most worried face she could muster.

"Chief Detective Vandenhoek, I'm so glad you could come yourself," she held out her hand which he shook with the very slightest pressure and a frown.

"Miss Anderson. I thought I was beyond the rank where I could be pulled from my bed in the middle of the night."

"Tell that to our intruders," she said. "I asked for you specifically because this is a matter with potentially serious consequences, perhaps even international."

"A coloured maid getting shot does not strike me that way, even if she is in a suite of the hotel." He took a deep breath and met her eye. "After all, Miss Anderson, you are the one that insisted on keeping that baby here."

She smiled without the slightest humour or goodwill. "Shall we sit down, Chief Detective?" She indicated an armchair for him and she took the sofa.

"If I were to tell you that the mayor's daughter is here and under my protection how would that affect your view?"

He leant forward. "Is that something you expect me to believe?"

"Ulrika Putnam is in the other room." She indicated the bedroom door with a nod of her head. "She could have been the one who was shot."

Vandenhoek followed her gaze and stared at the closed door. He rubbed his mouth with his palm and pursed his lips. He turned back to Maliha. "What about the baby?"

"Hers or mine?"

"Hers."

"She gave it away."

"Good."

Maliha knew she was tired; she knew she was overwrought by the events of the day; and she knew she should keep better control of herself. But she did not.

"*Good?* How dare you. That poor girl has been mistreated by her father; only her mother gave her any support at all. She has been forced to give away her very flesh. And you say 'good'?"

"The scandal would be terrible," he said calmly. "We have fought hard to become a nation that is as independent as the British will permit. To have a scandal like this affect such an influential person, it would make Johannesburg and our nations a laughing stock around the world."

Maliha sat back. "You're saying the father was black."

The chief detective remained impassive. "She did not tell you that."

"No, she didn't."

Vandenhoek's expression became smug, as if he had somehow won a crucial point in a game.

Maliha glared. "My parents were not of the same race, Chief Detective. So what in the world makes you think it would make any difference to me?" she toned down her venom. "The fact remains, the mayor's daughter could potentially have been the one shot."

"The only person for whom that would have been a problem, Miss Anderson," he got to his feet, "is you."

Maliha stood to reduce his superior position. "So you are going to cling to the idea that the attack was by offended citizens?"

He shrugged. "There is no other possible reason."

"Apart from the fact I visited Wit Nickells' house and confirmed that his family was attacked in the night," she approached the detective. "That his child was stolen in exactly the same way as the black children that have gone missing."

"Nonsense."

"Just how bad a policeman are you, Chief Detective?"

"Goodnight, Miss Anderson."

He strode to the main door and pulled it open. Halfway through it he stopped and turned.

"And what evidence do you think you found?"

"Marks of a hot container on the carpet emitting a sleep-inducing substance," she said. She could see the arrogant disbelief taking over his face. "If Mrs Nickells had not got up at the wrong moment, for whatever reason, she would still be alive and you would not be holding her husband for murder but looking for the child."

"You have a very active imagination, Miss Anderson," he said. "I hope our paths do not cross again."

The door shut with the sound of finality.

"Arrogant idiot," she said beneath her breath.

vii

The police left an hour later as the sun was rising and, shortly after breakfast, Maliha received a note from the hotel asking her to leave.

"As if it's my fault," she said to no one in particular. She knew there was no Sky-Liner to the Fortress for two days so she could agree to their request and still remain a little longer.

She leaned against the frame of the French window staring out into the increasing noise and bustle of the city. Valentine came to stand beside her and put his arm round her waist. Ulrika was with the baby and Amita in Barbara's bedroom. Between them they were tending both, though Amita was severely limited by the sling. Elder Barbara had indicated she was hungry, but needed feeding just like her young namesake.

"Of course it's not your fault," he said.

"I know that," she snapped and felt his hand tense on her hip. "Sorry. This place is just infuriating. It's like trying to get sensible answers from a calculating machine where the number five is stuck and adds itself into every sum." She adjusted her balance and leaned into him instead. He relaxed.

"I can't go back to India yet," he said carefully as if he expected her to attack again.

"I know," she said. "I don't suppose I will either but we need a plan."

"Let's take a walk," he said. "You know we haven't done that for a long time."

She thought of all the reasons why that would be a bad idea. "Thank you, I would be happy to accompany you."

* * *

They took a taxi north until the city was invisible behind a range of gentle hills. There was nothing but grassland marked off by fences.

"It's like Lincolnshire," said Valentine.

"But bigger, I would imagine," said Maliha.

They had the driver stop near a stand of trees. Valentine checked his revolver as Maliha raised her parasol against the intense sunlight.

"Worried about rabid hyenas?"

"That, and lions, rhinoceros and everything else here."

"I don't think that little gun would stop a rhinoceros," she said.

He placed it back into the holster at his waist. "No, but it makes me feel better."

She smiled. "There are snakes to worry about as well. Scorpions. Spiders."

"You don't seem concerned."

"I grew up in a place where such things are commonplace," she said. "But most of the lessons involved just not going where you might expect to find such things."

She took his arm with the parasol against her shoulder, and he guided them along the track instead of heading off across the grass.

"We did not have much in the way of poisonous insects in Boston."

"I never left the south coast except to go to London."

"It's near the Wash," he said.

She shook her head innocently.

"Just north of the bit that sticks out on the right."

She laughed. "Just south of Sleaford and north-west of Bury St Edmunds."

"I could hate you," he said grinning.

"I've only seen it on a map," she said. "I know a lot of facts, Valentine. And almost nothing that's real."

They walked on in silence for a while. Maliha looked out across the sea of grass. There was a light wind and the grass moved in waves like the sea. Just as she had seen it on the hills by the sea during the summers in England.

She let out a deep breath. If only life could be as uncomplicated as this all of the time.

"Why haven't the children of white families been taken?" she finally said.

"Do you really want me to answer or have you already worked it out?"

"I'm sorry," she said.

She smiled at the frown that appeared on his face even though she wasn't looking. "What for?"

"Being too clever."

He stopped, turned her to face him, and kissed her lightly. "I'm not sure you're all that clever," he said casually and headed off down the track.

"What do you mean?"

"Well, you agreed to marry me," he said. "Not sure that marks you as an intelligent woman."

"I think you're fishing for a compliment, Mr Crier."

"Would I do such a thing?"

"I would not have chosen you if you were not intelligent, kind, generous, and a gentleman," she said. "There, does that satisfy you?"

"For the time being," he said, "but compliments wear out and I will need additional supplies in future."

They walked on again, their steps synchronised.

"So," he said, "why haven't white children been taken? Except for the Nickells incident obviously."

"If a black child is stolen away, who cares?"

"The family."

"Of course," she said. "But not the authorities."

"Especially not when the family claim it was an evil spirit."

"Quite," she said. "And if a white woman has a child out of wedlock?"

"She is shunned, disgraced and disowned by the family, all the usual things."

"And she cannot keep the child."

"No, of course not," he said. There was a moment's pause and then, "Baby farming."

She stopped and glanced back down the trail. The taxi stood nearly a quarter of a mile away, steam and smoke rising gently from the furnace and boiler. She turned and faced Valentine. She looked into his eyes and waited.

She could see the realisation come over him just as she knew it would. And then the horror, as she expected. He gripped her by the shoulders; she did not resist. "You can't do it."

"I don't see what choice we have," she said quietly. "Has it occurred to you to imagine what might be happening to these children?"

He shook his head but she knew from the dread in his eyes he was lying.

"We could just leave," he whispered. "Go home."

It was her turn to shake her head. "Could you live with yourself?"

"Could I live with myself if something happened to our little girl?"

"It won't go that far," she said. "We just need to make the contact. Little Baba will add credibility if I need it."

"Could you stop yourself?"

She flared into anger and shrugged off his arms. "What in hell's name do you mean by that?"

His voice was almost a monotone. "Think of all the things you have done to yourself, Maliha. All the things you have willingly had done to you."

"But…" she trailed off. Thoughts flashed through her mind: putting herself in the power of a murderess; placing them both in danger with the Dutch spies; letting herself be abused by the guru; demanding Valentine beat her; and things he did not know about.

"Yes," he said as if he had watched the images in her mind. "All of those."

She nodded. "I understand what you are saying. My own body is my responsibility and I can do with it as I wish. I would not put an innocent child at risk," she took his hand. "But to ignore this would be to condemn all the ones yet to be taken and abandon the ones already gone."

His expression was tortured as if he wanted to believe but that the evidence denied it.

"I promise," she said.

CHAPTER 6

i

Amita jumped at the knock on the door and pain shot through her shoulder. She took a deep breath to calm herself. She glanced around to see if anyone had noticed. Ulrika was feeding the baby and Barbara was asleep again having slowly communicated her sympathy with Amita about her injury.

Ulrika had explained how the spelling board worked and Amita found translating for Barbara useful to practise her writing and reading. But she was still scared. The energy of her attack on the intruder last night was gone only to be replaced by a constant nervousness.

The knock came on the door again. Amita stood up straight and steeled herself. She went through into the lounge and forced herself to unlock the door.

"Hiya 'Meeta," said Ray as he strolled into the room, grinning from ear to ear. His gaze took in the table, which did not contain breakfast, then he saw her arm in the sling. The grin disappeared. "What the hell's happened to you? You all right?"

She flushed at his concerned attention, slightly embarrassed by him looking directly at her. "We were attacked in night."

"Bastards," he said. "What did they do to you?"

"I was shot," she said. "But I am not badly hurt."

"Bastards," he said again. He reached out and touched the back of her hand then withdrew it. Then as an afterthought. "Everyone else all right, yeah?"

"No one else is hurt."

There was a silence that stretched out embarrassingly too far.

"Sorry I weren't here," he said. "I'd've given 'em what for."

Amita frowned. "What for?"

"I'd've smashed their 'eads in," he explained.

Amita looked down at him. He wasn't very tall, just skin and bone without a significant muscle in sight. But she smiled. "I am sure you would have protected me."

"Right, anyway," he said looking round. "Any chance of something to eat? I'm starving."

Ray was sitting down to a breakfast of toast, bacon and tomatoes when Maliha and Valentine returned.

"I have to talk to Ulrika," said Maliha to Amita. "Send her into my rooms will you?"

* * *

Ulrika knocked on the door into Miss Anderson's room. The door was not shut tight and Ulrika could see through to where Miss Anderson was looking out through the French windows.

"Come in, Ulrika."

She pulled it open and went through, shutting it carefully behind her.

"Sit down at the table, please." It was hard to imagine that she was barely older than Ulrika herself. She carried herself with such strength and certainty. Ulrika sat. She did not sit back but perched, rubbing her fingers against her palms.

"I know you find it difficult to talk about what's happened, Ulrika," she said, still without turning. "But there is information I need to know."

"Yes, Miss Anderson." Ulrika swallowed hard. "I promise not to cry."

"You can cry all you like, just don't avoid the questions."

"Yes, Miss Anderson." She felt so pathetic; her eyes were burning with salty tears already. She was angry with herself for having no backbone. It felt as if her heart were fluttering behind her ribcage, like a bird trying to escape.

A shadow moved to her side. She looked up to see Miss Anderson dangling a kerchief for her. She took it and wiped her eyes.

"You did well last night, Ulrika," said Maliha. "You got little Baba away."

Ulrika sniffed. "It was Amita," she sniffed, "and your Mr Crier." "And you."

Miss Anderson sat down in front of her, across the table. "I am sorry that you were put in danger, and thank you for helping to save the baby."

Ulrika opened her mouth but did not know what words to say. Miss Anderson smiled at her. It was the kindest smile Ulrika thought she had ever seen. She sniffed again and wiped her eyes. Then she whispered "Thank you."

"Why didn't you tell me who your father is?"

Terror flooded Ulrika. She went cold and felt as if her every muscle and joint was paralysed. She flinched when Miss Anderson reached out and took her hand. But all she did was give it a gentle squeeze and release it again. The desperate desire to flee did not diminish.

Miss Anderson sat back and put her head on one side as if she was reading Ulrika's mind. Ulrika swallowed. The other woman pushed back her chair and stood slowly, making no sudden moves, then turned her back on Ulrika. She seemed to be loosening her dress and let the right shoulder drop down over her forearm. Then the left dropped too.

Ulrika stared. Whip scars criss-crossed the woman's back.

"Who did that to you?"

"It doesn't matter," said Miss Anderson. She covered up again and sat back down. "You have them too, don't you?"

Ulrika nodded. There was no point denying it; she already knew Miss Anderson could see into her heart. "What colour is your baby's skin?"

Panicking, Ulrika jumped up but Miss Anderson's hand was already round her wrist, holding her back, not letting her out of the chair. Ulrika gave up.

"Is Henry black?"

Ulrika nodded.

"You're lying to me."

"No, Henry is black. He's black, black as the night, black as sin, black as dirt." The words came out of her like a chant. She did not see the blow coming. It was not hard but the slap across her face snapped her back to the present.

"Henry is white, isn't he?" Miss Anderson's voice was not harsh but coaxing and gentle.

Tears burst from Ulrika's eyes. "No, no, no, not white, he can't be white."

"I know he's white."

"How can you know?"

"Because Henry's father is your father."

Ulrika wanted to scream that it wasn't true. But the fear and the shame filled her. The memories of every night that he came into her bed. From the first night that he hurt her, when she hid from him; being dragged across the floor. And every night thereafter. His threats against her if she dared try to tell anyone. How she would be locked up if she did. His endless blows. The things he did. What he made her do.

Grief and the suppressed hatred welled up inside her. She felt as if it would burn away her flesh. She sobbed with great tearing breaths as if her body were not strong enough for the pressure of the emotion to escape.

Miss Anderson held her hand. Ulrika clung to her as if she were the only thing that would not break.

Her throat was hoarse when the tides of emotions eventually subsided. Her eyes were dry because there were no more tears that could be shed. They felt red raw and gritty. But her hands no longer shook. She felt empty of the pain, as if it had been drained away. As if she was no more than a clay vessel.

Miss Anderson released her hand and went to the bureau. She returned with a glass of water. "Here."

Ulrika drank it down in one go.

"You're probably hungry," said Miss Anderson. Ulrika realised she was. Very hungry indeed.

"We'll eat soon but now you need to tell me exactly how you found the woman to take your baby."

And to her surprise Ulrika found that she did not want to cry anymore.

ii

Maliha, Valentine and Ray emerged into the light through the swing doors of the hotel. The air tasted dry and the few clouds dodged the relentless sun.

"We shouldn't leave 'em alone," said Ray. "Meeta can't protect all the others with her arm like that."

"There are only two reasons for the attack," said Maliha. "Either because we're non-whites in a white-only hotel who dare to bring in a black baby, or because we're making progress in the investigation. In the first instance we've made it clear we're leaving so that should prevent any further attack and, in the second, I'm the target and I'm not there."

She did not mention the third possible reason: that it was someone who had discovered Valentine's subterfuge and that he was the target.

"I need to go to the air-dock," said Valentine.

Maliha nodded. "We'll see you later."

"I don't know when I'll be back."

"I know."

They had said their proper farewells in a quiet moment alone in his rooms. She could still feel his lips on hers. But here in the present he touched his fingers to his hat and headed away at a brisk pace.

Ray hailed a hansom for them and Maliha gave instructions to take them out to the west border of the city. The interior of the cab was roasting in the midday sun and the smell of the sweating horse drifted in through the open window as they headed at a slow trot through the streets. They soon left the central shopping area and were heading through the business district.

"Where's he off to then?" asked Ray. His attitude was offhand but Maliha was sufficiently experienced with him to know how dangerous that was.

"He has some business to take care of."

"Bill Crier used to work for the Foreign Office at the Fortress," Ray continued casually. "He had an air-plane they gave him. He called it *Alice*."

"Really?"

"Your name."

"Our relationship is not exactly private, Ray," she said. "If he chooses to name a flying machine after a name I don't use because I don't like it that's not really my problem. He's a romantic at heart."

Ray was silent for a few minutes. "Except he's a spy," he paused for effect, "and I reckon he killed at least two men when you was in Pondicherry. How'd the French feel about that?"

"I have no idea what you're talking about."

"And that guru wossisname in Kerala."

"Do you have a point, Ray?"

"I reckon he's on the trail of something big, is all."

Maliha finally turned and faced him. "Even if that were true, do you think for one moment that I would tell you anything?" She sat back again. "And that's supposing he told me."

"'E'd tell you everything," said Ray.

Maliha said nothing and returned her gaze to the outside world. The people walking the streets reduced in numbers and changed from only white to a mix. The cab stopped.

Maliha let Ray pay the driver. If she was right he was going to learn everything he wanted in the next hour.

She then led the way along a side street with a high wall on one side and poor quality residential housing on the other.

"Christ, I recognise that stink," said Ray. He was not wrong; the air was filled with the putrid stench of sewage. He stared around, tried to jump to see over the wall but when that failed studied the buildings in more detail. "These are the same sort as Nickells' house."

"That's correct and, about a half-mile that way," Maliha said, pointing over the wall, "is where the black children were taken."

"You know where the children are?"

"No."

They came to an ornate iron gate in the wall. Moulded into its lattice of metal were the words "Treatment Works". The smell became even worse wafting out through the gap.

Inside they could see the great circles of the sewage beds with sprinklers rotating and letting the liquid effluent spill out on to the stones. Closer to them, off to the left, was a two-storey brick administrative building.

"Very modern," Ray muttered then laughed. "So we're going to be stirring shit this afternoon."

"Must you?"

"I thought it was funny."

"I'm sure you did."

Maliha took hold of the metal handle and turned it. The gate swung open on well-oiled hinges. They went in and closed the door behind them.

"Did you want a tour, then?" asked Ray. "I'm sure they won't mind us wandering round sniffing the flowers."

Maliha looked around. "There should be a series of tanks here where they let the effluent stand and liquefy before putting it out on to the beds."

She looked to the right. There was a slight incline up to a low brick wall. "This way."

She walked briskly up the slope towards the brick barrier. The beat of a thumping engine emerged from the background sounds as they climbed. As they got closer the walls resolved into a set of nine squares in a three by three pattern. Each square comprised a wall two feet high, and perhaps twenty feet on a side, while the inner space of each was hidden beneath corrugated iron panels. The stench of human waste grew worse at each step until Maliha felt as if she would have to eject the contents of her stomach.

There was the sound of retching behind her. She saved Ray's pride by not turning. Instead she rummaged in her bag and pulled out a bottle of lemonade. She set it on the edge of the wall and continued round.

The air throbbed with the sound of the pumping station; she could see it now, a small building amid a few bushed near the outer wall. It had a chimney that emitted a line of smoke. Wide pipes emerged from the building and each one ran to one of the nine tanks.

Maliha studied them thoughtfully. They would probably have to examine the contents of the tanks.

"Oi! What do you two want here?"

Maliha turned to face a red-faced man in an overall huffing up the slope towards them. He was overweight and the blue-grey overalls he wore did nothing to slim his figure. His moustache drooped at the ends but that was probably intentional.

"You can't be here. Tours on Thursdays only," he puffed.

"Tours? Are you serious?" said Ray, his voice sounded strangled as if he were still fighting the acidic taste. He had picked up the lemonade and was taking sips. *Pity*, thought Maliha as she had been hoping he would choose not to drink it.

Maliha smiled and held out her gloved hand. "My name is Anderson. I am pleased to meet you Mr…?"

"Oh." He wiped the palm of his hand on his overall and her hand disappeared inside his wide flabby palm. He did not grip her hand tightly but gave it the slightest shake. "Grummond."

"You're British?" she said.

"Yes, Mrs Anderson, Institute of Civil Engineers. On loan as it were, getting the new station running properly. Then it's back to Blighty," he paused as if uncertain. "Hopefully."

She smiled. "My father was Iain Anderson, the engineer. You might have heard of him."

"Well, goodness me," he said and grinned. "The Anderson valve? Such a useful invention, we have one—well several—in the pumping station." Then he remembered. "I heard about…I mean…I'm sorry."

"Thank you, Mr Grummond," she said. "You're very kind." She turned and indicated Ray. "This is Mr Jennings, he's a newspaperman." She could not help but notice the cloud that descended over Grummond's demeanour when she mentioned the press. "However, he is not here in any official capacity. I wanted to see the treatment works and he was willing to accompany me."

"Afternoon," said Ray giving a nod to Grummond, who seemed to brighten a little.

"Can we look inside the pumping station?" she asked to distract him.

"As it's you, Mrs Anderson—oh, Miss Anderson?"

"Yes, Mr Grummond, just Miss. My fiancé is otherwise engaged this afternoon which is why Mr Jennings is here."

"'E didn't fancy the stink," muttered Ray.

Mr Grummond led the way to the pumping station door and unlocked it. Hot, fetid air wafted out. He went in and Maliha followed.

"I'll stay out here if you don't mind?" said Ray. "I don't know how it's possible but that place smells even worse than it does out here."

"Don't wander off," said Maliha.

Ray scowled and said quietly. "I don't even know why we're here."

After the bright outdoors the interior was pitch black. Her eyes adjusted quickly and Grummond switched on a light. The outer part of the building did not rise very high but inside it had been cut into the ground and went down over thirty feet. The brickwork inside was covered in an impressive pattern of green and white tiles and brick columns rising up to a vaulted ceiling.

The pumping machines throbbed, hissed and gurgled in a complex rhythm of sounds. There were three in total, driven with steam from a furnace running in a chamber opposite the entrance. Under the electric lights the brass, copper and steel glinted brightly.

Each pump managed three wide inlet pipes that fed in from the walls. And the same three pipes then led up twenty feet and into the wall beneath her feet. She thought she knew which tanks were the most likely candidates but in the end she might have to check them all. She shivered involuntarily.

"It's beautiful, isn't it?" said Grummond proudly. Maliha looked up at where he stood leaning over the glistening rail and smiled.

"Does each of the inlets correspond more or less to the direction they come from?"

"Let's go down," he said. "I'll walk you through it."

She spent the next ten minutes half-listening to his description of the system. Most of the functionality was obvious; the only thing she was truly interested in was the source of the effluent from pipe to pipe. He knew them all and she linked them to the map of Johannesburg in her mind.

"I'd like to see in the tanks," she said after his explanation had wound down. They were standing on the painted floor of a cathedral to sewage. The pumps thudded around her and the disgusting contents.

"You would?" He had a pained look on his face. "They are not the sort of thing for a young lady's eyes."

"I know," she said. "But even so."

"I don't know if I should."

She turned towards him. "Mr Grummond, do you know what I do?"

He frowned uncomprehendingly, gave his head a slight shake.

"I investigate crime."

The fear returned to his eyes. He glanced at the stairs as if he intended to make a run for it.

"And you have a secret that you think would result in imprisonment, or at least serious trouble."

His knees buckled and he leant against the nearest pumping machine for support. Sweat broke out across his brow and he wiped his hand across it. "I have a wife, a son. Please don't…" He seemed at a loss to know exactly what it was he did not want her to do.

"Mr Grummond, what you do does not harm any other person." Maliha knew she was feeling her way in the dark. She had not the slightest idea what it was that drove the fellow's guilt but he did not give the impression of being a malicious fellow.

"No, I swear it. I never have."

"Then I see no reason to betray your secret." He sagged again, this time from relief. "However I want no more questioning of my requests."

"Of course, whatever you want."

"And," she said, "you really should cease those activities."

"Yes, I will, thank you."

She knew he meant his promise when he said it. And she knew he would fail to keep it. Sooner or later his compulsion would get the better of him and he would justify giving in to it. She hoped it would not degenerate into anything that involved anyone else. Whatever it was.

iv

The sun's light blinded her once more as they emerged.

Ray was not immediately visible; she finally spotted him standing in the shade of the bushes beside the pumping house. He emerged when she beckoned, the lemonade bottle dangling from his hand.

"I need you to help Mr Grummond lift off the covers on the tanks."

"You're not serious?"

"I'll get you some gloves," said Mr Grummond and headed off in the direction of the administration building.

Maliha looked at the nine tanks. The one in the top-left position was the best option. The centre of the nine would be her next choice but it would be better to deal with them systematically. Her guess could be completely wrong anyway.

"What did you see in there?" asked Ray.

"I just wanted to see where the pipes came in from and which tank they led to."

"Didn't know you had such an interest in crap."

"Must you use that language?"

Ray grinned. "Does it upset you?"

"Inasmuch as it's inaccurate, yes."

"Sorry, your majesty."

"Shut up, Ray," she said. "Or I'll pass on details of your behaviour to Amita."

He had been poised to utter some retort or other, but he shut his mouth. A result that Maliha found quite satisfactory and enlightening.

Mr Grummond returned a few minutes later carrying two sets of gloves. He handed one pair to Maliha. They were far too big. "In case you need them," he said. "They're the smallest ones we have."

Ray pulled on the other pair and Grummond handed him a T-shaped tool with a hook at the other end. "Called a *tau*," he explained. "Put the T in your fist and use the hook to lever up the sheet so you can get your fingers under it.

They stood at either end of the first panel. Ray had a few false starts but finally got the *tau* underneath the panel and lifted. A cloud of flies, tens of thousands of them, erupted from the gap. Ray dropped his end in shock and ran back a dozen paces. Maliha and Grummond waited while he recovered himself and returned. Together they managed to get the whole panel off to the side and leaning against the wall. Ray choked and retched again. There were three panels to each tank and a couple of minutes later they had all been removed.

Bracing herself Maliha judged the breeze, such as it was, and approached the open top from the windward side to reduce the appalling malodorous stench. She looked down. The surface was a few feet below. The top of the brown and grey liquid was an oily slime with patches of foam. Tiny bubbles were constantly rising and popping releasing their miasma. Thankfully unidentifiable lumps floated here and there while others rose and sank. The air was thick with flies.

She forced herself to scan the surface taking in everything trying to identify items. There was the occasional stick or twig that were almost comforting as she took it all in. Finally she stepped back, she turned away and sought air that was at least a little cleaner.

"Have you finished?" said Ray.

She didn't respond. There was something nagging her, an image in her mind.

"We'll put it back then, yeah?"

"No," she said abruptly.

"What?"

She turned and came back to the tank. She knew where she needed to look but the thing she had seen that nagged at her was no longer visible. It must have sunk. She kept her eyes on the place.

"Mr Grummond, do you have such a thing as a boathook?"

"I'll get it."

He set off again.

"You want to fetch something out of this?"

"No, Ray," she said. "I want *you* to do the fetching. I'll do the guiding."

"You know I've already thrown up four times, right?"

"I know," said Maliha. "It means you'll have nothing left to come up. Right?" She mimicked his accent with the final word.

"Think you're funny, do you?"

She was distracted by Grummond hurrying back. He was now dripping with sweat but showed no sign of slowing down. She wondered whether he could even smell what it was like here anymore. Ray took the boathook without any further question.

"Where do you want me then?"

Maliha went back to the tank and closed her eyes. The piece of knitted material she had belatedly recognised, though it was covered in filth, had been about three foot in from the side opposite her.

She opened her eyes and pointed. The material had not resurfaced but she was sure of the location now. Ray knelt on the edge of the wall, then jumped as Mr Grummond grabbed his jacket.

"Don't want you falling in, Mr Jennings."

Ray gave an unconvincing laugh. "Yeah, no, me neither." He glanced up at Maliha's pointing finger and dipped the five-foot pole down until it was just above the surface.

Maliha called instructions to him. He always seemed to overshoot and it took a while before she was happy with his position, taking into consideration the length and angle of the hook itself.

"All right, put it in, but slowly," she ordered. She saw Ray screw up his face as he slowly dipped the pointed end of the boathook into the disgusting morass. He stopped before the hook part had touched the surface. "There's something in the way," Ray shouted.

"Pull up a bit, take it to your left a few inches and down again."

This time the head of the boathook went all of the way in and down. She saw him leaning further over with Mr Grummond holding tight. When it looked as if it had gone in about a foot she called a halt. "Move it back to your right."

He did so. The surface around the pole swirled and eddied. Something with rounded surfaces lifted up and then sank out of sight. Ray choked. "Don't be sick now!" Maliha shouted.

"Got something," he said with a gulp. "Something's there."

"Pull up a little so the hook engages, then stop."

He did so, then looked at her with a frown on his face.

"Ray, Mr Grummond, whatever you pull up, don't let it go. It's important." They just stared at her. "Do you understand?" Mr Grummond nodded.

"No, I don't bloody understand," said Ray. "I do understand that you hate my guts and this is your revenge."

"Ray, if I'd wanted revenge I could have done it a dozen other more effective ways than this," she said. "I need you to trust me."

He looked at her with a face full of disdain. "Yeah, whatever you say, Miss bloody Anderson."

"When you're ready then."

Ray focused on the bubbling liquid below them. He moved his hands down the pole a further few inches and then drew it up slowly.

Something broke the surface, and Ray stopped pulling. As the liquid of the tank drained away it resolved into the corner of a knitted blanket. It had a smooth edging that Maliha guessed was probably satin.

"Just the corner of a blanket," shouted Ray.

Maliha raised her hand to her neck. She felt cold despite the heat. "Keep pulling." She realised that the words had caught in her throat and she had made no noise at all. "Keep pulling."

Ray did as instructed. More of the blanket came up out of the mire. It was getting heavier and Ray was straining. He paused for a moment to let the liquid drain, then lifted again.

Then Maliha saw it. A lump, no more than a couple of inches long, emerged. The liquid ran off it.

"Don't drop it!" Maliha screamed moments before Ray let the rod slip momentarily. The lump sank.

"Fucking Christ, Maliha!"

She looked into his face. It was drained of colour.

"Tell me you've still got it hooked. For god's sake, Ray!"

He nodded. "Yeah, still got it."

"You have to bring it in."

He nodded, his face filled with fear.

"What are you two talking about?" said Grummond.

"Close your eyes, Mr Grummond," she said.

"Don't be silly."

"Fucking close them, Grummond, and don't fucking let go of me."

"Do as he asks, Mr Grummond," Maliha said in more consoling terms. "Please, it will be for the best."

Grummond frowned but followed her direction.

Ray looked at Maliha with despair in his eyes.

"You have to, Ray," she said. "I'm sorry."

He nodded and sighed. He pulled again.

And the bloated body of the dead baby rose from the mire.

v

Ray had not passed out but his body had tried to eject his stomach's contents repeatedly, except there was nothing more to come up.

Grummond had panicked when he realised what was lying on the stone slabs at the side of the tank. Maliha told him to fetch a cloth and a bucket of water. And when he had done that and they had covered the body she sent him to fetch the police.

The flies still filled the air. Thankfully the disgusting stench of the place kept the vultures away.

The battered body of Lochana Modi, crushed skulls, poisoned husbands, beaten and broken friends, poisoned girls and caesarean births. Never mind the leprous poor of India. Her experience with those things did not compare to this. She felt numb, and her fingers were cold.

She shook herself. She must look at the body and there was only a limited amount of time.

"Want any help?"

Ray's voice came from behind her. She realised she had not heard the sound of his convulsing body for a minute or two.

"No," she said. "I'll do it."

"My mother was a martyr," said Ray. "Just like you. Never accepted help, always had to do everything herself. Died at thirty-five."

"Disease brought on by exhaustion and overwork?"

"Nah, she was hit by some drunk toff in a steam carriage," said Ray. "Probably would've outlived me. She was tough as nails."

Maliha felt like laughing but it was not appropriate.

"Yeah, it's funny," said Ray. "We all had a laugh about that. Eventually. She was like that though, always liked to 'ave a laugh. Joker to the end."

"Is that even true, Ray?"

"Every word." He came up beside her and stared at the form under the cloth. "Better wash that crap off before it dries hard or you won't be able to do your thing."

"My thing?"

"Your magic, Miss Anderson," he said. "Whatever it is, right now we're just prevaricating, ain't we?"

He was right. Why did the fact that it was a child make it harder? She shook her head and knelt down beside the body.

"Should've asked him for a tin bath."

Maliha couldn't decide whether it would be better to start at the feet or the head. Ray plunged his hand into the bucket and pulled up a cup. He grabbed the bottom of the cloth and pulled it past the small bare feet. He doused them with water and started to wipe.

She looked at him. His face scrunched up in concentration, perhaps holding back the horror, and she found that, suddenly, she did not hate him. When push came to shove, Ray Jennings did the right thing. And that's all anybody could ask.

* * *

The child was black, male, about eight months old and had been dead a couple of days. There was post-mortem damage to the skin probably from the battering as it passed through the sewer system. But there did not seem to be any other wounds on the body. That indicated the child had not been tortured or otherwise harmed, then thrown into the sewer alive, for which she was grateful.

The boy's head had been hidden inside the wool blanket with the satin edging and when they unwrapped it it provided the final confirmation the child had been dead before being disposed of. But Ray's strength deserted him one final time. The top of the skull had been sliced off. The brain was missing as were the eyes. Ray fell back.

"Fetch some water to drink, Ray."

He did not answer but climbed to his feet and stumbled away.

Maliha did not wipe away the tears that fell from her eyes. She blinked to clear the blurriness and moved round to examine the wound in more detail. The bone of the skull had thousands of tiny serrations indicating a mechanical cutting tool. She covered the body again and sat back on her heels.

Ideas as to why someone would do this, how they *could* do this, fought with how she could possibly tell Ulrika the likely consequence for her son, even if he were the incestuous get of her own father. Or how Wit Nickells could be told. Or the black families, one of whom was family to this child.

She stood up and stared out into the city.

What was happening here?

After a while Ray returned with a tin mug of tea and another bucket of water.

"Clean yourself up," he said and put the bucket down under the bushes by the pumping station. She washed her hands and face. The water was refreshing and she felt herself recovering a little.

He handed her the tea. It looked intensely brown. It tasted as if he had used three spoons of tea in that one mug and then emptied the sugar bowl into it. It was completely stewed and she hated tea with sugar. She drank it all down and felt the strength returning to her.

"Nothing like a good cup of tea," said Ray. "Good job our mate Grummond is a proper Brit."

"This is nothing like a good cup of tea, Ray," she said. He looked hurt. "But thank you. It's what I needed."

The first Johannesburg uniformed police officer hurried through the gates with Mr Grummond and Maliha sighed. "Here we go."

vi

"Well, Miss Anderson," said the chief detective. "You have really done it this time."

"I beg your pardon?"

She looked out through the window of the office in which she and Ray had been put after the police took over the area. There were nearly twenty officers in uniform and half a dozen in plain clothes combing the grounds.

Pointlessly.

"You had to keep digging."

"I think that's a fairly poor turn of phrase under the circumstances."

"What did you think you would achieve?"

She turned away from the window. The chief detective looked as if he'd aged twenty years. Given that he could be expected to have several sleepless nights ahead of him she did not expect he was going to be looking much better for a long while.

"I am investigating the disappearance of children," she said. "And you can add to that their murder and mutilation." She did not want to save his feelings since she had yet to find any. "Hopefully after they were dead."

"If you had left it alone as I told you—"

"What, and allowed these murderers to continue kidnapping and killing children?" she stopped for a moment. "Or is killing black babies not a crime?"

"Of course it's a crime," he said hotly. He approached her, emphasising the foot of height he had over her. "We were investigating."

"Really? When did that start? You told me yourself that you didn't believe it was happening."

"Your evidence in regard to Wit Nickells—"

"Oh, so you believed me? That's a novelty—Mr Jennings? Do make a note of that, won't you?"

Vandenhoek glanced across at Ray who was perched on a desk with his notebook and a pencil. He looked up with a malicious grin and waved at the chief detective.

"You will not print any of this!"

"I am a member of the press, Chief Detective Vandenhoek. You spell that with an oh-ee, doncha?"

"I'll have you in jail, and I'll throw away the key!"

Jennings' grin became wider. "Embarrassed Crusher Jails Innocent Journalist."

Vandenhoek's face had become so red it looked as if he were going to explode. Maliha decided she had done enough.

She turned her back on the chief detective. "Am I under arrest?"

"No," growled Vandenhoek.

"What about Mr Jennings?"

"No."

"Good," she said. "Now, shall we sit down? You can ask me anything you like about the case and I will attempt to answer those questions to the best of my ability."

Vandenhoek growled again but pulled up one of the straight-backed chairs and sat facing the window so he could see what was going on. Ray stayed on the desk while Maliha brought a chair close to the window and sat also facing out.

A number of water treatment engineers had turned up, some of them were black.

"How did you know to look here?" asked Vandenhoek in a forced calm.

"I didn't really," she said. "It was just a guess."

"Are all your guesses like this?"

"Usually."

"I see." He paused and she glanced at him. He was staring out at where a doctor was examining the child's body before moving it. "I have never had to deal with anything like this before."

"Neither have I," she said. "It is an abomination."

He turned his gaze on her. "Yes, that is the word." His face hardened. "But you still have not explained why you came here."

"It was possible, of course, that the children were being shipped away in which case we would have no chance of discovering them," she said. "But the method by which they were being kidnapped seemed too sophisticated for simple slavers, and very young children don't make good slaves."

"They have other uses," said the chief detective darkly.

"I know, but again that route would be much harder to trace, so I went for the simpler option."

"Simpler? What are you talking about?"

"They were being taken one at a time, used in some fashion, and then disposed of," she replied.

"It would be simpler to take the bodies into the grass and leave them for the animals," said Vandenhoek.

"Yes, and the fact that they did not tells us a great deal."

Vandenhoek's face relaxed. "You mean they are not locals so the best idea they had was to put the bodies in the sewer."

Maliha did not respond and looked out.

"Lucky you found the right one first."

"Yes," she said absently. "That was lucky, wasn't it?"

He got to his feet and went to the door.

"We are free to go?" asked Maliha, standing as well.

"Yes," he said. "I understand you have booked passage back to India."

"That's right."

He turned to go then stopped halfway through the door. "I should thank you for your assistance."

"Yes," she said. "You should."

"I know you think of us as primitive and uncultured, Miss Anderson," he said. "But we can be the bigger man, so I want to thank you for your help and I hope your journey home is uneventful."

Maliha smiled as he left and shut the door. She allowed the sound of his footsteps to disappear before she turned to Ray with no sign of the smile she had been wearing.

"What a nasty bloke," said Ray. "And I thought the police back home were bad."

Maliha did not disagree.

"We're not leaving, are we?" he said.

"We? Mr Jennings? You are not one of my party; what you choose to do is your business."

He put his head on one side. "All right. Yes. I know. But you're not leaving, are you?"

"I am not."

Ray's face fell. "But you're sending Meeta back?"

"With Barbara, Ulrika and the baby, yes. Someone needs to look after them." She turned away and moved the chair back to where it had come from and then the chair the chief detective had used.

There was a map on the wall showing the route of the main sewers through the city. Maliha studied it for a few moments and then said. "She likes you."

"What?"

"Amita likes you, Ray."

There was a long pause. "She punched me."

"Everyone wants to punch you, Ray."

Another long pause. "I like her."

"Even though you know what she is?"

The next pause was even longer. "Because of what she is."

Maliha smiled at the map. She knew it was difficult for him, and what he had admitted was a crime that would get him locked up.

"You could go back to India with them."

"Nah, the story's here," he said. "And you were right; it's a bloody good story. I'll steal the front page from that Winifred Churchill cow."

"We better get you to a place you can write it up and send it then, hadn't we?"

She turned back and Ray was grinning like a cat that had got the cream.

vii

Valentine took his room key from the desk clerk who slouched back into his chair once his duty was discharged. The foyer of the hotel was empty. Valentine strode across it to the stairs and was about to push through the worn door.

"Hey."

He turned to see the desk clerk waving a letter. Valentine retrieved it from the man, who said nothing further and relaxed back into his chair, and headed upstairs.

The room was as he had left it as far as he could tell. The bed still unmade, the wardrobe door closed tight, the half-consumed whiskey bottle still on the bureau.

He opened the cupboard and looked at the screwed up paper in the corner behind his suitcase. He pulled it out and opened it carefully. The hair was missing. Valentine smiled.

The sun was on the other side of the building so he did not have to suffer its intense heat but the room was stuffy. He pulled up the window letting the sound of the city in with the slightly fresher air.

He sat on the bed leaning against the wall with the pillow supporting his back and examined the envelope. His fake name and the hotel address were typed and there was no stamp. He might be able to get a description of the person who delivered it from the desk clerk. He tore through the top of the envelope with his finger and extracted the thin paper from the interior.

Mr Jonathan Dyer esq.

We are pleased to confirm that our enquiries in regard to your bona fides have been successfully concluded. Your appointment will commence this coming Thursday. We lift at midnight. You will be informed of the location separately.

Yours sincerely,

Capt Blake

Valentine put his head back against the wall and closed his eyes. He had done it at last. He would be aboard one of the vessels that should not even exist.

And then he thought of Maliha.

He still had some time with her but that would be all. And then they might never see one another again. There was a good chance he would end up dead. If not from the slavers themselves then in a fight, or even by an attack by the Royal Navy.

He toyed with the idea of simply going to the consulate with this information and staying with Maliha. But he could not; he had to bring down Timmons. Not just for Maliha but for Riette and Marten and every other person enslaved or taken by them.

And he could discover the secret of their Faraday device that could lift a ship the size of a Sky-Liner as if it were a feather.

These things were so much more important than his relationship with a woman he had met on a passenger ship. He remembered the way she had moved the previous night and smiled.

Valentine rolled over on the bed. He had not realised how tired he was. But the night had been long on action and short on rest. A quick nap would do him the world of good.

* * *

He jumped to being fully awake.

His arm was hot. The brightness through his eyelids told him that the sun was now shining through his window directly on him. He must have been asleep for hours.

A shuffle of movement on the floorboards behind him told him there was someone else in the room. Without thinking he rolled over and up into a sitting position. He got his feet on the floor and launched himself at the dark figure by the bureau. Even as he did so he caught sight of someone crouched down by the door.

He landed on the intruder and bore him to the ground. There was a childlike squeal from the one by the door. He got his knee in the back of the one under him when something hit him over the head. It was a surprise but no damage was done.

"Get off my brother!"

Valentine lashed out with his arm to grab the other assailant round the knees but found a waist instead. A thin, childlike waist. *Brother?*

He stood up and jumped back to the wall.

Izak lay on the floor. Lilith's face was pulled into a very serious expression of anger with her fists curled into hard and dirty balls. Izak turned over and grinned. "Good fighter, boss."

"What are you two doing here?" he demanded. "And how did you get in?"

Lilith glanced at the open window. "Open windows invite snakes."

"Not on the third floor."

She smiled. "Some snakes got legs."

"What are you doing here?"

Izak's face grew serious. "Goddess wants you. Bad business."

Valentine panicked. "She's not hurt?"

"She's not hurt," said Izak. "But she found babies."

"That's good."

"Dead babies."

"Oh god," said Valentine. Izak and Lilith crossed themselves like Catholics though Valentine guessed they'd probably never been in a church—except perhaps to steal something. He also knew Maliha was not as strong as she pretended to be. "Is she really all right?"

"The goddess is angry," Lilith said simply.

Yes, that was her other emotional setting. She could burn with an anger that would scorch anyone who stood too close. Most people did not see it in her, but he had felt it.

"All right," he said. "I need to get back to the hotel. You go back the way you came, I'll just go out through the front."

Lilith put her hand on his wrist. He looked down into her brown eyes. "You be careful. Danger outside."

"Why, what's wrong?"

Lilith glanced at Izak who answered. "Goddess found black baby in white people's toilet. Black baby had head cut open. Black people angry. Mama Kosi say white people use bad magic. She make black people fight."

He looked back at Lilith who had squeezed his wrist. "Black people want to kill white people dead and dead."

"You come hard way with us," said Izak. "Goddess said we have to help you find your way."

Valentine nodded. He looked around the room; there was nothing here that he needed. He was paid up for a week so no one would come checking on him. He looked at the window. Well it wouldn't be the first time he had to leave a room that way.

"Won't you be in danger if you're with me?" he said.

Izak grinned showing a lot of white teeth. "If that happens, we just knock you down and kick you."

Valentine matched his smile with a wry grin.

"Lead the way," he said.

CHAPTER 7

i

"Did you have to tell her?" asked Valentine. He was looking through the doorway into Maliha's bedroom. Ulrika was curled up in the opposite corner. He could not see whether she was crying but her body was moving rhythmically with her heavy breathing.

"What else was I supposed to do?" she said. "Let her read about it in a newspaper? Or overhear our conversation?"

"Yes, but…"

"There was no easy way, Valentine," she said and turned her head to look in on the girl. "Sometimes you have to do something bad in order to do right."

He looked at her profile in the light, her straight nose and delicate lips. "You don't always have to be the one to do it."

She turned back to him. "I may not be the one who committed the crime but I am the one who uncovered the truth of it. Who else has the responsibility?"

He sighed. He knew she was right, and he was sure she would have been as gentle as she could have been.

As if they were one person they moved away from the door to save any further embarrassment to the poor girl.

"Are you sure her Henry will be dead?"

The dark streets were empty; even the gentle background susurration of the city was absent. The mayor had announced a curfew. Anyone breaking it would be shot. Of course, they meant any blacks found breaking it.

She shook her head. "No, of course I can't be sure but it is most likely," she took a deep breath. "And even if he is not there is no telling what condition he might be in. He might be better off dead."

There was the crack of a gun in the distance.

"Izak said they cut the top off the head." Valentine said the words yet he could still barely believe it, let alone imagine it. How could someone do such a thing to a child?

"Yes."

"Why?"

Maliha sighed. "It was reminiscent of post-mortem examination or a surgical demonstration."

"That still doesn't explain why."

"Do I have to spell it out, Valentine?" she turned on him. "Do you have to make me say the words?" He tried to put his arm around her to provide some comfort but she shrugged him off. "Why don't you just think for a change?"

Her words hurt but he knew it was because of what she had seen. What he did not want to see.

"Someone is carrying out experiments. Why?"

"It may be related to the eugenics work of Galton."

"I don't know what that is." he said.

"That humans can be bred like dogs to produce desirable traits and weed out the undesirable ones," she said quietly. "It is a popular hypothesis in some quarters. They might be looking for evidence of a difference in brain development between blacks and whites."

"Oh," he said. "And where would you fit into that scheme?"

"I'm sure you can work it out, Valentine."

She turned on her heel, crossed to the connecting passage and went through into Barbara's suite.

* * *

Maliha tried to force herself into calm. She was not angry at Valentine, just the perpetrators of this monstrosity. But they were not here, and Valentine was. She still did not treat him well. Absently she turned the engagement ring on her finger. She wanted to act right now but she could not.

She must get Barbara and the rest away from here first and there was an entire day to be filled before that could be done.

The chief detective had insisted on providing them with guards. It was clear to her that the discovery of the dead child, and the public awareness of it, had decreased their danger but it was his attempt to atone for his earlier behaviour so she did not argue.

On the other hand the rioting was not something that could be determined by logical thought. Mobs were like rabid hyenas; they were entirely unpredictable.

She pushed through the second door and into Barbara's lounge. "Amita—" she started "—oh."

Amita and Ray were in a tight embrace. Maliha's immediate thought was that Amita was squeezing the life out of him, except that their lips were locked together. Amita was considerably taller than Ray and leaning down to him.

Ray opened his eyes and glanced sideways at Maliha. He tore himself away from Amita, stepping back. "Miss Anderson. I… we…"

Amita looked angry then followed his gaze and her face fell. "*Sahiba*, I am sorry."

They looked like naughty school children caught with their fingers in the chocolate box. Maliha smiled when she really wanted to laugh, but that would hurt their feelings.

"It is of no concern to me," she said, waving her hand as if to dismiss the issue. "But I think perhaps you should be more circumspect."

Ray did not seem to know where to put his hands. He finally shoved one in his pocket and used the other to punctuate his speech. "Yeah. You're right, sorry. Got carried away."

Maliha found their embarrassment awkward. "Amita, please go and check on Ulrika. Does the baby need feeding?"

"Soon, I expect."

"Well, take little Baba with you."

"That will make her more upset."

"Yes, but she needs to snap out of it. She's no use like this," said Maliha. "Feeding the baby will help her." *I hope.*

She waited while Amita fetched the baby. Amita was just crossing the room when she turned back. "*Mem sahib* spoke words today."

Maliha's heart leapt. "Is she awake now?"

Amita shook her head. "She made herself tired with talking." She turned back and went out.

"You're a hard woman, Maliha Anderson."

"I'm barely twenty, Ray. Hardly a woman."

"Goin' on eighty."

"Well, thank you for the compliment, so now I'm older than Barbara?"

"You know what I mean."

Maliha sighed and sat on the sofa, putting her feet up for the first time in nearly sixteen hours. She closed her eyes.

"Am I really hard?" she asked, almost in a dream.

"You drive people."

"Sometimes they need driving."

"Control them."

"Some need control," she muttered.

If he said anything further she did not know it.

When she opened her eyes it was dark. For a moment she did not know what had woken her but then the sound of shouting, screams and gunshots filtered into her consciousness.

Hundreds of voices. Indistinct, merged one into the other yelling, screaming in anger, shouting in pain. Men and women. And the guns, cracking again and again.

Maliha stood up. Her shoes had been removed but nothing else. There was the dark silhouette of someone standing at the French window, leaning forward on the rail.

She padded across the carpet, on to the floorboards and out to the metal grid of the balcony. She put her arm around Valentine's waist. He did not jump; he must have heard her.

"Barbara is asleep. I closed her window so she wouldn't hear this," he said.

Maliha looked down into the street. Immediately below them it was empty but looking west she could see the walls of buildings illuminated by flickering orange lights. In the open air the shouts and screams were louder, and the gunshots more distinct.

"They're setting fires," he said. She shivered.

"What can they possibly hope to achieve?" she said almost to herself.

"Their land is stolen from them; they are forced into ghettos and prevented from owning anything; and then their children are murdered," said Valentine. "How would you feel?"

"I've experienced some of it," she said. She leaned her head against his shoulder for comfort. "You want to fight back even if you don't know what you're fighting against."

They watched together for a while. The fires did not seem to be getting any closer; the screams and shouts were less regular. The sound of running feet echoed between the buildings below them. A black man emerged from an alley two hundred yards in the direction of the riot. He pounded up the street. As he drew opposite the hotel he stopped and looked directly up at them. There was a shout of anger below them and he set off again running hard.

Maliha looked down and saw the night porter holding a shotgun.

"Let's go to bed," said Maliha.

"Can't," said Valentine. "Ray's in my room. Ulrika and Amita with the baby in yours."

Maliha did not respond but stared back at the flickering lights, listening to the noise.

"I should have just gone home when I realised that Marten Ouderkirk's family would not take the baby."

"And if you'd done that children would continue to die."

"People are always dying. Children and adults. It's what happens in the world. We can't do anything about it. Look at them," she said nodding at the fighting.

"In which case, you have done no harm either."

She was silent again for a few minutes. "Do you believe in God, Valentine?"

"I suppose so," he said.

"Why?"

"Because otherwise there's no point," he said. "Do you?"

"In Hindu gods and goddesses? Not really. In the Christian god? Well, he's a lot nicer than the Jewish one, and if I had to believe in one I guess he'd be the one I'd prefer."

"But you don't believe in Him."

"Most believers have never read their basic text book, or if they have they don't understand it. All they do is blame him for anything bad and congratulate themselves for everything good. They take the parts that support their own actions and so claim what they are doing is God's will. He gave them free will, he doesn't guide their actions.

In war both sides claim he's on their side, but ignore the fact they aren't supposed to kill at all."

"So you despair of humanity?"

"Yes."

"But still try to make things better."

She sighed. "Yes."

"Because to do nothing is an even worse crime."

"And then this happens," she said waving her hand at the disturbances.

"They did not have to riot," he said. "That was their decision. The person who chose to kidnap children and murder them did not have to do it. It was their decision. None of that responsibility is yours. You have revealed the truth and people make their own decisions."

She was silent.

"They would have found another reason to riot eventually," he said. "As you pointed out they have enough justifications."

She turned towards him and put both arms around him. She rested her head against his shoulder and breathed in his hot, musky scent. In his turn he wrapped her in his arms and held her tight.

They clung to one another for a few minutes then Valentine guided her inside and sat her on the sofa. He went back and shut the window to block the noise.

"I'm going to have a drink," he said. "Do you want one?"

"What's the time?"

"One in the morning."

"Too late for tea. Just some water."

She perched on the edge of the seat and watched him pour a whiskey for himself. He brought over the two drinks and handed the water to her. Then he sat down with his leg touching hers but leaning back.

"You should try to relax," he said.

She took a sip of the water. She felt his hand wander across her back and across the skin of her shoulders. "Don't you have some kind of ritual that will dispel the worries and the tension?" he asked.

"If I sat on a mountaintop for a hundred years and rid myself of all worldly concerns," she said. "Apparently that works."

She heard him put his glass down on the side table. Then he pulled himself up on the sofa behind her. Both his hands came down on her shoulders. He began to rub and squeeze them rhythmically. She sighed as he forced the muscles to relax. She let her head droop forwards. His thumbs dug into the muscles on each side of her spine.

"Where did you learn to do that?" she asked.

"You probably don't want to know the answer."

There was a time when she would have demanded to know but it probably didn't matter. You didn't have to know everything. And knowing as much as she did had not led to a happier life as far as she could tell.

"A woman?" she asked.

"I would not let a man do this to me," he said.

"What about Amita?" she said with a laugh in her voice, gently reminding him of when he had kissed Amita thinking she was a woman.

"Perhaps Amita," he said.

"Françoise?"

"I doubt she would even want to touch me."

She wriggled. "Can you reach further down?"

"Not without removing your armour."

His fingers stopped moving against her skin, waiting for her decision. Maliha considered what events might occur in the morning. She was not concerned about Ulrika finding them but Ray coming in uninvited would be awkward. Amita was not a problem. If Barbara needed her she would be able to hear from in here.

"Lock the connecting door to your rooms and pull the curtains," she said.

He jumped off the sofa to carry out her instructions. She put down her glass, stood up and unfastened her dress. It slipped down to pool around her feet leaving her in satin bloomers with matching chemise.

She saw him moving across to switch on the light. "Don't," she said.

"You're not shy," he said.

"How would you know? But right now I'd like to be in the dark."

She kicked her dress off to the side and sat down again. She waited while he shucked off his clothes, not quite sure what degree of déshabillé he had reached. His shadowy form climbed behind her on the sofa and manipulated her back again. This time he rubbed all the way down her spine and up again.

It was very relaxing.

Then he kissed her neck. It tickled. Then he bit her gently. His arms snaked round and cupped her breasts. "Is this part of the treatment?"

"I understand it is an excellent way to relax the muscles."

"I love you, Valentine," she said.

She felt him shift his weight, no longer pressing against her. "But?"

"Not tonight, we need to sleep."

"You, Miss Anderson, are far too sensible for my good."

He released her and lay down along the sofa. She lifted her feet on to the cushions and wriggled into position, he with his arms around her.

He went to sleep before she did.

iii

Her modern French-styled dresses were an armour of sorts, thought Maliha as she stepped out of the hotel and into the sun. Wearing a sari made her vulnerable; like this she was the same as all the other Indian women that walked the streets of Johannesburg. Another potential victim to hatred and ignorance.

It had taken a lot of work to convince Amita that she must not accompany her. For someone who was supposed to be just a servant, who had arrived so timid and uncertain, Amita was growing into a formidable person in her own right.

Maliha was glad, of course, she just wished Amita would remember who was in charge. And appreciate that she could not ignore the fact she had been shot in the arm.

They had made her outfit quite modest, but only the *pallu* hid the lower marks on her back which could be revealed "by accident" for added effect.

There was very little traffic, far less than one would normally expect on a Wednesday, and Maliha made her way across the road without difficulty to where Izak and Lilith loitered in the alley. She ignored them and moved down the road and then up a side street before stopping to talk.

"You found her?"

"Auntie Flo, yes, we found her," said Izak. He was serious, and Lilith mimicked him, there was no laugh in her.

She almost wished they had not found the woman but her course was set.

"Take me to her."

They made the journey across the city on foot. Izak led her north at first before heading west in order to avoid the destruction of the night before.

Their circuitous route may have avoided the worst of the damaged streets but as they travelled towards the west they came across buildings with shattered windows. Men were busy hammering boards across the broken windows. The ground was littered with rocks and bricks.

They passed a building with blackened window frames and smoke still drifting from it. The smell of burnt wood and melted metal hung in the air around it.

They crossed a main road, still with almost no traffic, and the landscape changed abruptly. The buildings here were older and bore the old scars of the war but no new ones. Maliha kept her head down as they walked on until finally they reached a church, or at least the remains of one. It had been constructed of brick but nothing of it above ten feet remained in place. Grasses and moss grew from the mortar joints while bushes were scattered through the untended graveyard and inside the remaining structure.

The ironwork fence was still intact near the entrance but had been ripped away from everywhere else. The place was not deserted; it had been infested with the dregs of humanity. At a guess from looking at their faces, most were half-breeds with perhaps the colour of the Europeans but the facial structure of the natives, or the other way around.

There were makeshift tents and fires burning. Old people and young. Some children chased one another among the gravestones.

Izak and Lilith came to a stop near the gate. The arch that led through to the old entrance was intact.

"Auntie Flo is in here?"

"This is her place," said Izak. He shifted his weight from foot to foot and looked uncomfortable.

"You don't need to come in," said Maliha. "But if Auntie Flo comes out I need you to follow her, carefully."

Izak nodded.

Maliha walked up to the iron gate, pushed it open and stepped through on to the smooth flagstones. She knew from Ulrika's description what sort of person to expect. Someone round and smiling, someone who exuded pleasantness, sympathy and concern. Someone who loved children and wanted to see them given the best possible life she could.

Maliha adjusted the cloth about her neck so that it hid her face. The entrance to the church had no door to go with the lack of a roof. Despite that it seemed to become quieter when she entered and looked around.

The enclosing walls, such as they were, were scarred and burnt. Towards the far end of the ruin the stones were not overgrown and reflected the sun's light, like glass. She ran her fingers over what remained of the door frame. Where the hinges would have been were twisted pieces of metal.

The story of the church became clear to her. It must have been used as a munitions store during the war and been hit. The resulting explosion obliterated the roof, scored the insides of the walls and the heat of the explosion had partially melted the surface of the sandstone floor at one end, turning that part to glass where no plant could get purchase and grow.

There was no baby farmer here. There was nobody here. The only life was the plants and the buzz of insects.

But to her right there was a dark hole in the floor where stone steps led down. She took them, counting fifteen steps as she descended. Despite the light filtering from outside the dark seemed all-enveloping. She gave her eyes a few moments until she could discern the short corridor that ended in a door with a faint light escaping beneath it.

She knocked.

There was no response.

She knocked louder.

"*Wie is dit?*" the voice was quite deep in tone, to the point where Maliha was uncertain if the speaker was male or female.

"Auntie Flo?" Maliha gave her voice as much Indian as she could muster.

"Who?"

"I need help."

There was a long delay. Maliha could hear someone moving around inside. At one point something was knocked over; it could have been a chair or an empty wooden box.

A bolt slid back on the other side of the door. It opened a little and then the bottom of it scraped on the ground and it came to a halt. A shadowy figure, shorter than Maliha and much rounder, stood on the other side, a silhouette. The figure coughed deep in its lungs.

Maliha summoned a sob. "Please, are you Auntie? I need help."

The figure yanked harder on the door which scraped across the ground.

"I am Auntie Flo," she said. "Come in, *jong frau.*"

She moved back and Maliha stepped over the threshold.

iv

The crypt in which Auntie Flo made her home stank of her sweat, cigarettes and an underlying odour of beer. The room contained a small table and two chairs, one threadbare armchair of unknown vintage and a child's cot.

Maliha went straight over to the cot but it was empty except for dirty sheets.

"I do not have ladies in my rooms," said Auntie Flo and coughed again.

"I am desperate, Auntie Flo," said Maliha. "My father beat me for bringing shame to the family. I ran away but I cannot live alone. Someone said you can help."

Auntie Flo had not moved from the door, and was in darkness. But as Maliha turned towards her she stepped out into the light. Her skin was dark but not black, her features European and her dark hair was streaked with white. She walked with a limp. It seemed one of her legs was a different length to the other.

The sight of the woman's halting step made Maliha flinch. It had been a while since her injury had bothered her enough to make her limp, but the sight of Auntie Flo moving in hesitant jerks caused Maliha's old injury to ache in sympathy.

Auntie Flo smiled. It was a convincing smile, and her teeth were in good condition.

"Sit down, dear, and we'll talk about your problem."

She pointed to the chairs by the table. Maliha crossed to the table and took the chair nearest the door; it also afforded her the most complete view of Auntie Flo's lair.

Auntie Flo sat with a groan and pushed herself back into the chair so her twisted back was supported.

"Drink?" she asked.

Maliha shook her head. The crypt had no hearth, though it was not cold, but there were four sets of wrought iron fire tools lying by the partition. As her eyes adjusted more she could make out dozens of baby pictures lining the walls.

"All the children I have helped," said Auntie Flo. She conjured a stained glass from somewhere beside her, along with an open beer bottle. She emptied the contents of the bottle into the glass. Maliha cast her eyes down as if she had been caught out being bold.

"Can you help me, Auntie Flo?"

"Of course," she said with her wide toothy grin. "But I have to ask you some questions, but I don't want you to be upset. All right?"

Maliha nodded.

"Is your baby a boy or a girl?"

"She is a girl."

"And what colour was the father?"

"He is Indian like me."

"Hmmm," said Auntie Flo in a disappointed tone.

"Is something wrong?"

"Not a lot of call for Indian girls," said Auntie Flo. "You know how it is with your people. Boys are a blessing and girls only a burden."

"Yes," said Maliha sincerely. "I do know. Does that mean you cannot help me?"

"Oh no, not that I can't help you, no," she said and grinned again. "It just means it is harder. Might take a bit longer. Might cost a bit more."

"I do not have much money," said Maliha.

"I wish with all my heart I did not have to ask for money, little one." Auntie Flo's face became the epitome of sadness and sympathy. She stretched across and rested her fingers on Maliha's hand. "I know this is hard; you have to give away your heart; that is so much more difficult than giving away money."

Maliha said nothing but allowed herself a sob. She imagined that Ulrika would have been crying like the monsoon by this time. It was hard to imagine how she could even have got this far. The terror of her father must have exceeded the pain of giving away Henry, or seemed to have exceeded it, at first.

"What's your little girl called?"

"Sita."

"And how old?"

"Three months."

"So she is not yet weaned?"

Maliha was aware that her body would not pass that test. It was clear she was not feeding a child from her own breast. She sobbed. "I was not able. I could not…"

"So you found someone."

Maliha nodded then jerked her head up. "How will you feed my Sita?"

Auntie Flo smiled comfortingly. "You see how many children I have helped, there's always someone to be a wet nurse. You don't have to worry on that count."

"So you can help me?"

"Of course I can. I said I would and I will," she said. "But there are expenses while I find someone."

"I understand," Maliha slipped off a plain silver ring and placed it on the table between them. She could see Auntie Flo's eyes light up. "I hope this will be enough."

The woman almost snatched it up as if Maliha might change her mind and take it back.

"That will do for beginnings," said the woman. "There will be a fee for feeding and clothes."

"Can I see her afterwards?"

Auntie Flo's smile could not have been bigger and more generous. "Of course, it is important for you to see your little one."

"Thank you."

Auntie Flo climbed off the chair. "Don't you worry, sweetness, Auntie Flo will make everything right for you. You'll be able to go back to your family with your head held high and see your Sita whenever you want to."

Maliha stood and went to the door. "Thank you."

"Give it a good pull, sticks a bit," said Auntie Flo indicating the door.

"How will I know when you've found someone?" said Maliha then sobbed again. She hid her face in her hands.

"I will place an advert in the personal columns of the Johannesburg Gazette and address it to Sita's father. There will be an address and a time. You bring Sita."

"How long?"

"I will make enquiries immediately and we'll see what we can find."

Auntie Flo gave Maliha a final goodbye and pushed the protesting door closed behind her. Maliha climbed the steps and blinked in the sunshine. She went out through the gates but could not see Izak or Lilith anywhere as she turned back the way they had come. She heard the sound of children playing and glanced into the cemetery. Her two spies were chasing the others around the gravestones. Maliha caught Izak's eye and he nodded.

Maliha headed into the city.

v

The rooms were in uproar when Maliha returned. Amita was issuing orders in the middle of a confusion of cases, trunks and hotel staff. When Maliha entered Amita smiled at her and shouted at a young maid who happened to have stopped packing.

Maliha made her way across the room to where Amita stood with her arm in its sling. "I understood the ship was not leaving until tomorrow."

"It is so, *sahiba*," Amita said. "But the Sky-Liner lifts early in the morning. We must be aboard this evening."

Maliha nodded. "You are packing for everyone?"

"Yes, *sahiba*," then she frowned, "is that not correct? You are travelling also?"

"Let's go out on to the balcony."

Amita paused at the French window to allow Maliha to go out and then followed. The traffic levels were increasing at last as the pressures of trade and life forced scared people out of their homes to deal with those matters that would brook no further delay.

Maliha switched to Hindi so their conversation would not be understood even if it were overheard. "We will pretend that I and Mr Crier are accompanying you back to India. However we will not be."

"Then I must stay with you."

"No. You must go," said Maliha. "You must look after Barbara, Ulrika and the baby."

"Ulrika is coming?"

"She can't stay here."

"But her child?"

"If Henry is alive I will bring him," said Maliha. "But he isn't."

She did not add that, even if he was, she feared something terrible was being done to him.

"But I am your maid, *sahiba*. You saved me; I cannot leave your side."

Maliha smiled and put her hand on Amita's. She squeezed it gently. "You have been a most wonderful maid, and also a good friend. But that must come to an end."

Amita's expression turned to fear. "You are releasing me from your service? Have I done something wrong?"

"Of course not," said Maliha. "I am promoting you."

"I do not understand."

"What you have been doing here," she waved her hand towards the hustle and bustle in the suite, "and the responsibilities you have been taking. It is time for it to be official. You will receive an increase in wages, of course."

"*Sahiba*, I do not care about wages. I only want to serve you to the best of my ability."

"And your abilities are far greater than you consider them to be."

Amita fell silent as if she were absorbing this new idea.

"What will be name of my position?"

Maliha smiled again. "That is an excellent question. Housekeeper is entirely the wrong idea, although you will be responsible for that as well. In the very big houses they have a House Steward but I do not have a large estate nor many staff."

Maliha got the impression that Amita's head was spinning with such terms and none of them fitted. She needed to think of something more suitable.

"You would also oversee Naimh O'Donnell and the new school."

"You want us to return to Pondicherry, not Fortress?"

"Yes. That would be best, I think."

Maliha paused and watched as Amita took it all in. Then she could see a suspicion growing.

"Why do you need me to do this?" said Amita. "You will be there."

"I want someone who can ensure I am not bothered with day-to-day concerns," she said, and convinced herself it was not a lie. If she gave even a hint of the truth she would never be able to persuade Amita to leave. "Perhaps if we just call you my Executrix."

"Executrix?"

"A woman who gets things done," said Maliha. "I will write letters for you so you have the necessary administrative and financial control." *And I will write my will. Ray can witness it; he's used to keeping secrets.*

"You are too kind to me," said Amita, dropping her eyes and turning away. "I do not deserve this reward."

"I cannot think of anyone I trust more."

Amita sniffed. Maliha handed her her handkerchief.

"Have you thought about how we will move Barbara?" said Maliha switching to English.

Amita nodded and wiped her nose. "Yes, *sahiba*. A Faraday wheelchair has been ordered. It has been measured and will fit in the lift."

"Good, is she awake?"

"She was awake before you arrived."

"Good."

Maliha entered Barbara's bedroom where two trunks lay open on the floor and some clothes had already been packed away.

Barbara had been lifted into a sitting position on the bed and was surrounded by pillows to support her. Her eyes were open. Maliha felt the tingling border of the Faraday field as she sat on the edge of the bed angled to face Barbara. She looked so old and tired; it was as if Maliha was seeing her for the first time. Perhaps the last time.

Barbara twisted her body and her left hand came up and then down, landing on Maliha's. Maliha felt her eyes burn with nascent tears. She wiped them quickly.

"You're recovering well."

"Too slow," Barbara said. The words were slurred and the consonants lacked force but she was understandable. "Didn't see lions or zebra."

"Nor me."

"Dead babies."

Maliha nodded. She did not know where to look. The more she thought about it the angrier she became.

"The police are still looking," she said. "There have been no reports in the press but I know they will have found more."

"How many?"

"Five, ten, twenty. What does it matter?" Maliha brushed away the tears that now just hung on her eyelashes; the reduced gravity was insufficient to force them to detach and roll down her cheeks. "I want to kill the people who did this," she said almost in a whisper.

"You should."

"I want truth, not judgement," she said. "I just want to shine the light on them, bring them out of the shadows so everyone can see. But I do that and people riot. People die because of the truth."

Barbara did not answer immediately. Maliha looked up to make sure she was still awake and met a pair of eyes that defied the illness and paralysis.

"You are *Durga Maa*."

Maliha wanted to shout her protest but Barbara was ill.

Instead she whispered. "I am not." Though even as she said it the consequences of all her enquiries and investigations came to her mind. All the murderers, save one, dead or incarcerated.

"Perhaps you need to be, daughter."

vi

"You cannot take Ulrika Putnam, Miss Anderson."

The chief detective had arrived while the trunks were being wheeled out by porters. Barbara was about to be relocated into the bulky Faraday wheelchair, running on battery power for the time it was inside the hotel. Its compact diesel motor would be started up once they were outside.

Maliha gave an exhausted sigh. She glanced over to where Amita was waiting. "It's all right, Amita, just get everybody out."

"Perhaps you did not hear me, Miss Anderson," said the chief detective. "Miss Putnam remains here; I will return her to her family."

It seemed as if she spent half her life on the balcony in this damn hotel, Maliha thought to herself. She looked outside to where rain was drenching the city. The pouring rain did nothing to relieve the temperature; it just made the atmosphere stifling.

"Come with me, Chief Detective," she said. "Let us find somewhere a little more private."

"You cannot distract me," he said. "My men will not let her leave the hotel."

"I assure you that thought did not even enter my mind. Now if you will come with me."

She did not wait for his response but crossed to the door that linked through to her rooms which she knew had already been cleared. There was a flash of lightning as she entered her lounge area. The electric lights in the hotel flickered in response. The crash of thunder rolled through the building and she thought she could feel the floor vibrate.

She closed the French window to keep the noise of the rain out. The chief detective closed the door behind him. She turned and faced him.

"How many more babies did you find?"

He shifted uncomfortably. "Half a dozen so far."

"In various states of decay."

He nodded. "You seem remarkably calm about the matter," he said. "For a woman."

"Do I?" she said. "I suppose I could break down in tears. I could weep and throw myself about the place just satisfy your antediluvian concept of how a woman should be." She paused for a breath. "But that would hardly bring the perpetrator to justice, now would it?"

"You've done your part, Miss Anderson," he said ignoring her insult; but she could see by the glint in his eye that her barb had struck home. "You should leave the rest to the police. Let us do our job."

She let her head drop to one side and allowed the scorn to seep into her voice. "You haven't done much of a job up to now have you?"

Turning her back on him before he could reply, she went to the drinks cabinet and poured herself some water. She did not offer him a drink.

"I did not come here to discuss the case."

"No," she cut in, still with her back to him, "you have come here because the mayor ordered you to retrieve his daughter before she could reveal his nasty little secret."

She faced him and could see from his expression she was right.

"Yes," he said. "The mayor wants his daughter back. Of course he does."

"Oh, I'm quite sure that's true," she said sitting down at the table and crossing her legs, revealing her ankle and calf. She noted with satisfaction that he could not prevent himself from looking. "After all, he must be getting quite frustrated." She emphasised the last word.

"Yes, he wants his daughter back."

"And why is that, do you think, Chief Detective?"

He frowned. "She's his daughter."

"Who made the mistake of having a black baby by a black servant."

The chief detective looked very uncomfortable. He did not seem to know what to do with his hands and finally landed on rubbing the fingers of his left hand with his right.

Maliha smiled with a malicious glint in her eye. "He told you not to believe anything I or she told you. Didn't he?" She nodded. "Yes, I can see it in your eyes. But has it not occurred to you, Chief Detective, to ask yourself *why* he would say such a thing?"

Vandenhoek looked past her at the French window and the rain beating on it.

"Clearly she has already told her lies to you," he said, regaining some confidence.

Maliha stood up and placed the glass of water on the table. "You strike me as an honest man, Chief Detective Vandenhoek."

He puffed out his chest. "Of course."

"If short-sighted and half-blinded by your antiquated views."

"Miss Anderson, that is quite enough!" he strode to the table and loomed over her. "You will desist from insulting me at every turn."

"The child that Ulrika Putnam had was the product of a union between her and her father."

He barely paused. "I cannot accept that."

"There are dead babies in the sewers because you wouldn't believe children were being stolen away either," she shouted up at him. "When will you stop denying the truth that is as plain and as large as the nose on your face?"

He looked about to explode but she saw him focus and suppress the rage. He took a deep breath and withdrew to the exit.

"Miss Anderson," he said. "Perhaps you are right. However, Ulrika Putnam is not of age; her father is her rightful guardian. I cannot deny his wish to have his daughter returned to him."

"Even if all he's going to do is misuse her?"

"If she wishes to state her grievance I will listen."

Maliha smiled but she felt no pleasure or humour; it was more a reflection of the sad faith that he had for the system of justice under which he lived. In a land that considered all women chattel, subservient to men and the source of evil according to their religious beliefs.

"I'm sorry, Chief Detective," she said. "But I forbid it."

"And I too am sorry, Miss Anderson, but you are in no position to dictate my actions."

"I will keep this simple," she said. "If you take Ulrika Putnam back to her father, the world's press will carry the story about his behaviour."

He stared at her. "You cannot."

"I can, and I will." She settled herself on a sofa and arranged her dress demurely over her legs. "And it will be made quite clear that you abetted him by returning his daughter when you knew what would happen."

"That is blackmail."

"There are four possible situations, Chief Detective. Let me enumerate them for you: I am right, or incorrect. He abuses her, or he does not. The choices where you return her weigh far more on your soul, and her well-being, than if you let me take her with me."

She said nothing but simply waited expectantly, watching him.

"You might be wrong," he said.

"You being wrong carries far more risk," she replied. "If I take her the worst outcome is that he is angry with you, and has lost a daughter already disgraced."

"You put me in an impossible situation."

"No, Chief Detective. Only you do that."

He paused as if he were going to say something then, somehow deflated, he opened the door to the corridor and left without further word.

The door closed with a firm click. Maliha waited a few moments then said loudly.

"You can come out now, Ray."

The door to the bathroom opened and the little rat of a man emerged. He had not the slightest look of embarrassment on his face. He had a pen and his notepad in hand.

"How did you know I was there?"

"I could smell you."

He grunted then looked her in the eye. "Great story."

"Yes, it is."

He hesitated and frowned. "You haven't told me to keep it quiet."

"No."

"You want me to run it?"

"Yes."

His face lit up. "Really?"

"Well it might be eclipsed by the story to come, but yes send it to your paper. Every paper." Maliha stood up and yawned, placing her hand over her mouth but with no attempt to suppress it. "However," she added.

"I knew it."

"Leave out the chief detective," she said. "After all, he did leave Ulrika behind."

vii

Valentine went out into the pounding rain first. He pulled his hat further down over his eyes and his coat up round his neck. He shook out the umbrella and opened it. The porter held the door open as Maliha emerged and put her arm through his so she was sheltered from the rain. Amita followed with her own umbrella already opened.

Ulrika, the baby and Barbara in her wheelchair—carefully covered with an oiled cape—were already aboard a puffing ambulance. He could see the ambulance staff had engaged the Faraday by the way the rain slowed and collected into broad drops above its roof.

The vehicle he and Maliha would be using was parked in front of it. A German diesel vehicle by its appearance.

"What are those?" Maliha demanded pointing at the three police vehicles, one in front and the other two behind the ambulance.

"I understand that the chief detective insisted on giving us an escort," he said as they headed down to their transport. "For our own safety after the disturbances last night."

"He just wants to make sure we are gone," she replied.

"Can you blame him?" said Valentine.

She made a disapproving noise. "If he had done his job right in the first place, it wouldn't be an issue."

Valentine opened the door to the vehicle and held the umbrella up as she climbed inside. He closed the umbrella, getting a further wetting as he did so, and shook it out a little before getting inside and pulling the door closed. He took off his coat so as not to make the seat wet and sat down beside her. He tapped on the glass between the front and back compartments with the handle of the umbrella.

The seats vibrated as the engine started up. Beams from the headlights illuminated the police vehicle in front which then moved off and their limousine followed. He glanced behind to make sure the ambulance was moving.

There was an awkward silence as he tried to think of a way to broach the subject uppermost in his mind, knowing only too well how she would react.

"You could just tell the police where to find them."

"I could."

"This is insanity."

"Oh? And are you going to have your fiancée sent to Bedlam because she is not behaving the way you wish?"

He sighed. It was going as badly as he had predicted. He tried again.

"I love you," he said. "I do not want to lose you."

"I have no intention of becoming lost."

"Then explain to me why you think this is a good idea."

"Because if I just tell the *crushers*," she used the term Izak had for the police, "they will go in with their hobnail boots, and will learn nothing of any lasting value."

"Let me come with you."

"If anyone accompanies me I will lose my advantage."

"What advantage does a young unarmed woman all alone have against child murderers?"

"Precisely the advantage you have just expressed, Valentine," she replied. "They will underestimate me."

She fell silent for a moment as if reflecting on the past, then said almost inaudibly. "They always do."

Valentine reached out and took her hand. It was cold and he knew she was afraid. He felt so frustrated but he could do nothing. Even following her closely was more likely to put her at risk than help. She turned her hand in his palm so they were holding hands.

He stared at the grey rain-drenched buildings drifting past like ghosts, with only the occasional light burning in a window. It took less than fifteen minutes to reach the gate of the air-dock.

Above the police car ahead of them he saw the arch of the gate but they came to an abrupt stop some distance from it. He tapped on the dividing glass and shouted "Why have we stopped?"

The driver half-turned and mimed his ignorance.

Uniformed police piled out of the vehicle in front and into the rain. They had their truncheons in their hands. Maliha gasped and grabbed the door handle. She flung it wide and stepped out into the rain.

"Hell's bells," said Valentine and followed her out.

Without the police vehicle in the way the grey light revealed what at first glance were perhaps fifty black men and women blocking the gate of the air-dock.

"Get you sorry black arses out of the way," shouted one of the crushers. "Or we'll beat you to Kingdom Come!"

Eight more police rushed past them from the rear vehicles to reinforce the ones already standing there.

Ignoring the rain that soaked her completely and turned her dress into a slick second skin, Maliha walked forwards. Valentine hurried after her. In the middle of the crowd there was an old woman supported by a younger one, with Izak and tiny Lilith in front of them.

The police were advancing, truncheons at the ready. The crowd shuffled a little but did not retreat.

"Disperse and go back to your homes. There is a curfew in force, no blacks allowed in the city. If you don't go home you will be arrested."

He raised his truncheon above his head menacingly. At which point Maliha reached him and stood in front of him. "Put it down, Sergeant."

"Get back to the vehicle, miss. You might get hurt." He grabbed her arm and the crowd surged towards them.

Maliha turned to them and raised her free arm. "Stop!" They came to a halt ten yards away.

Valentine reached them, pushing past the police who tried to block his approach. "Sergeant, kindly unhand my fiancée."

The man loosed his grip. "You should keep better control of her."

"In case you had not noticed, Sergeant. She has a better control of this situation than you do."

Maliha faced the crowd. "Please step back, the police will not hurt me."

The majority of the crowd shuffled backwards except for the old woman, her support and the children. Valentine stepped round further. "Sergeant, please move your men back. Miss Anderson will deal with this."

The policeman looked at Valentine, then Maliha and the crowd. Valentine could almost see his mind working.

"All right men, move back to the car. Keep your sticks handy."

They did so with ill grace, keeping their eyes on the crowd. No doubt hoping they would not lose an opportunity to teach the blacks a lesson. Maliha turned to Valentine. Rain was running from her loose black hair in rivulets. And her face was covered in water droplets. He could feel a trickle of water making its way down his back. He had his hat but his coat was back in the limousine.

"If you would also step back?"

"Really, Maliha?"

"Please."

He sighed and did as she asked but only halfway to the police line.

Maliha approached the old woman. They conferred for a few minutes. The rain lightened somewhat but as they were all wet through it made little difference.

Finally the old woman turned to the crowd and made a dismissing gesture with her fingers. The people turned and headed away into the grey rain and shadows. The old woman and the others went too, leaving the gate to the air-dock free and open.

Maliha turned and went back to the limousine. He followed and helped her inside where they dripped on to the leather seats.

"What was that about?" he asked.

"Mama Kosi thought the police were forcing us to leave," she said.

"And you disabused them of that idea."

"Yes, I explained we were leaving of our own free will."

"And they would not oppose the desires of the goddess."

"As you say."

The vehicle bumped forward and the convoy made its way through the gates and into the air-dock.

CHAPTER 8

i

The *RMS Morea* was a sister ship to the *Macedonia* built at the same time and to the same specifications but constructed in Glasgow by Barclay, Curle & Co Ltd.

The five vehicles drove up the ramp directly into the first class boarding area in the bottom of the vessel. Valentine climbed from the limousine and opened the door for Maliha while he scanned the cavernous room. Since boarding had been going on all day they were the only passengers embarking at this time.

Amita appeared. She intercepted one of the deck officers who had been heading in their direction armed with a clipboard. She extricated what Valentine assumed must be their tickets and other documents from her bag and handed them to him.

Once those formalities were complete the officer waved over the porters who began to unload their bags. He glanced in the direction of Maliha and Valentine. If he noticed they were dripping wet he gave no indication.

Amita came over and handed them the keys to their staterooms.

"We'll need to change," said Valentine. Maliha nodded. She did not meet his eye.

Unlike the *Macedonia* this vessel possessed a Faraday lift to Deck 'A', one of the features that no doubt contributed to the rumour that this was the better vessel.

Pity we won't be travelling on it, Valentine thought as he unlocked his door. Maliha was doing the same in the next room down. Hers was adjacent to the hull and had portholes while his was inboard with only a window on to the companionway.

The facilities were as he remembered them. Everything was of the finest quality from the rugs to the furniture. He found the drinks cabinet and poured himself a whiskey.

The baggage arrived and he tipped the porter a half-crown. He opened the trunk and began to strip off his wet clothes.

There was a knock on the partition door from Maliha's cabin. He unlocked it and pulled it open. She had undressed, the electric light in her room shone through the sheer fabric of her dressing gown highlighting her shape. She threw herself at him and wrapped her arms around his chest as if she never intended to release him. He enclosed her in his arms.

"I love you," she said. He felt the warmth of her words on his chest.

Feeling guilty he glanced at the clock. She must have noticed.

"I know," she said. "We cannot delay."

She gently tore herself from him and looked up at him. Holding her shoulders he bent down and crushed his lips against hers. She kissed him back for a few moments then pulled back.

"Don't," she said. "Please don't make this any harder than it is. I would rather stay aboard and simply go home."

"But we cannot," he said.

She shook her head and looked him directly in the eye. "I love you with all my heart, William Albert Valentine Crier. Bill."

He smiled. "I prefer it when you call me Valentine."

She kissed him then went back into her room. She shut the door without turning back.

Valentine sighed and went back to his trunk. He pulled out his disguise and set about getting dressed. He heard Maliha's door open and close. He listened as Maliha and Amita talked—he couldn't make out the words but there was no strong emotion. He had thought

Amita would put up more of an argument with Maliha leaving the ship without her.

He glanced at the clock. It was getting on for eight. They needed to be going. He found his cheap overcoat and put it on, then picked up his hat. Finally he pulled his revolver from a pocket in the trunk and shoved it into an inside pocket along with spare ammunition

Amita opened the door to his knock. There may not have been high emotions but he could see from her face that she was very unhappy, almost enough to slam the door in his face. But she did not. Instead she stepped aside and allowed him in.

Maliha had her back to him and was adjusting her hat in the mirror. It was a lady's hat unquestionably but sewn from leather that gleamed with oil. It had a wide brim that came down low over her neck at the back. Very practical in the rain. She wore a heavy dark dress but then she turned and he saw that it was split at the side and her legs were encased in trousers. She wore boots with almost no heel and laced up her calf. It would allow her to run if it was needed.

"When did you get those?" Valentine asked.

"In Pondicherry, before we left."

"How did you know you would need them?"

Maliha shrugged. "I checked the almanac. It can rain a lot here; I wanted something practical."

"I've never see anything like it."

"Amita designed them," she said. "Do you like them?"

"Yes, I particularly like the…" he waved his hand to indicate her leg which was visible to an inch above the knee, though completely covered. "…skirt."

Amita came over with a coat, again shaped for a woman but of leather like the hat, and the same shade of dark brown. She held it for Maliha and she put her arms in, did up the buttons and belt. Her leg was no longer on show; it looked like she was wearing a dress.

"We're ready," she said. Then turned to Amita. "The letters are in my document case."

Amita nodded. "Will you say goodbye to Barbara and the baby?"

Maliha glanced over then concentrated on her gloves. "No. Everyone will get teary and that will upset the child. There's a letter for Barbara."

Valentine felt a wave of cold. She believed she might not return from this journey.

He had lived with that danger for years and he realised that in all that time he had never considered the effect it would have on others. Now, presented with the fact he might lose the one person in the world he loved, he felt dread running in his veins.

But their path was set.

"Valentine?"

He realised she had spoken his name several times. He looked up and grinned. "Sorry, miles away," he said. "You ready to go?"

"I'm ready."

Amita strode to the door, her body moving as if she were made of wood. Maliha went to go through and then paused. She put her hand on Amita's arm and squeezed it.

"Thank you," she said simply then went up on her tiptoe and kissed Amita on the cheek.

Valentine followed her to the door. He felt awkward. Maliha had explained that she had promoted Amita to a senior position so that she could handle Maliha's estate. As such she was certainly deserving of respect, besides they had been through an interesting time together, and Amita had saved his life on one occasion.

But no matter how she dressed, and regardless of her apparent habits, Amita was still not a woman even if he had come to tolerate her presence in the bed chamber. He accepted that Maliha treated Amita as if she were completely female to the extent of being her personal maid. Yet Amita was not a woman and he had felt the bristles on her face on the occasion that he discovered the truth.

He reached out to shake her by the hand. There was a hint of disappointment in Amita's eyes as she placed her hand in his. Gently and delicately, just as a woman would, even if her hand was rather larger than most. Valentine clasped her hand and drew her in; he kissed her on the cheek.

When she pulled back he could see the slight moisture of a tear in her eye.

"*Shubh Kaamnaayein,*" Amita said. "Good luck."

Valentine heard the door close behind them as he and Maliha headed towards the main companionway.

ii

They descended through the ship using one of the staff stairwells and came out in the disembarkation lounge for the second and third class passengers. There was a steady trickle of people entering though the main hatch on the port side, and a few others heading out—those who had accompanied friends and family but were not taking the journey themselves.

Valentine and Maliha joined that group and went out on to the airfield. It was still raining though not as heavily as before. Valentine pulled up his coat collar. Maliha was perfectly dressed for the weather and the water simply rolled off her hat and coat. It took five minutes to cross the muddy field by which time water had seeped into Valentine's boots and soaked his socks. He might as well not have bothered changing at all.

They rounded the main administration building and joined a whites-only queue waiting for a taxi. The rank where taxis waited for fares was empty.

"Where are they all?" Valentine muttered.

"They're afraid," said Maliha.

Valentine looked at his watch. "I have to go."

"I'll be fine."

A large man with an umbrella that was not doing a good job of keeping him dry joined the queue behind them.

Valentine hesitated. She turned towards him. In the dark the contours of her face were only vague highlights and her eyes where bottomless. Her hat hid her face from the man behind and the others in the queue were facing away from them.

He took her hand. She was tense and resisted him.

"Don't," she said quietly as he moved closer.

He turned his head away in annoyance; she was always telling him what to do and what was appropriate.

"Remember where we are."

He sighed, lifted her hand and kissed it instead. She squeezed his fingers. Standing back he released her hand. "I'll see you later then."

"Later? Yes."

He touched his fingers to his hat brim in salute then, with the greatest force of will, turned his back on her, and strode along the road towards the air-crew building. He felt empty. When she had driven him away after the incident with the guru he had been able to console himself with the fact that it had been what she wanted, even if he did not agree with it.

This was not the same. He wanted to run back to her and take her back aboard the Sky-Liner—carrying her if necessary—and escape from this damned place. But he could not, of course, she would cut him to pieces with the lash of her tongue. And she was right; she could not leave children to this terrible fate and he could not abandon the opportunity to get inside the operations of the devious Terence Timmons.

He signed in to the air-crew hostel under his assumed name then went into the lounge. Nobody would be on the roof in this weather.

He looked around, peering through the cigarette and cigar smoke. He spotted Keighley in a corner nursing a pint.

Valentine went to the bar and paid for two. He carried them to Keighley's table and placed the spare in front of the old and battered man.

"I got the captain's message," said Valentine as he sat down.

"The captain is happy with your qualifications and told me to tell you the meeting place." The old man downed the dregs from his original pint pot and pushed it aside. He pulled the new one closer.

"All right," said Valentine and took a sip of his drink. "So where do I meet him?"

"Where is easy enough but the time has been changed." Keighley glanced up at the clock behind the bar. "Twenty-two hundred, tonight."

"It was going to be midnight."

"Something's come up," he said. "They're lifting early."

"Where do I have to go?"

Keighley supped from his pint pot. "Place called Delmas."

"Where the hell is Delmas?"

"About forty-five miles due east."

Valentine jumped to his feet. "How in God's name am I supposed to get there in an hour, in this weather?"

Keighley leaned back in his chair. "Not my problem, Dyer."

Valentine jumped to his feet, his mind spinning. A taxicab could never get him there in time; it would be impossible to make the necessary speed over what would be little more than a track in the rain and dark.

He needed a plane. He could use his position with the British government to commandeer a vessel. It might reveal his true nature to Keighley but he had no way of communicating with Timmons' ship. Unless he had a radio. It would work over short ranges. Too risky.

There was nothing for it; he would have to steal something with enough speed.

"How will I know when I find the place?"

"Fires around the ship," said Keighley with a smile. "Think you can do it, sailor?"

Valentine downed the rest of his pint and wiped his mouth with his sleeve. "Oh, I'll get there."

* * *

He strode out into the rain and headed at a fast pace towards the hangars for the small independent aircraft. He passed the first hangar because it was completely closed up. The second had light filtering around the doors. Without hesitation he stepped through the door into a wide, dimly lit space. The air was filled with constant thrumming of rain on the curved, corrugated iron roof.

The deck was packed with planes. The owners and small companies shared the hangar to reduce costs. He glanced around rejecting most of the planes immediately as too slow or too far back inside the hangar, though his eyes lingered on a big ornithopter. That too he rejected: they were a nightmare to fly and he had no idea how to do it.

A voice echoed through the man-made cavern. "Hey!"

Valentine kept moving and pulled out his gun from the inner pocket.

"Hey! You can't be in here."

One ship attracted his attention: it was like a miniature version of the Sky-Liners or the massive Royal Navy assault carriers. It had two rotors for lift which would also rotate forwards, short wings for lift in flight and a rear prop for main thrust. It looked like it would take a dozen passengers or a decent cargo. And there was no smoke

- 244 -

stack so it was a diesel which meant it was ready to fly and didn't need a stoker.

"Stop right there, mister!" The voice was very close to him now. Valentine turned and pointed his gun.

"You can help me, or not. The first way is healthier for you," said Valentine. "Either way I'm taking this ship."

iii

The driver spent time insisting he had to take her to a hotel since the curfew was still in force. It had taken a considerable bribe to make him drop her off at the junction she requested in the rundown northern quarter of the city.

The rain had not let up and the gaslights in the streets were not lit—why waste money on the poor?

"You really shouldn't, miss; this area is not safe for a young woman even in daylight."

She handed him the promised coin, more than double what was displayed on the taximeter, and climbed out. "You don't need to worry, I'm meeting someone."

He took the money and with an uncertain glance in her direction, turned the vehicle around and disappeared into the mist and rain. Maliha withdrew from the edge of the street into the shadows, her clothes blending in to the darkness.

She stared around into the wet and the dark. *What am I doing here?* The thought surprised her; she seldom questioned her own actions. Was it a sign of maturity? Or just responsibility. She had acquired so many people that were now dependent on her. But she had dealt with that. Amita was perfectly capable of continuing in her stead. That could not be considered the reason. Though she knew in her heart it was part of it.

This was the trap her Buddhist studies warned against. If you cared about material things, if you attached yourself to the so-called real world it became a trap. You could only be free by detaching yourself.

Except she did not want to be alone. She liked having people around her. She had experienced a life of utter loneliness when she was at boarding school. But now she had Barbara, Amita, the baby and even Ulrika.

And Valentine.

She longed for him. The memory of holding him, and being held by him in the cabin. Of lying with him. Of touching her skin. Even just holding hands. She closed her eyes. She never wanted it to end; she wanted him by her forever.

But they were apart. Perhaps forever.

"Goddess?"

"Hello, Izak."

The boy emerged from the rain, just a dark shadow, with a small dark shadow beside him.

"You shouldn't have brought Lilith."

"He didn't bring me," said Lilith in her little piping voice. "I brought myself."

Maliha was not going to argue. She wondered what the time was; it was too dark to see her watch. She wondered briefly where Valentine was. There were too many imponderables to be able to guess. He might even be lying on his bed in the hotel. Or lying dead in the rain. She shook her head to clear that image from her mind. Whatever he was doing he was on his own path. Hers led in a different direction.

"Goddess?" Izak's voice seemed concerned.

"Yes," she said quickly, she needed to stop being maudlin. There were children to save. "You have checked the location?"

"This way," said Izak and heading north across the junction.

They travelled along a road with single storey buildings on either side, each one with considerable space between them. Most of them had light showing in the windows with the occasional figure moving about inside.

The three of them moved like shadows. The light from the windows reflected on the wet road highlighting the splashes from the rain that continued to pour down. Some of it had begun to seep through her defences and a cold trickle had found its way down her neck.

The buildings thinned out and disappeared behind them. The road turned into a ridged trail. There were wide tracks made by large vehicles criss-crossing each other. Rain had collected in the furrows.

From her memory of the map Maliha knew they were outside the city and heading into one of the disused diamond mines. Eventually the ground fell away beneath them, the track turned to the left and descended into the deep opencast mine. They stopped. Their eyes had adjusted to the dark but even so there was almost nothing to see despite the rain reduced to spitting and the cloud thinning out a little.

"You wait for Mama Kosi and the others," said Maliha.

"What will you do?" asked Izak.

"Will you kill them with lightning?" asked Lilith.

Maliha sighed; she had stopped arguing with them calling her a goddess but that did have complications.

"No, I want to talk to them. I want to know why they're doing it."

"Then you'll kill them?" asked Izak with more enthusiasm than seemed healthy.

"They will be brought to justice."

She decided further discussion was pointless and headed down the track.

It took five minutes to reach the bottom while the perspective of the place changed around her. The floor of the mine rose up to meet her as she descended. The top of the huge crane that had been at her eye level now towered above her.

An administration hut stood at the bottom of the ramp but there were no lights on. In the rock wall opposite a faint gleam emerged from deep inside a tunnel. For a moment she stared at the entrance, a faint mist drifted from it and mingled with the rain.

She heard the squeak of a rat and a rustle of movement beneath the administration block. She did not like rats. She walked towards the tunnel opening ahead of her. Her pace quickened even while she berated herself for acting like a scared child. But around her was the damp dark and ahead was the warmth of light.

iv

With his arm resting on the window ledge Valentine held the gun steady on his reluctant assistant. The poor fellow was terrified but it was not in Valentine's interests to ease his mind. The hangar doors rose with excruciating slowness as the man pulled the raising mechanism. The light from the interior flooded out, illuminating the pounding rain.

Valentine had the rotors powered up but the Faraday still disengaged so there was insufficient lift. He adjusted the power to the propeller and the machine crept forwards across the smooth concrete floor. As soon as there was space for the rotors he gunned the engine and the vessel lurched forward into the rain. He pulled in his hand and dropped the gun on to the passenger seat.

The chronometer in the dashboard gave him forty minutes. It had to be enough. The airspeed of this machine must be at least one hundred miles per hour. Rain struck the canopy as it bumped out into the dark. He glanced behind; the man had disappeared, no doubt wanting to warn the authorities. It didn't matter. With rotors and propeller at full power he engaged the Faraday.

The plane leapt into the air and accelerated fast. It reached a hundred feet in no time at all and kept rising. He reduced the power to the rotors in stages but had reached a thousand feet before he managed to bring it under control. He reached up to the rotor attitude control and wound it. The rotors turned from horizontal and providing lift, to vertical and adding to his speed.

A side effect was that he lost altitude steadily. He checked the compass and adjusted his course. At five hundred feet he used the rotor control to wind the rotor back a little more to provide a little lift. He was sure that wasn't the best method but it was all he had.

He was flying blind at night, using only dead reckoning to find his destination. The airspeed indicator suggested he was travelling at a little over two hundred kilometres per hour. He did the sum in his head and concluded it was something over a hundred and twenty miles per hour which meant he could do forty miles in twenty minutes.

Keighley had said he would be able to spot it by numerous fires. At five hundred feet he should have enough of a view. He had to allow five to ten minutes to get down. Landing this crate would be far more difficult than getting it into the air but still, at worst, he could switch off the Faraday and come down hard.

If he could find the place. And if they did not decide he was a threat and shoot him down. He would have to cross that bridge if he came to it.

He shivered. He was soaking wet and it was cold in the cockpit.

How long had he been in flight? Only five minutes according to the clock. He had travelled a quarter of the distance. He tried to force himself to relax, to accept that he had plenty of time and would make it in time.

There was nothing to suggest he wouldn't.

Every so often he passed a light glowing beneath him. Farmhouses like the one belonging to Ouderkirk, and the one with the dead bodies. To distract himself he thought it through. Ouderkirk had not really responded about the hyenas but both his and Maliha's reaction told him that a pack of hyenas did not attack a human settlement no matter how hungry they were. And when some of them had been shot the rest kept on coming like troops ordered to attack despite the odds.

And children with their brains removed. Maliha had said it was must be an experiment. What sort of experiment did you carry out on children? Were they madmen? Eugenicists? Something else? He had trouble thinking past the point of murdering children. How could anyone do that?

What if the two items were connected? How could they be connected? What if the experiments being carried out on children had been carried out on the hyenas first?

But the hyenas were running free. Perhaps they escaped; hyenas were strong and dangerous.

While children were weak.

Had Maliha already worked this out? Had she not told him the truth because if she had he would not have left her? Would not have let her go alone, if at all?

He was on the verge of changing direction and returning to the city when he caught sight of lights up ahead. Far more numerous and brighter than any he had seen. He had found it.

He circled overhead, steadily reducing the power to the rotors while adjusting them back to the horizontal position. He cut the power to the driving propeller so it provided just enough to give him steerage.

In the clearing below, the huge bulk of one of Timmons' secret vessels lay in the lee of a large *kopje* as the locals called hills. There were camp fires and people moving from them to a huge ramp that led up into the side of the vessel. A trip to "Australia" no doubt.

He stopped circling and commenced a run parallel to the ship on the side away from the loading. There were too many people there and he was likely to hit someone. But on this side he could barely see anything. He could only guess the position of the ground by the bulk of the ship.

He brought the air-plane over the space at the lowest possible speed he could manage. He cut power to the thrusting propeller. And reduced power to the rotors. The altitude indicator was not accurate enough to show his height and indicated he was on the ground.

The air-plane lurched and there was a violent cracking coming from beneath him. He had hit a tree. There was a long drawn out scraping that set his teeth on edge. Then his forward motion ceased completely. He was hooked. He judged his options; none of them seemed good.

He cut the power to the rotors and the ship began to lean to the right as it descended. The left side must be hooked on a branch. As it leaned the less of the vehicle's mass was within the Faraday field. Valentine could feel himself getting heavier.

So he cut the Faraday completely. The entirety of the weight ripped the branch from the tree and the plane crashed to the ground. Valentine was thrown against the controls. Rhythmic thuds announced the rotors were ploughing into the ground with the remainder of their power then ended in a metallic screech.

Everything went silent.

V

Back in England, when Maliha had gone into the caves along the beaches of the south coast, even in the height of summer, it had always become colder. This confirmed everything she had read about tunnels and cave systems.

This tunnel did not; it grew warmer and the moisture in the air was very noticeable. It was like the monsoon but underground. She pressed on and picked her way along the double tracks for mine carts laid into the floor. The wall and ceiling were supported by sturdy timbers. Electric bulbs at twenty foot intervals illuminated the way but still created deep shadows in the uneven walls.

As she pressed on slowly and carefully she became aware of a throb in the air. At first it was a simple pressure against her skin but then the sound of it pressed against her. A machine of some sort perhaps driving the generator for the electric lights.

She came alongside a side tunnel. It too was lit. She heard the whimper of a child float gently from the passage. She froze with the heart-stopping horror of it. It was not her imagination; she had seen what had been done to the child dumped in the sewer, but she had read Poe and his nightmarish visions flooded through her mind.

It was nothing but the fear of the unknown. On the one hand she could rationalise her fear and understand it. On the other she was desperate not to know but a lack of knowledge could be fatal. There was another whimper and she turned to follow it down the side passage.

The walls, floor and ceiling glistened with moisture from the humid air. The passage opened up into an ellipsoid space about thirty feet in length and twenty wide. The ceiling was twice the height of the passage but lit by the same electric bulbs so the overall effect was that the cavern was darker.

The whimper came again. Along one wall were five cribs made of iron—more like cages—on the other was a long bench that had food containers at one end and empty tool racks on the wall behind it. At the other end of the bench were empty bell jars, some upright others lying on their side. One was broken on the floor. An adult-sized examination chair, discarded on its side, lay in the half-light furthest from her at the end of the room.

Maliha closed her eyes. Once more she felt the intense desire to simply run and never come back. The child cried again. Not the full-throated demand for food, or the simple complaint of discomfort; this was a child without hope.

She braced herself and opened her eyes. The sound had come from the second bed. She forced her legs to move and walked hesitantly across the room. As she approached the high solid end of the bed she saw deeper into the cot. Her nerve almost deserted her. She resisted the desire to close her eyes again as she moved forward.

A dark-skinned child of less than six months lay on its back in the cot, pressed up against the bars on the further side. It wore a simple smock with streaks of dirt across it. It was very thin. Each of the digits of its hands and feet were perfectly formed. Its hair was short and bristly. The proportions of its head seemed a little too large but that might have been a trick of the dim light. Its eyes were closed.

It opened its mouth and whimpered again, showing its white teeth. The child looked normal and seemingly unhurt.

"Hello," Maliha said quietly. The child gave no indication it had heard her. After a few moments it waved its feet a couple of times then stopped. It had not moved its arms at all.

"Hello," she said again louder. There was still no response. She tapped on the metal of the end of the bed with her fingernail. It did not make much of a sound so she rapped on it using her engagement ring from Valentine.

The clink of metal penetrated the room and she glanced at the entrance instinctively then back at the child. There was no reaction, until it whimpered again but she was sure it had not been because of the sound. Was it deaf?

The child appeared normal but there was something about its behaviour she found unnerving. She felt guilty about it but could not shake the curious loathing she felt for the whimpering creature. She had no desire to touch it. She cast around until she spotted a pole lying near the broken chair. She fetched it and wiped the excess moisture from it.

She checked the ends and chose the smoothest one. She rested the length against the end of the cot and let it down. She guided the end and touched it against the sole of the child's right foot.

The moment the end of the pole made contact its eyes snapped open and it made a kind of straining sound. There was something wrong with its eyes. Instead of irises surrounded by white the ball was completely black with pin-prick dots of white in the middle.

Maliha barely suppressed her own cry of horror. Panic hit her. Still clutching the pole she ran from the cavern. The creature still uttered the guttural growl that should never come from a child's throat. One part of her watched in a detached way as she fled back up the passage and, when she reached the junction, it was that part of her that forced her to stop.

She leaned against the wall. The thing that had once been a child was now moaning. She pushed her fingers into her ears to block the sound but the memory of its alien eyes would not move from the forefront of her mind. Once again she thought about simply leaving then she remembered the sounds of the rats, and Valentine's hyena. And the men that were doing this.

Now she knew that Timmons' fleet of secret vessels carrying colonists to who-knew-where were connected to the strange hyenas and the killing of children here. The colonists were most likely being taken to either Venus or Mars. Mars had very limited life, being as cold as it was; Venus was the complete reverse and teemed with plants and fungi. Both places, not to mention other planets, were so unexplored it would be easy to create secret colonies.

As she thought it through she recalled a reference in a report by a Dr Sidor Mikhalkov about the similarities in structure between certain types of Venusian fungus and the brain. This was the same scientist who had suggested a technique for copying mental patterns from one brain to another for the purpose of pacifying violent criminals.

She wiped the combination of perspiration and condensation from her face. They kept this place hot and damp and the only reason for that would be to emulate the conditions on Venus. The child was deaf and blind. If one were to introduce a fungus directly into the brain one would do it by the most direct of routes: through the ears and eyes.

Whatever their purpose this was not about eugenics; they were experimenting on combining the human brain with these fungi. Their monstrous behaviour must be stopped, but she needed to understand why.

vi

Valentine found himself face down against the windscreen of the flyer. His arms ached and there was a pain in his forehead. Though he found that by lifting his head from the lump of metal pressing into his forehead the pain reduced.

He pushed himself up. His lower body and legs were higher than his head and resting on the central control panel. He was disoriented until he realised the air-plane had come to rest nose down and he had fallen forward. He untangled himself from the controls then reached up to the door lock and unlatched it. The door fell open to the sound of breaking twigs. He crawled out across it and on to the soaking wet ground. The rain had stopped but the air was heavy with moisture.

"Give me one good reason not to shoot you, mate."

The voice was Australian.

"Jonathan Dyer, able seaman, reporting for duty," he said and climbed unsteadily to his feet. "Sorry I'm late."

The man was a shadow against the massive dark bulk of the voidship behind him. Faint light shone through its portholes.

"You wrecked your plane," he said with a laugh in his voice.

"Wasn't mine," Valentine growled.

"Ha! March, limey," said the man. "We'll see whether you're wanted for duty or not. And if not, you'll be out the hatch faster than a roo with a dingo on its tail."

"Thanks."

"Thanks for what, mate?"

"Not shooting first and asking questions later."

"Move it."

"Which way?"

"There's a service hatch in the hull closest to us," he said. "You walk, I'll guide."

Two minutes later, after cycling through two sets of airtight doors, Valentine stepped out into a companionway. It looked as if it stretched the entire length of the ship. He was within twenty yards of one end but the other end was too far away to estimate. He shook his head; nobody built ships like this.

The paintwork on a pipe running floor to ceiling caught his eye. It was painted in the same uniform grey as the rest of the vessel. There was rust around the joints but contours of the paint ran into deep holes and out again in rounded curves, where you would expect the edges to be sharp. There must be dozens of layers of paint on the pipe which meant this ship was very old indeed. With that in mind, the style of the hatches and the bulkheads, the size and shape of the rivets all made a kind of sense—though it was nonsense.

If he had to guess, this vessel had been built before the 1870s, which was impossible. The first ship to enter the Void had done so in 1874 and that had been a modified atmosphere plane with a crew of three. This machine could not have existed any earlier than the 1890s.

"All right, that's enough gawking," said his captor. "Start moving. That way." He indicated the closer end of the companionway. Valentine walked ahead; he did not think he was likely to be shot but he did not plan on taking any chances. At the end of the companionway was an airtight hatch marked Bridge. This led into a small passage and another airtight door which would not open until the other door had been sealed.

Valentine had only been into the Void twice and both times it was as a passenger, but he appreciated the need for airlocks when the hull might be breached at any moment by the debris that circulated through the emptiness.

The bridge itself was a wide area with a crew of at least seven. Valentine recognised Captain Blake who was in discussion with the navigator. The captain glanced at them for a moment and then went back to his discussion. While he and his guard waited Valentine took the opportunity to memorise everything he could.

The helmsman was at his post and there was a navigator working an ancient-looking Babbage—its cogs were well-polished but much larger than one saw in modern machines. He guessed it had originally been steam-driven but the side of the machine was now penetrated by the drive shaft from a large electric motor at its side.

On the far side of the room were the Faraday controls; for a huge ship like this it was more than just a single switch. By the look of it sections could be energised separately, a technique popular with the Germans for their big ships. Next to that panel was another with multiple switches and lights. He could not fathom their function although their proximity to the Faraday panel suggested some relationship.

The Captain finished his discussion and strode over.

"Dyer. You're late."

"Yes, Captain," he said as meekly as he could. "I am sorry but I did not receive your message until an hour and a half ago."

The captain's eyes narrowed. "So you flew here at night, in the rain just to join my crew?"

"I was keen to serve under you, sir," he said with a hint of embarrassment which he hoped the captain would notice.

"You mean you got yourself into trouble."

"Yes, sir."

"What sort of trouble, Mr Dyer?"

"Woman trouble, Captain."

The captain nodded and laughed. "Welcome aboard Mr Dyer. Loading of the main cargo is complete but we're lifting ahead of schedule because we have a little pick-up to do before we head out."

"Yes, sir."

The captain addressed Valentine's captor. "All right, Benson, you can take your gun off him. Show him the way down to cargo and hand him over to Mr Cazarez."

Once they were off the bridge Benson turned to him and held out his hand. "Jim Benson."

Valentine shook it. "Jonathan Dyer."

Benson headed back along the companionway as a klaxon went off, sounding three times. "Going light in three," said Benson. "You been on a company ship before?"

Company ship? Valentine wondered, he shook his head. "No."

Benson grinned. "Been up there, in the black?" He gestured skywards.

"Couple of times."

Benson continued grinning. "Well this should be interesting for you."

"What?"

"You'll see."

They continued down the companionway. The klaxon went off again, twice this time. *Two minutes.*

Benson stopped by a hatch and undogged it. "Through you go." It was another airlock system and they used up the next minute cycling through. The klaxon went off again. The other side of the airlock opened on to another companionway but this one had thick glass ports that looked down into a huge hold.

Valentine had seen one of these ships before, on the ground with its hatch open—big enough to swallow a large fishing boat and have room to spare. The hatch was closed and a hundred men, women and children were camped out on the floor of the cargo bay. Some by themselves, some couples and the others by family.

"We'll wait here until we go light," said Benson grabbing hold of a leather strap attached to the wall. "Watching the farmers when that happens can be a laugh. Though we got fewer than usual this trip due to the rush."

The klaxon rang out three times in quick succession and on the fourth beat the Faraday cut in.

Valentine found himself floating off the floor.

"Better grab a strap."

Valentine had experienced the sensation of no gravity but this was not quite the same. There was gravity but it was far less than you expected from a Faraday device. That settled it; the slavers could generate a Faraday effect that nullified almost all gravity.

The British had their complete nullification effect but, as far as Valentine understood, it was completely different to the usual technique. This was a normal device but more effective. He found himself settling back to the deck. He bent his legs to avoid a rebound.

Benson smiled and nodded. "Yeah, you've been up there. Good one." He changed hands on the straps and pulled himself towards the door. "Let's find Caz for you."

Valentine glanced through one of the ports into the cavernous hold and glimpsed at least one person ejecting the contents of their stomach. Then he followed Benson through the next door.

vii

Maliha took a deep breath and looked at her watch. The cavalry would be arriving soon so she needed to move on. She continued along the tunnel deeper into the mine.

The heat and humidity intensified. She was sweating under her layers of clothes.

The next opening was on the other side of the passage and contained several beds. They were in good condition but stripped of linens. Each bed had a locker at its side of which two were open. The floor showed drag marks in the damp dust that coated everything.

They were moving out, or had already gone.

"Who the hell are you?"

She turned to face the speaker. He stood beneath a light: a thirty year old man with a small moustache and wearing a rough tweed suit that had seen better days, a shirt and tie. He looked like a professor from a university. His skin was pallid and glistened with moisture.

"Anderson," she replied slipping her hand into the pocket of the coat. "And you?"

"Are you our transport?" He sounded as if he was trying to make sense of contradictory information. He was expecting someone but that someone should not be a woman.

"Are you ready to leave?" she improvised.

"Yes, Dr Lang is just securing the samples and the rest of the equipment," he said. "Everything else is packed."

Not only was he expecting someone but around about this time. "Take me to him."

After a moment's hesitation he half-turned and gestured for her to go ahead. "Haven't you forgotten something?" she said.

He shook his head. "What do you mean?"

She smiled. "You were here for a reason, not to meet me."

For a moment the confused look returned to his face then a realisation. "Oh yes, I was checking the nursery for anything left behind."

"Like a baby?" she suppressed any emotion in her voice.

He snorted. "Another failure. It'll be dead in a few hours."

"You could kill it."

"Too risky," he said. "Tried that a couple of times but that strain of mycorrhiza generates spores when the host is threatened. We don't have time to dispose of it properly."

"Doesn't starvation count as a threat?"

He shook his head and hesitated as if choosing his words carefully. "There is a different bodily response."

"The *hormones* of Bayliss and Starling?"

He grinned. "You know their work? Yes, we think that's what it is but we need many more tests and subjects to be able to confirm it. It seems the fungus only responds to a direct threat, if the host just dies the fungus goes with it."

She nodded and said. "Where are your associates?"

"Third on the right," he said and headed up the tunnel the way she had come.

She sighed. In some ways she had hoped for a crazed and wild-eyed madman. That these crimes were committed by someone apparently sane was somehow more disturbing. She glanced at her watch again. She was running out of time but had most of the information she needed.

With proper directions she moved forward with haste and ignored all other passages and openings—one of them was the source of the heat and air-bound moisture—until she came to the third entrance on the right.

It was a cavern cut into the rock about the size of the main assembly room in Brighton: sufficient for one hundred and fifty couples to waltz at one time. Crates were piled near the entrance and marked with labels that she could not read but she guessed those would be the scientific equipment. A further pile of smaller crates stood near it. The samples perhaps. And finally a third collection made up of trunks for travelling.

There were five men in the room still working at clearing the numerous benches of equipment.

The sound of a gunshot echoed along the passage and rang through the cavern. Almost as one the men jerked their eyes towards the entrance and saw Maliha in her long dark coat and hat. Maliha herself was confused; she had not expected firearms. "Take cover!" She shouted and hurried across to the crates.

More gunshots. Screams.

Maliha checked the labels on the boxes and shook her head in annoyance. They named the contents of the crates and the name of Dr Lang but they had no destination.

A black man staggered through the entrance holding a spear, the light reflected from the bloodied blade and the red pouring from his chest. He collapsed.

There were further gunshots, shouting in both English and, as far as Maliha could guess, one of the African tongues. There was a battle being fought in the tunnel and it must be between the Africans that Maliha had seconded for assistance through Mama Kosi and the people coming to collect the scientists.

Despite the gunfire in the tunnels the cavern seemed relatively safe. Maliha looked around for the eldest of the scientists and spotted a white-haired fellow cowering behind the trunks. She listened to determine whether the battle was getting closer. It did not seem to be; if anything the gunshots were reducing in number. She doubted the natives had won the day. Her plan was in pieces; she would have to improvise.

She stood and walked calmly across to the trunks and remained standing. "Dr Lang?"

He stared up at her in astonishment though whether that was because she was apparently challenging death, or merely that she was a woman, she could not tell but he did not deny the name. She held out her hand. "My name is Anderson. I am here to assist your evacuation."

"About time," he said. "I requested rapid removal."

"These things take time to organise, doctor," she said.

"And I want it understood that I consider the attack on the hotel to be ill-conceived."

"Duly noted."

Two Europeans with guns ran in through the entrance.

With her hand still out Maliha smiled. "Shall we proceed, doctor?"

viii

Valentine had not served in any war though he had seen his fair share of action. But the slaughter of the blacks left him horrified and speechless. The ship had touched down inside the excavation of the mines and immediately come under assault from at least one hundred men with spears.

They achieved nothing, of course. The only evidence of the attack was some banging on the hull that filtered inside. Orders had come through to allow the squads of armed men out first to deal with the problem. They clearly enjoyed their work. The ship may have been old but their weapons were not. Spotlights shone from the portholes illuminating any pockets of attackers who were summarily killed with gunfire.

The attackers did not get away unscathed but lost only four or five men before the remaining blacks retreated.

The cargo chief, Cazarez, spoke English in the broken way that confirmed his nationality as Spanish, or perhaps Portuguese. The entire cargo crew was about twenty men and they waited at a smaller cargo door next to the main area in which their passengers were kept.

When the fighting had died down Cazarez ordered his crew out, along with three diesel trucks with Faraday loading beds. They drove round the ship and headed into the tunnel with six or seven men to each truck. Valentine was one of three riding on the back. He stared at the bodies, and the crewmen moving among them with their guns. Just before they entered the tunnel he saw one of the crewmen fire three shots into the head of a black who had had the audacity to groan.

"Don't take no notice," said the man beside him. His name was Dix. "If you say anything they're just as likely to shoot you. No one cares."

Valentine nodded his response then ducked as the vehicle slowed down and entered the tunnel.

*   *   *

The caverns echoed to the roar of engines. She forced a smile on to her face. "We had better finish up the packing, doctor." She pointed at the benches where their work had been interrupted. "Quickly now."

Inside she was trembling. If she could keep up the pretence the scientists would think she was with the ship and the crew would think she was with the scientists. Dr Lang got to his feet and went back to his bench; the others followed his example. Maliha squeezed in between them, reached over and picked up a container marked "microscope lenses". The lenses themselves were piled up in individual leather bags on the bench.

The sound of the engines reached a deafening climax and then cut off. There was no echo but the noise kept ringing in her ears. She glanced up as if disinterested and saw a dozen or so men entering.

One of them gave orders to start the loading. She recognised his accent as from the Iberian Peninsula.

She finished placing the lenses in the box lined with straw and closed the lid. She added the box to the pile of instruments. She stood back as the crewmen went in and out, carrying away the boxes and trunks.

Which was when she saw Valentine. He did not look at her and she was unsure whether he had seen her. She stopped herself from staring and turned back to the bench. The Timmons organisation must be related to this experiment. They might be funding it, or simply acting as couriers.

What does this mean?

The noise around her was distracting and made it hard to concentrate. Apart from his legal fleet Timmons operated a rogue fleet of secret vessels that carried cargo and passengers at least to Venus if not elsewhere. The fungi in the experiments also came from Venus. But she could not go to the British and claim these things without proof. She knew perfectly well that Timmons was part of the British establishment and that gave him security from investigation.

It was hopeless. How could she possibly make any headway against this much power? How could she expect to get out of this situation alive?

"Miss Anderson?"

She jerked her head round. It was Dr Lang.

"We're ready to go."

In surprise she looked about: all the baggage was gone from the room and the scientists were filing out into the tunnels. The engines of the trucks roared.

Dr Lang offered his arm and she took it. Trying not to remember that these hands had dissected and killed children. He seemed so reasonable, so normal.

She climbed on to the remaining vehicle. It carried the personal luggage and all the scientists were on it, seated on trunks and bags. They helped her up and one of them relinquished his position for her. She smiled her thank you. Valentine must have been on one of the other trucks. Had he seen her?

She was facing the rear and saw the body of the man she had spoken with lying dead on the ground as they passed. There was a flash of white light from the tunnel's entrance which highlighted the bloody wounds on his back and abdomen.

"Poor Jacobs," muttered Lang. Then there were other bodies, all black men, some in European-style clothes, others in their native costume. All with spears, not a gun among them. The sound of the machines quietened as they left the tunnel to be replaced by a deafening crack and roll of thunder. And they were drenched in the downpour. Maliha turned her head.

Where before there had been empty space on the floor of the mine workings, now there was a massive ship curiously squared off. It was unlike any style of flyer she had ever seen in life or in a book. It was exactly as Valentine had described the one he had seen near Pondicherry.

She schooled her expression since Dr Lang thought she had come from the ship itself. But she could not control her heart that raced in her breast. Her mind flashed from possibility to possibility but still there was no way out. There were armed guards posted around the perimeter of the ship and others at strategic points around the mine.

The vehicles splashed through puddles and turned as they reached one end of the voidship. They wove in and out of the dead bodies and occasionally over them. She stared up at the ship's vast bulk. High above her there was a line of windows with light behind them. In all probability the vessel's bridge.

The trucks came to a halt on the far side. A brightly lit ramp led up into the ship but they were being shepherded to a smaller ramp up to a single door. Once they had all dismounted, the trucks drove up the larger ramp and disappeared into the vessel. They made their way up the smaller one and Maliha was worried there might be checks on the personnel.

She even thought she might make a break for it, perhaps hide in the shadow of the ship until they left. The mere fact she considered such a thing revealed how desperate she was. She suppressed such foolish thoughts. There would be a way through this. There always was.

The outer hatch was shut and they were passing one at a time through an inner door. Maliha hung back at the rear. She was about to step through when it was slammed in her face, knocking her to the floor.

ix

So much for subterfuge, she thought. Her arms and left knee were bruised—along with her pride and faith in her own abilities. She should leave the undercover activities to those who were experienced. Like Valentine. The klaxon sounded again, just once. They would be going light within the next minute.

Considering Valentine led her to a new thought. She was absolutely certain the scientists were completely taken in. She had not at any time lied. Simply omitted the greater part of the truth. There was no reason for any ordinary crew member to know that she was not part of the scientists. It might be unusual that she was a woman but it was not so uncommon as to be a red flag.

And while it was possible they had been examined invisibly against a checklist of expected staff she knew that their departure was premature—caused no doubt by her revelations in the treatment works. So this would most likely have just been the nearest available vessel. Having a list of the scientists was unlikely.

Which meant the most likely possibility was—the klaxon emitted three short sharp bursts and on the fourth count Maliha found herself lifting from the deck. She had experienced reduced gravity many times but it had never been like this. Valentine had been right: the slavers had a more effective form.

There were straps in the wall. She grabbed hold of one and forced her feet to the deck. There was gravity here, just not very much of it. If she was careful she could avoid flying off into space. She focused on her previous train of thought.

Valentine was the one that must have told them who she was. Or at least that she was an interloper.

The inner door opened and three men floated in.

"Yeah, that's her." Valentine said. "Told you I had woman trouble."

The swarthy aspect of the second man suggested he was the one who had been giving the orders to the men handling the baggage and instruments. The third man had a gun. She was not an expert on guns, but the dangerous end was pointing in her direction. The swarthy man shut the inner door.

"Bitch tried to seduce me," said Valentine with a harsh grate in his voice.

"Reckon she must really like you to follow you," said the one with the gun.

"Don't be stupid, Benson. She was with the scientists; how'd she know about them? I didn't even know about them—who did?"

"*Si*, she is a spy. We must report to the captain." He turned and headed for the inner door.

"Let's have some fun first," said Valentine. He went to the outer door and unlocked it while the one called Benson kept his gun trained on Maliha.

The Iberian stared. "What are you doing?" he tried the inner door but it would not open.

Valentine grinned maliciously and pushed the outer door. "Better we get the information out of her before we go to the captain."

Wind slashed through the external hatch as it swung wide. The wind-driven raindrops penetrated the room and then hung in the air. Maliha clung harder to the strap.

The interior lit up with a brilliant flash of lightning turning the men's faces into masks of white and black. The ship lurched and heeled over. A surge of real gravity went through it and the rain in the air splashed to the deck creating a slick sheet.

Maliha swung out towards the open door but clung tight to the strap. She could see the city lights of Johannesburg hundreds of feet below and for a moment there was nothing between her and the ground.

The ship righted itself and the Faraday effect re-established but it was not as strong as before. Maliha looked at Valentine; he was soaked to the skin and his face was twisted in either anger or desperation. She could not tell which.

Valentine pushed himself over to the wall between her and the open hatch. He hooked his hand through a loop. "I'll make the bitch talk." He reached into his pocket and pulled out a folding knife. He flipped the catch and the blade opened. In one quick move he slashed the strap she was holding and it fell away.

She slumped to the deck and tried to reach for the next one along.

"What are you doing, Dyer?" shouted the Iberian from the other side of the room.

"Making her talk."

Then, to Maliha's horror, Valentine grabbed her damp wrist and, in the reduced gravity, swung her out of the hatch. He grinned maniacally.

As her feet went out the door the wind caught them and dragged her harder. With her free hand she grabbed his jacket. Terror coursed through her. What was he doing? He could kill her. Another lightning bolt lit up the sky and shone off the soaked hull of the ship. If anyone was looking up they could not fail to see the massive machine.

"Think you can trick me, bitch? I hate you half-breeds. You didn't stand a chance with me," he shouted above the noise of the wind and rain.

She knew he was lying but it still hurt. He was dangling her out of a voidship hundreds of feet up and her fingers were slipping and she knew he could not hold her. He was in reduced gravity, but she was only in the periphery of it. She was heavy.

"Who you working for?"

Blinking against the rain she looked up through the hatch. The two heads of the other men were visible behind Valentine's silhouette. "Myself!"

He jerked his arm and she screamed in terror.

"Liar! Who are you working for?"

"The blacks!"

"Pull the other one, bitch!"

Lightning exploded around them again. The ship lurched once more. Maliha stared down. She saw a strange circle of lights. The ground was closer now. The ship must be having trouble in the electrical fields of the storm.

She felt his fingers loosening. "Please!" she screamed. "Please don't."

She stared up into his eyes reflecting the lights of the city but he wasn't looking at her. He was staring past her at the ground.

Then he focused on her.

"Die, bitch!"

He released his grip on her wrist.

She clutched the sleeve of his coat.

He yanked his arm free from her grip.

She watched his face fall away from her. Then the great vessel came into view lit by lightning and reflecting the lights of the city. It spun away from her.

Finally the dark turmoil of the storm filled her vision.

For a moment she wondered how long it would take to fall.

~ end ~

Read **UNDER THE BURNING CLOUDS**
The breathless conclusion to the **Maliha Anderson** series.

Steve Turnbull was born in the heart of London to book-loving working-class parents in 1958. He lived with his parents and two older sisters in two rooms with gas lighting and no hot water. In his fifth year, a change in his father's fortunes took them out to a detached house in the suburbs. That was the year *Dr Who* first aired on British TV, and Steve watched it avidly from behind the sofa. It was the beginning of his love of science fiction.

Academically Steve always went for the science side, but he also had his imagination—and that took him everywhere. He read through his local library's entire science fiction and fantasy selection, plus his father's 1950s *Astounding Science Fiction* magazines. As he got older he also ate his way through TV SF like *Star Trek*, *Dr Who* and *Blake's 7*.

However, it was when he was 15 he discovered something new. Bored with a maths lesson, he noticed a book from the school library: *Cider with Rosie* by Laurie Lee. From the first page he was captivated by the beauty of the language. As a result he wrote a story longhand and then spent evenings at home on his father's electric typewriter pounding out a second draft, expanding it. Then he wrote a second book. After that he switched to poetry and turned out dozens, mostly not involving teenage angst.

After receiving excellent science and maths results, he went on to study computer science. There he teamed up with another student and they wrote songs for their band, with Steve writing the lyrics. However, they admit their best song was the other way around, with Steve writing the music.

After graduation Steve moved into contract programming but was snapped up a couple of years later by a computer magazine looking for someone with technical knowledge. It was in the magazine industry that Steve learned how to write to length, to deadline, and to style. Within a couple of years he was editor and stayed there for many years.

During that time he married Pam (who also became a magazine editor), whom he'd met at a student party.

Though he continued to write poetry, all prose work stopped. He created his own magazine publishing company which at one point produced the subscription magazine for the *Robot Wars* TV show. The company evolved into a design agency, but after six years of working very hard and not seeing his family—now including a daughter and son—he gave it all up.

He spent a year working on miscellaneous projects including writing 300 pages for a website until he started back where he had begun, contract programming.

With security and success on the job front, the writing began again. This time it was scriptwriting: features scripts, TV scripts and radio scripts. During this time he met a director, Chris Payne, who wanted to create steampunk stories, and between them they created the Voidships universe, a place very similar to ours but with specific scientific changes.

With a whole universe to play with, Steve wrote a web series, a feature film, and then books all in the same Steampunk world and, behind the scenes, all connected.

Join the mailing list at http://bit.ly/voidships